Praise for *Shiver*

"If you... ...wean...
...methad... ...co...
Traveller's... *Twilight*. Yes it's a supernatural thriller,
but re... ...ly free of clichés ... all consuming"
Sunday Telegraph

"This bittersweet tale had the publishing world buzzing"
**Glamreads 2009's best books – Best Book
to Curl Up With,** *Glamour*

"*Shiver* has a sense of unfolding mystery, a genuine
quest and threats from humans and wolves alike"
The Observer

"An engrossing story of teenaged love ... humorous
and witty, with wry observations of suburban existence.
Even without the mystic enrichment, the book can be
appreciated as a romantic story of youthful anomie"
Books for Keeps

"If you are a fan of *Twilight*, then you will love *Shiver*.
Beautifully written, with alternating chapters from
Grace and Sam's points of view, this a wonderful debut"
Waterstone's Books Quarterly

Maggie Stiefvater

Lament

SCHOLASTIC

Scholastic Children's Books
An imprint of Scholastic Ltd
Euston House, 24 Eversholt Street
London, NW1 1DB, UK
Registered office: Westfield Road, Southam, Warwickshire, CV47 0RA
SCHOLASTIC and associated logos are trademarks and/or
registered trademarks of Scholastic Inc.

First published in the US by Flux, an imprint of Llewellyn Publications, 2008
This edition published in the UK by Scholastic Ltd, 2011

ISBN 978 1407 12031 7

A CIP catalogue record for this book is available
from the British Library.

Printed and bound in the UK by
CPI Bookmarque, Croydon CR0 4TD
Papers used by Scholastic Children's Books are made from wood
grown in sustainable forests.

1 3 5 7 9 10 8 6 4 2

www.scholastic.co.uk/zone
www.maggiestiefvater.com

To my dad, because he's like me,
And Ed, because he's not

Prologue

He didn't know how long he'd been clinging there. Long enough for the bone-cold water to drive the feeling from his legs. Long enough for his fingers to tire of holding his head above water. Somewhere in the distance, the eerie wail of the hounds quickened his heartbeat.

He closed his eyes, concentrating on keeping his hold on the old well's uneven sides, willing his heart to slow. *They can't smell you in here. They'll lose your scent in the stream and they'll never find you here.*

The water's chilly touch crawled further up his neck and he tightened his grip, looking up to the clear night sky. Sighed. Weary. How long had he been doing this? As long as he could remember. Above the well, the howls fell away; they'd lost the scent.

Just leave me alone. Haven't I paid enough? He prayed for Them to go back where They came from, but he didn't expect an answer. God's attentions were for those with souls, a status he'd lacked for a thousand years or more. He swallowed. Deep in his chest, he felt the soft and curious rustling that meant They'd entered the cage room. He reached down through the water to his pocket, withdrew two old, rusty nails, and held them tightly. All he had to do was not cry out. He could do this.

Somewhere else, in a small, round, grey room of stone and moss as soft as a fox cub's fur, a dove beat furiously in a cage made of a net of the hair-fine wires. Wings crashed into the bars, and claws scraped at the perch only to unsuccessfully seek purchase on the thin wire sides. It was a frenzy not of a desire to escape – the cage had no door – but rather of fear. It was the worst kind of fear – the hopeless kind – and it sent the bird's eternal heart racing until it seemed it would burst out of its breast.

Somehow, slender hands took the pale dove from where it trembled at the bottom of the cage and held it out to a bright lady, oddly golden in this grey-green room.

When she spoke, her voice shimmered in the room, beautiful enough to draw tears. "The wing," she said softly, holding up a candle. The fingers gently tugged the dove's wing outwards from its body and offered the prone bird to the lady. The candle she held reflected the colours of the sun in the dove's eye.

The lady smiled thinly and held the pale flame beneath the bird's wing.

The boy in the well shuddered. Biting his lip, he pressed his forehead into his arms, willing himself quiet.

The pain in his chest gnawed and burned, squeezing his heart with a fiery touch. As quickly as it began, it abated, and he gasped silently.

The lady in the grey room held the candle beside her face, illuminating her beauty: beauty that looked at the beauty of a perfect summer day and scoffed that they should bear the same description. "He always chooses the hard way, doesn't he?" The dove began to thrash wildly at the sound of her voice. This time, she held the candle closer, and the flames seized the feathers, twisting and blackening them like shreds of paper. The dove froze, beak parted in silent pain, eyes fixed blankly on the ceiling.

In the well, the boy gasped again, audibly, and tried to remember to hold his head above water. His heart writhed within him, and as he squeezed his eyes shut as tightly as he could, his heartbeat stopped. Feeling curiously hollow, he slid silently under the water, fingers limp, the nails he had been holding tracing a slow line into the dark below him.

His head jerked back, his neck seized in an inhuman grip. He was pulled into the night and dropped to the clover-scented ground, water trickling from his mouth.

"You're not to die quite yet, old friend." The Hunter looked down at him, neither angry nor happy with his captured quarry. The chase was done, so the entertainment was over. Hounds milled around the body in the clover. "Work to do."

Book One

. . . you've left my heart shaken
With a hopeless desolation, I'd have you to know
It's the wonders of admiration your quiet face has taken
And your beauty will haunt me wherever I go.

—"Bridgit O'Malley"

One

"You'll be fine once you throw up," Mom said from the front seat. "You always are."

Standing behind our dusty estate car, I blinked out of my daze and tugged my harp case out of the back, feeling nauseated. It struck me that Mom's statement was just about the only reason I needed to avoid a career in public music performance. "Keep that pep talk coming, Mom."

"Don't be sarcastic." Mom tossed me a cardigan that matched my trousers. "Take this. It makes you look more professional."

I could've said no, but it was easier just to take the sweater. As Mom had already pointed out, the sooner I got into the auditorium and threw up, the easier it would be. And once I got this over with, I could return to my ordinary life until the next time she decided to take me out of my cage. I did refuse Mom's offers to help me carry my harp, though plenty of the other students heading inside had parental retinues. Somehow it was easier to be utterly insignificant without anyone you knew watching.

"We'll park the car, then. And find a seat. Call if you need us?" Mom patted her dove-blue handbag, which matched her plunging dove-blue top. "And Delia should be here soon, too."

The thought of my diva-aunt pushed me slightly closer to the vomit end of the sick scale. *Oh Deirdre,* she would say loudly, *can I help you run through those scales? You really are a bit flat on the upper range.* And then I would throw up on her. Hey, maybe that wasn't a terrible plan after all. Though, knowing Delia, she'd probably correct my form. *Deirdre, dear, really, you need a better puke arc if you're going to ever blow chunks professionally.*

"Great," I said. My parents waved and left me to find the competitors' area. I shielded my eyes and scanned the broad concrete side of the high school. Shining brightly in the early afternoon glare was a huge canvas sign that said *Competitors' Entrance.* I'd sincerely hoped I wouldn't have to return to the school until my junior year started. Yeah. Farewell, mine dreams.

Man, it was hot. I glared up at the sun, eyes narrowed, and my eyes were drawn to the moon hanging in the sky next to the sun. For some reason, this appearance of the ghost of the moon gave me an odd prickle in my stomach – nerves of a different kind. It had a sort of magic, magic that made me want to stay and stare at it until I could remember why it enchanted me. But staying outside in the heat wasn't helping my nervous stomach, so I left the pale disc behind and I hauled my harp over to the "Competitors' Entrance".

As I pushed through the heavy doors, it occurred to me that, before my mother mentioned it, I hadn't wanted to puke at all. I hadn't even been thinking about the competition. True, I'd had my familiar glassy-eyed, all-attention-devoted-to-not-hurling look on my face on the drive over, but not for the reason my mother assumed. I had still been lost in last night's dream. But now that she'd brought it up, and with the competition in sight, all was right again with the world and my stomach was a disaster.

A woman with two chins and a clipboard asked for my name.

"Deirdre Monaghan."

She squinted at me – or maybe that was her normal expression. "Someone was looking for you earlier."

I hoped she meant James, my best (only) friend. Anyone else, I wasn't interested in them finding me. I wanted to ask what they looked like, but I was afraid that if I talked much, I'd lose my tenuous control over my gag reflex. Mere proximity to the competition area was definitely antagonizing the whole bile thing.

"Tall, light-haired woman."

Not James. But not Delia, either. Puzzling, but not really a priority, all things considered.

The woman scribbled something next to my name. "You'll need to pick up a packet at the end of the hall."

I held a hand over my mouth and asked carefully, "Where can I practise?"

"If you go down the hall past where you get the packet, the big double doors on the—"

I couldn't wait much longer. "Right. The classrooms down there?"

She wagged her chins. I took that as a "yes" and walked further inside. My eyes took a minute to adjust to the light, but my nose operated immediately. The familiar smell of my high school, even without any students nearby, pricked my nerves. God, I was so dysfunctional.

My harp case rang. The phone. I fished it out and stared. A four-leaf clover was stuck to the back of it, damp and fresh. Not one of the ones where the fourth leaf is stunted, either, and you can obviously see it's just a mutation of a three-leaf clover. Each of these leaves was perfectly formed and spread.

Then I remembered that the phone was ringing. I looked at the number, hoping it wasn't Mom, and flipped it open. "Hi," I said tightly, peeling the four-leaf clover off the phone and putting it in my pocket. Couldn't hurt.

"Oh," James said sympathetically, picking up on my tone. Though his voice was thin and crackly over the line, it still had its usual calming effect. The bile in my throat momentarily retreated. "I should've called earlier, huh? You're puke-a-rella already."

"Yeah." I headed slowly towards the double doors at the end of the hall. "Distract me, *please*."

"Well, I'm running late," he said cheerfully. "So I'm probably going to have to tune my pipes in the car and then run in shirtless and half-dressed. I've been lifting weights. Maybe they'll score high for a defined six pack, if they aren't awed by my mere musical genius."

"If you manage just your skirt, at least the judges'll give you *Braveheart* points."

"Don't mock the kilt, woman. So, did you have any entertaining dreams last night?"

"Uh. . ." Even though James and I were just friends, I hesitated to tell him. My intensely detailed dreams were usually a source of great amusement for us – two nights ago, I'd dreamt I was being interviewed by a Harvard college counsellor who was up to her neck in cheese (Gouda, I think). The mood of last night's dream still lingered with me, in a sort of appealing way. "I couldn't really sleep well enough to dream," I finally said.

Oh. The moon. It suddenly occurred to me that my dream was where I had seen a moon in a daytime sky – that was where the sense of déjà vu came from. I was disappointed that it was something so normal.

"Well, that's typical," James was saying.

"Delia's coming," I told him.

"Oh, so it'll be the whole sister-on-sister catfight thing today, huh?"

"No, it's the whole 'my kid's more talented than you are' thing."

"Neener neener," James added helpfully. "Oh, damn. I really am late now. I have to get my pipes into the car, but I'll see you soon. Try not to pass out."

"Yeah, thanks," I said. The phone went silent, and I stuffed it back in my case as I arrived at the double doors. Behind them I could hear a vaguely muffled cacophony. I waited in line for my competition packet, pulling my harp behind me. Finally, I accepted my crisp manilla envelope and turned to go. I was so eager to get out of there that my harp tipped precariously. Next thing I knew, the student behind me was stumbling under the weight of it.

"Uh – *God.*" He carefully set the harp back upright and I realized I knew him: Andrew from the brass section of the school orchestra. Trumpet, maybe. Something loud. He grinned hugely at me – boobs first, then face. "You have to be careful. Those inanimate objects will get away from you."

"Yeah." If he got much funnier, I was going to throw up on him. I pulled my harp a few centimetres away from him. "Sorry."

"Hey, you can chuck your harp at me any time."

I didn't know how to respond to that, so I just said, "Yeah." Effortlessly, I became invisible and Andrew turned away. Funny how it was just like any other day in high school.

Except that it wasn't. Standing next to the double doors, listening to the roar of voices and instruments behind it, I couldn't forget why we were all here. Tons of students were warming up for their turn on stage. Warming up for their shot at winning a prize at the 26th Annual Eastern Virginia Arts Festival. For their chance to impress the college and conservatory representatives who would be watching from the audience.

My stomach turned again and this time I knew there was no going back. I fled for the girls' bathroom, the one in the basement below the gym, so that I could puke in private. Leaving my harp by the sinks, I barely made it in time, arms resting on the old grey-yellow toilet seat that reeked of too much cleaner and too many students.

I hate this. My stomach gurgled more. Every time I played in public, this happened. I *knew* it was stupid to be afraid of crowds, and I knew that the throwing up and nerves were all my fault, but I still couldn't stop it. James had looked up "the fear of public humiliation" for me (katagelophobia), and one afternoon we'd even tried hypnosis, complete with self-actualizing pamphlets and soothing music. We'd just ended up slap-happy new fans of New Age music.

I still wasn't done. My stupid hair was falling in my face and my choppy haircut was too short in front to pull back into my ponytail. I imagined going onstage with chunks in my fringe. I cry only when I'm frustrated and I was getting dangerously close.

And then, I felt a cool hand gently pulling my hair back from my face. I hadn't even heard anyone come in to the bathroom. But somehow I wasn't surprised – like I'd expected someone to come find me here. I knew without looking that it was definitely a guy's hand, and definitely not James.

I started to pull my head away, embarrassed, when the owner of the hand said firmly, "Don't worry about it. You're almost done."

And I was. I finally couldn't throw up any more and I was left shaky and utterly empty. And for some reason, I wasn't totally undone by the idea of a guy standing behind me. I turned around to see who had witnessed the most unsexy thing a girl could do. If it was Andrew, I was going to punch him for touching me.

But it wasn't Andrew. It was Dillon.

Dillon.

The guy from my dream. Here to save me from public humiliation and lead me triumphantly to a standing ovation.

He held out a handful of paper towels and smiled disarmingly. "Hi. I'm Luke Dillon." He had one of those soft voices that oozed self-control, a voice you couldn't imagine raised. It was, even in the context of a barf-filled bathroom, amazingly sexy.

"Luke Dillon," I repeated, trying not to stare. I took

the towels with a still-trembling hand and wiped my face. He had been hazy in the dream, like all dream people, but this was definitely him. Lean as a wolf, with pale blond hair and eyes even paler. And sexy. The dream seemed to have left that bit out. "You're in the girls' bathroom."

"I heard you in here."

I added, in a voice more wavery than I wanted, "You're blocking me in the cubicle."

Luke moved to the side to let me out and turned on one of the taps so I could wash my face. "Do you need to sit down?"

"No – yes – maybe."

He retrieved a folding chair from the cubby behind the cubicles and put it next to me. "You're white as white. Are you sure you're OK?"

I sank down on to the chair. "Sometimes after I'm done – uh – doing that, I pass out." I smiled weakly as my ears started to roar. "One of my – uh – many charms."

"Put your head between your knees." Luke knelt beside the chair and watched my upside-down face. "You know, you have very pretty eyes."

I didn't answer. I was going to pass out in front of a perfect stranger on a bathroom floor. Luke reached between the tangle of my arms and legs and pressed a wet paper towel against my forehead. My hearing came back in a rush.

"Thanks," I muttered, before very slowly sitting up.

Luke crouched before me. "Are you sick?" He didn't seem particularly concerned about me being contagious, but I shook my head vigorously.

"Nerves. I always throw up before these things. I know I should know better – but I can't stop it. At least I won't throw up on stage now. Might still faint, though."

"How Victorian," Luke remarked. "Are you done fainting for now, though? I mean, do you want to stay in the bathroom, or shall we go out?"

I stood. I stayed standing, so I must have recovered. "No, I'm better. I – uh – really need to warm up, though. I think I've only got forty-five minutes or something until I play. I'm not sure how much time I've wasted." I pointed to the cubicle he'd found me in.

"Well, let's get you outside to practise. They'll let you know when you need to go on, and it's quieter."

If he were any other guy in the school, I would have given him the brush-off there. I think this was actually the longest conversation I'd had with someone other than James or my family in the last two years. And that wasn't even counting the puking as part of the conversation.

Luke shouldered my harp case. "I'll take this for you, as you're Victorian and feeble. If you'll carry this for me?" He held out an exquisitely carved little wooden box, very heavy for its size. I liked it – it promised secrets inside.

"What's in here?" Right after I asked the question, I realized that it was the first one I'd asked him since he touched my hair. It hadn't even occurred to me to question anything else about him – as if everything up to now was unquestionable and acceptable, part of an unwritten script we both followed.

"Flute." Luke pushed open the bathroom door and headed for one of the back exits.

"What are you competing in?"

"Oh, I'm not here to compete."

"Then why are you here?"

He looked over his shoulder and flashed me a smile so winning that I got the idea he didn't smile like that very often. "Oh, I came to watch you play."

It wasn't true, but I liked his answer anyway. He led me out into the sun behind the school and made his way to one of the picnic benches near the football field. A student's name blared across the grounds from the speaker near the back door, and Luke looked at me. "See? You'll know when you need to go."

We settled there, him on the picnic table and me on the bench next to my harp. With the sun fully on them, his eyes were pale as glass.

"What are you going to play for me?"

My stomach squeezed. He was going to think I was

completely pathetic, too nervous to play even in front of him. "Um. . ."

He looked away, opening his flute case and carefully putting the flute together. "So you're telling me you're a great musician and you won't share it with anyone?"

"Well, you make it sound so selfish when you put it that way!"

Luke's mouth quirked on one side as he lifted his flute. He blew a breathy "A" and adjusted the slide. "Well, I held your hair. Doesn't that deserve a tune? Concentrate on the music. Pretend I'm not here."

"But you *are*."

"Pretend I'm a picnic table."

I looked at the muscled arms beneath the sleeves of his T-shirt. "You are *definitely* not a picnic table." Man, he was definitely not a picnic table.

Luke just looked at me. "Play." His voice was hard, and I glanced away. Not because I was offended, but because I knew he was right.

I turned to my harp — *hello, old friend* — and rocked it back on its ten-centimetre legs to settle it into the crook of my shoulder. A moment's attention to the strings showed me that they still held their tune, and then I began to play. The strings were lovely and buttery under my fingers; the harp loved this warm and humid weather.

I sang, my voice timid at first, and then stronger as I realized I wanted to impress him.

The sun shines through the window
And the sun shines through your hair
It seems like you're beside me
But I know you're not there.
You would sit beside this window
Run your fingers through my hair
You were always there beside me
But I know that you're not there

Oh, to be by your side once again
Oh, to hold your hand in mine again
Oh, to be by your side once again
Oh, to hold your hand in mine—

I broke off as I heard his flute joining in. "You know it, then?"

"Indeed I do. Do you sing the verse where he gets killed?"

I frowned. "I only know the part I sang. I didn't know he died."

"Poor lad, of course he dies. It's an Irish song, right? They always die in Irish songs. I'll sing it for you. Play along so I don't wander off tune."

I plucked along, bracing myself for whatever his voice might sound like.

He turned his face into the sun and sang,

Fro and to in my dreams to you
To the haunting tune of the harp

For the price I paid when you died that day
I paid that day with my heart
Fro and to in my dreams to you
With the breaking of my heart
Ne'er more again will I sing this song

Ne'er more will I hear the harp. . .

"See, he gets killed—"

"—sad," I interjected.

"—and it's a very old song," continued Luke. "That bit you sang – 'oh to be by your side,' that bit – must have been added on somewhere along the way. I've not heard it before. But what I sang – that's always been part of it. You didn't know it?"

"No, I didn't," I said, adding truthfully, "You have a wonderful voice. You make it sound like something you'd hear on a CD."

"So do you," Luke said. "You have an angel's voice. Better than I expected. And it's a girl's song. The lyrics are girly, you know?"

My cheeks flushed. It was stupid, of course, because all my life I'd been told – by highly qualified professionals and people who should know and folks "in the business"– that I was good. I'd heard it so often that it didn't mean anything any more. But my heart leapt at his words.

"Girly," I managed to scoff.

Luke nodded. "But you could do so much better.

You're not pushing yourself at all. So *safe.*"

My mood immediately shifted from pleased to irritated. I'd practised "The Faerie Girl's Lament" for months – I had arranged it with so many impossible embellishments and chord changes that even the most cynical of harpists would be awed. I didn't think I could take the designation "safe", even from the enigmatic Luke Dillon.

"Any less safe and it'd be impossible," I managed to say evenly. I get my temper from Mom; like her, though, I never show it. I just get frostier and frostier until I freeze the person out entirely. I think Luke's comment sent me to somewhere between "pretty damn cold" and "frostbite warning".

Luke gave me an odd little smile. "Don't be angry, pretty girl. I just mean that you could really write a nice little interlude in there that was all yours. Improvise a bit – be spontaneous. Make something happen. You've got the talent for that; you just aren't trying."

It took me a moment to get past his flirting to realize what he was trying to say. "I've written some tunes," I said. "But it takes me a while to do it. Weeks. Days, anyway. I guess I could see where I could put something in there."

He slid closer on the table and lifted his flute up. "Not what I meant. Write something *now.*"

"I couldn't. It would be slop."

Luke looked away. "Everyone says that."

I sort of had a strange sense then that a lot rode on that moment, on whether I gave up or tried. I just wasn't sure what. I just knew I didn't want to disappoint him. "Then play it with me. Help me think of something. I'll try."

He didn't look back at me, but he lifted his flute and played the opening notes. I joined in with my harp half a measure later, and together we played. The first time through, my fingers automatically found the notes, as I had trained them to for months. Just like I'd automatically followed along with Luke and all his strangeness for the last half hour, taking the script as it was written for me.

But the second time through, my fingers plucked out a little variation. Not just a few notes, either. It was something more – a decision to take control and make the tune my own. For once, I was calling the tune and it felt amazing. No regrets. No second-guessing.

By the third time through, Luke dropped out after the first verse and I coaxed eight measures of something brand new from the harp.

Luke smiled.

"Gloating is very rude," I told him.

"Very," he agreed.

I bit my lip, thinking. Now I was in completely unfamiliar territory and I didn't know any of the rules. "If – what if – would you play with me this afternoon? If I switch my name over from solo to duet?"

"Yes."

"I'll go do it now." I started to rise, but he reached out and caught my arm.

"They already know," he said softly. "Would you like to practise some more?"

Apparently, I wasn't in control. Frozen by his words, I slowly sank back down, looking at him with a puzzled expression. Something in me prickled with either a warning or a promise. I had a choice – the power to decide which one it was. In a safe world, it would have been a warning.

I nodded firmly. "Yeah. Let's practise."

"Dee – there you are."

Distracted, I turned to find James standing behind me. It took me a moment to remember the last time I'd spoken to him. "I threw up."

Luke said, "Nice kilt."

James looked hard at him. "Haven't I seen you somewhere before?"

"Parking lot," Luke said mildly. "Of the music store."

It was peculiarly difficult to imagine Luke some place else, some place ordinary, but James seemed to believe him. "Oh – right. What happened to that fiddler you were playing with?"

"He had to go home."

I had the curious sensation both were leaving things unsaid. I resolved to ask James about it later.

"Are you playing soon?" I asked.

"They've just finished up the *a cappella* or whatever it's called and they're starting the duets now. Jason Byler – you remember him – and I decided to do the pipes with his electric guitar, just to see if we can get a rise out of the crowd. So yeah, soon. I'm going to head inside and find him. I'll listen for your name, though." James was still staring at Luke as if he were some sort of rare plant specimen.

"Good luck," Luke said.

"Yeah. Thanks." He held out his hand, brushing my fingers with his. "Later, Dee."

After he had gone, Luke said, "He likes being different."

I agreed.

"Unlike you," he added.

I frowned. "That's not true. I like being different. But somehow everything that makes people outside of high school notice me makes me invisible *inside* the school." I shrugged. "James is my only real friend." Immediately I thought I'd said too much, that I'd go invisible to him as well.

But he merely rubbed his flute absently before looking at me. "Their loss."

"Deirdre Monaghan. Luke Dellom."

I jerked at the sound of my name over the loudspeaker.

"Easy now," Luke said. "We don't need you passing

out. They'll wait." He got up and shouldered my harp, offering me his flute case again. Then he held the door open for me. "After you, my queen." I closed my eyes briefly as the door shut behind us, waiting for nerves to slam me again.

"Do you know how some people can do anything?"

I opened my eyes. I realized he was waiting for me to lead the way to the auditorium, so I started walking up the stairs. "What do you mean?"

As we got closer to the auditorium, there were more students waiting in the halls, all talking noisily, but I heard Luke's voice behind me without difficulty. "I mean, you tell them to write a tune, they give you a symphony right there. You tell them to write a book, they write you a novel in a day. You tell them to move a spoon without touching it, they move it. If they want something, they make it happen. Miracles, almost."

"Uh, not really," I said. "Except for on the Sci-Fi Channel. Do you know anyone who can do that?"

Luke's voice dipped. "I'd ask them to do a few miracles for me if I did."

We pushed our way backstage; the previous duet, two trumpets, was still playing for the judges. They were revoltingly good.

Luke persisted. "What gets me is you could walk right by someone like that on the street. That you'd never know if *you* were like that unless you tried."

"This is about the improvising on the tune, isn't it?" I scanned heads for someone in charge. I was starting to get that light-headed, too-warm feeling that meant I was going to either hurl or fall down soon. "I get it. I wouldn't have ever known I could improvise like that if you hadn't made me."

"Deirdre Monaghan and Luke Dillohm?" It was another lady with a clipboard, horribly mispronouncing Luke's last name. "Good. You're up next. Wait until these guys get offstage, and they'll introduce you. You can say something brief about your piece if you like. *Brief.*" With a harassed expression, she turned to the musicians behind us and began repeating the speech.

"I just think you don't push yourself enough," Luke said, continuing exactly where he'd left off. "You settle for ordinary."

This struck a chord with me, and I turned to look at him. *I will call the tune.* "I don't want ordinary."

Luke smiled at me, or at something behind me, his expression unreadable. Then he pulled a small, unmarked bottle of eyedrops from his pocket.

"Dry eyes?"

"I have strange eyes. I'd like to be able to see everything tonight." He blinked, his eyes shiny with the drops and his lower lashes filled with small tears. A swipe of his arm and his eyes and lashes were dry, though no less bright. Something about them made me want to see the *everything* he was going to see.

"Deirdre? Ah, I thought that was you." Mr Hill, the school's music teacher and band director, touched my elbow. He had acted as my musical mentor since I began high school; I knew he thought I was destined for greatness. "How are you doing?"

I contemplated the question. "Actually, not as bad as I expected."

Mr Hill's eyes smiled behind his wire frames. "Great. I wanted to wish you good luck. Not that you need it, of course. Just remember to avoid pinching the high notes when you're singing."

I smiled back. "Thanks. Hey – I'm playing in duets. Did you know?"

Mr Hill looked at Luke and his smile vanished. Frowning, he asked, "Do I know you?"

Luke said, "Nobody knows me."

I looked at him. *I will.*

"Deirdre? Lucas? You're on." The clipboard-woman took my elbow firmly and pointed me in the direction of the stage. "Good luck."

Together we walked into the too-bright lights of the stage. Luke's hair was lit to white. I looked out, off the stage, trying to see where my family was, but the audience was cast in shadow. It was better that way – I wouldn't see Delia's invariably smug expression. I gave the darkened faces one last glance before sitting on the folding chair; it was unpleasantly warm from the last nervous performer.

Setting down the harp, Luke crossed behind me and

whispered, "Don't be ordinary."

I shivered and gathered my harp to me. Something told me "ordinary" wasn't possible when Luke was involved, and that thought was more exciting and terrifying that anything the competition could offer.

"Deirdre Monaghan and Luke DeLong on lever harp and wooden flute."

I leaned to Luke and whispered, "They all say your name wrong."

Luke's teeth made a thin smile. "Everyone does."

"I didn't, did I?"

The stage lights reflected off his eyes like the glow off a lake; I was dazzled in spite of myself. "No, you didn't."

He adjusted the microphone and addressed the crowd, his eyes running over the people's faces as if he expected to see someone he knew. "Excited to be here, folks?"

There was some mild clapping and calling from some of the louder dads.

"You don't sound excited. This is the biggest musical event for students in a eight-hundred-kilometre radius. We're playing for great prizes. These are your children and the peers of your children, playing their hearts out, folks! Now, are you excited, or not?"

The audience clapped and hooted, distinctly louder. Luke gave a wild smile. "Now, Dee and I will be playing an old Irish song called 'The Faerie Girl's Lament'.

I hope you like it. Let us know!"

This was where I would normally either throw up or fall down, but I didn't feel like doing either. I felt like grinning as big as Luke. I felt like kicking some music-geek ass. It was the best feeling I'd ever had. Where had the real me gone? Because I didn't want her back.

"Ready, Dee?" Luke asked softly.

His smile was infectious and for the first time in my life, being on stage felt *right*. I smiled hugely at him and began to play. The strings were still buttery-soft from the heat outside, and the acoustics of the stage made the harp sound ten metres tall. Luke chipped in and began to play, and the flute was low and breathy like his singing voice, full of expression and barely suppressed emotions. Together, we sounded like an orchestra, albeit it an ancient, untamed one, and when I began to sing, the auditorium became as still as a winter night.

Did I really have the voice of an angel? The voice that filled the room didn't sound like mine – it sounded grown-up, complex, as agonized as the Faerie Girl in the lyrics.

The first verse ended and I *felt* the flute hesitate for the barest of moments, waiting. I began to play a counter-melody, something that had never been heard before. Only this time, I'd done it before and I *knew* I could wander from the melody without getting lost. This time

I attacked the counter-melody with sweet savagery. It climbed up the scale, bitter and lovely, and Luke's flute came back in, low notes that climbed with mine to an almost unbearable intensity.

Then I began to sing the last verse, the one I had just learned from Luke. Any other day, I would've forgotten the lyrics, but not today, with the memory of his voice singing them. The words seemed to take on new meaning as I sang them; they were real.

I *was* the Faerie Girl.

> *Fro and to in my dreams to you*
> *To the haunting tune of the harp*
> *For the price I paid when you died that day*
> *I paid that day with my heart*
> *Fro and to in my dreams to you*
> *With the breaking of my heart*
> *Ne'er more again will I sing this song*
> *Ne'er more will I hear the harp.*

By the time we got to the last refrain, Luke was grinning so widely he almost couldn't play. I let my voice fade softly, vanishing with the flute's last note, returning to wherever that amazing counter-melody had come from.

The room was completely silent.

Luke smiled a small, private smile, and then the audience leapt to its feet, clapping and whistling. Even the judges in the front seats were on their feet. I bit my lip, colour flushing into my glowing face, and exchanged a look with Luke.

We let ourselves be directed offstage for the next performers and Luke seized my hand, his face shining as if from within. "Good girl!" He released my hand. "Good girl! I have to go – but I'll be back for the reception tonight."

"You have to what?" I repeated, but he had already disappeared into the throng of people backstage. I felt strangely lost.

TWO

"Don't wear something trashy," Mom advised, shutting my bedroom door behind her.

Thanks for the hot tip, I thought, staring at the pile of clothing she'd put on my bed. I didn't know what I was going to wear to the reception, but I already knew it wasn't going to be any of the items she'd taken out of my wardrobe.

I was still holding her last suggestion, a dress that made me look like a runaway from a nursing home. I chucked it on top of the pile of other too-formal dresses and trouser suits, and looked out of my bedroom window. Patchy white clouds slid across the afternoon sky, taking the edge off the heat and obscuring the faint sliver of the moon – if it was even still out there.

Instead of getting dressed, I stuck a CD into my player, shoved the mound of clothing over to the other side of the bed, and crashed on top of the covers. The wild set of reels on the CD whirled through my brain, bringing back the vivid memory of playing on the stage earlier today.

Holy crap. Luke Dillon was real. I couldn't really wrap my brain around it. People didn't just walk out of dreams.

For a few minutes, I allowed myself the luxury of lying on the bed and remembering Luke. The careful way he spoke, delivering each word as if it were something precious. The breathy voice of his flute, whispering secrets and longing. His super-pale eyes, like glass. I could imagine him holding my hand and making me one of his secrets. I kind of felt guilty for lying around, letting myself crush on him when I should've been getting ready, but I hadn't ever had a crush on a boy before.

Well, that was a lie. Back in seventh grade, I'd been in a class with Rob Martin, a slight, dark-haired guy with a face like a brooding dark angel. Or at least, that's how I imagined it. With my superpower of invisibility, I watched him every day at school without ever working up the courage to speak to him. I knew he was a saint of some variety, because he spoke out loudly against animal cruelty and picked all of the meat out of the cafeteria's offerings. He once berated our teacher in front of the entire class for wearing a leather jacket. He used words like "anathema" and "pogrom".

He was my hero.

Then, a few days before the summer holidays when I was shadowing Rob during break, invisible, I watched him take out a lunch box and eat a ham sandwich.

I hadn't had a crush on anyone since then.

On the CD, the reels ended and the next track started, a sweet, sad ballad and one of my favourites – "If I Was a Blackbird". As I hummed along, a sudden, familiar phrase stuck out like a sore thumb. Oh. So much for magical improvisation. My counter-melody wasn't exactly like the one the band was playing now, but it was close. I listened hard as they repeated the verse. OK, not that part. But there – wait – those few notes? And maybe those? Oh yeah. It was painfully obvious to me where my inspiration had come from.

I sighed heavily, but some part of me was a little relieved. If there was a plausible explanation for my sudden ability to improvise, then there was probably one for Luke, too. Because the fact of it was, people *didn't* just walk out of dreams. I was recognizing him from somewhere – heck, the way he'd played the flute, maybe he even had a band that I'd heard before. I didn't know anything about him except that he was cute, played music, and was interested in me.

Did anything else matter?

Well, he did just show up in the bathroom—

"Deirdre!" Mom shouted. "Have you picked something?"

I stood up and looked at the CD player for a long moment before shutting it off. "Yeah!" I shouted back. "I've just decided."

★

By the time we got to the reception, I was pleased that I hadn't given in to any of Mom's suggestions. Nobody was wearing jeans, but nobody was wearing anything worthy of the little-black-dress numbers she'd put in my hands. My light blue sundress and strappy white sandals fit the dress code perfectly, and the halter top on my dress showed off my neck and shoulders in case Luke really did come back for the reception.

"I hate when they hold these things outside," Delia said loudly as she stepped off the sidewalk and her pointy heels sank five centimetres into the turf. "Thank God they at least have chamber music. I was afraid they'd have something awful, like that bagpiping earlier."

I disagreed entirely. Nothing was worse than being shut in a room that smelled like carpet cleaner with one hundred strangers. Instead, I saw students, parents, teachers, and judges roaming between large white tents set up for food and the quartet that provided the music. The food smelled great and reminded me of Saturday nights at home. And the hot summer air had given way to a cool breeze as the sun slipped down towards the treeline.

"What is that *smell?*" Delia demanded. She was just being nasty, of course. She knew darn well that Mom's catering company was here tonight. Dad always called Delia "my least favourite sister-in-law". He was being funny, of course, since Delia was Mom's only sister.

But I agreed. Delia was an overbearing cake with condescending frosting, and frankly, I was on a diet.

"Dee, you survived!" James sauntered up and paused half a step when he saw Delia. "Oh, I didn't realize you were busy."

Delia surveyed his kilt, his unkempt hair, and his hands scrawled with various messages to himself.

"You're the piper, aren't you?" she asked coldly.

James smiled firmly. He had already identified her as a piper-hater. "Yes, but I do it against my will. The aliens won't let me stop."

Delia's smile was iron. Not amused.

I said, "This is James, Delia. He's the number two piper in the state of Virginia this year."

"Soon to be number one," James said with a charming smile. "I hired a hit man."

Delia's face remained exactly the same.

James exchanged a look with me. "Well, it was nice to meet you. I'd better find out if the food's lonely."

I gave a little wave as he retreated, mouthing *later*, and Delia frowned deeply. "What strange people always come to these events. We'd better find your parents."

"I'll catch up with you." I edged away from her. "I think I see some of my friends." I wasn't a very good liar, but Delia wasn't a very good listener, so we parted amicably, her towards the tents and me definitely away from them. I glanced quickly towards the food tent crowds but didn't see any sign of Luke, so I headed around the side of the chamber group's tent.

Here, the sun came slantwise through the trees across the road and made long gold stripes of light across the grass. I walked along one of the gold stripes, watching my incredibly tall shadow walking before me. I hadn't gone far along the stripes when I smelled herbs.

The scent was so strong and came on so quickly that I checked the ground under my sandals to see if I had crushed something. There was nothing but clover beneath my feet. But the leaves caught my eye, and I crouched. Sure enough, there was a bunch of four-leaf clovers, a few among many three-leaf. I picked one and straightened up, looking at it. For luck.

"I heard you play."

I blinked and focused beyond the clover. Unnoticed by me, a young man with ginger hair had approached. His face was a riot of freckles, but he was still amazingly handsome – like a magazine ad. He had the beautiful, cared-for look of kids with trust funds.

I wasn't sure how to reply, so I just said, "You did?"

He ducked around me in a circle, as if studying me. "Yes." He circled again; I spun to keep my eyes on him. "Very impressive. Quite better than I expected."

Better than he expected for *what*? For a girl? For a student? For a harpist? For me?

"Thanks," I said, voice guarded. He circled again, a smile on his face. I got another whiff of the herbal scent, and I had an idea that it must be him. Something he was wearing.

"Quite impressive altogether."

I asked politely, "Did you play?"

He grinned. "Do I ever stop?"

He kept circling, ceaselessly moving, and then his smile changed in some subtle way that made my stomach drop to my feet. "You smell good."

A familiar voice made me spin the other direction. "Deirdre."

Luke grabbed my hand abruptly, knocking the clover out of it as he did. Relieved to be rescued, I said, "I'm glad you're here. This guy—" I turned to look at the weirdo, but there was nothing there, only the lingering scent of rosemary or thyme. There were a dozen places he could've hidden as soon as my back was turned. It only meant that he really had been up to no good. Why else would he hide? "There was a guy right here."

Luke looked behind me. "There's nobody there." His eyes narrowed. "*Nobody*."

Goosebumps prickled on my skin. It would've been easy to just believe Luke, but the freckled boy was impossible to forget. "There was," I said unhappily. "Some freak."

"I don't doubt it," Luke said loudly. "C'mon. Let's get back to civilization. What were you doing way out here, anyway?"

I glanced around. All my spinning had taken me

surprisingly far from the tents. The chamber music was only a faint music-box sound from here. "I – I was just trying to get away from my annoying aunt."

"Well, let's get closer to her and further from invisible freaks," Luke suggested. He turned me with the barest touch on the small of my back and we headed towards the noise. "I like your dress, by the way. Suits you."

I secretly preened, then surprised myself by saying, "I know."

Luke said, "It's not polite to gloat," but he grinned. "So, tell me about your annoying aunt."

I sighed as we approached the food tent. "That would be her, over there. Aggravating my mom by the food tent."

He stood with me and quietly observed Delia and Mom. I was beginning to like that about him. He listened. He watched. "She's quite awful, isn't she?"

"The sort of aunt that's in storybooks," I said. "If they put evil aunts in storybooks. She and my mom have never got along."

Even from here, I could hear Delia's loud voice as she told someone how Mom had been quite talented in her youth, but had never done anything with it. *Bitch*, I thought uncharitably.

"I just thought a very uncharitable thing about a family member," I admitted.

Luke leaned in, close enough that I could smell his faintly musky odour – nothing like a herb, nothing like any high-school boy – and whispered, "Did it start with a *B*? I thought it, too."

I laughed, loud enough that Delia looked up at me. She made motions for me to come over, but I pretended to be looking past her into the food tent. "Hurry. Pretend you're pointing something out so I can pretend to not see her."

Luke put a hand on my shoulder and pointed with the other towards the sky. "Look, the moon."

"That was the best you could come up with?" I demanded. But I looked at it anyway – pale, mysterious, hanging in blue instead of black. Once again I felt I could look at it for ever, or at least until I could remember why I wanted to look at it. "It's beautiful, though, isn't it?"

I didn't think he was looking at the moon any more, but he said, "Very."

I kept gazing up. "This will sound stupid, but – it makes me feel funny." The same way Luke made me feel funny.

"That's because it's from the night. The night keeps secrets."

Luke kept secrets as well, didn't he? Secrets we both pretended he didn't have.

"Very poetic."

"I can be very literary when I want to be. I'm a very complex person. Like yourself, I have hidden depths."

I looked down. "Awww, you think I have hidden depths? That's awfully sweet." His eyes shifted from me to a point just behind me, and I turned to see what he saw.

A very tall, very blonde woman was approaching us with a modelesque stride. She was as fair as an Easter lily, with perfect blue eyes and a perfect snowy neck. My dress suddenly felt shabby.

"Eleanor," Luke said, face expressionless.

"Luke. How wonderful to see you again." She placed her hands on his shoulders and kissed him on the cheek, running a finger down to his chin. I looked away. "It seems like for ever."

"Yes."

"Well, you're not in a very good mood tonight, are you?" Eleanor said. "I'd have thought you'd be in heaven with all this good music."

Luke didn't reply.

"Especially you, Deirdre. You played beautifully. We *all* were amazed by how you played."

I looked up at the sound of my name and was blinded by her radiant smile. Still, for all her beauty, it was just another compliment. "Thanks. Luke helped a lot."

Eleanor turned her smile to Luke, who still had that strange, expressionless face. "Oh yes, Luke helps out a lot." She smiled at him. "Luke, dear, you don't believe in small talk?"

Luke's voice was flat. "How's work."

She laughed. It was annoyingly beautiful. "Going *very* well."

He raised an eyebrow. "How's the boss?"

Eleanor studied her gently sculpted nails. "Oh, more like a co-worker these days, I should say."

"That must be thrilling."

"The masses appreciate someone like them." She gestured to herself. "Someone like me."

Luke said, "How lucky for both of you."

"Oh, I think so, lamb." She turned to me. "Well, you're certainly a rising star. I'll be watching you."

Beside me, Luke stiffened.

"It was very nice to meet you, Deirdre. Have a lovely evening." She touched Luke's cheek again. "And I'll see you again, Luke."

After she'd gone, I looked at Luke, biting my lip before speaking. "Ex-girlfriend?"

Luke's eyes widened and he laughed. "That," he said, "would be a terrible thing to wish on a man. No. Remember that storybook that would have Delia in it? Eleanor belongs in it as well. Think of her as an evil godmother."

I relaxed. I shouldn't be thinking of Luke that way at all, considering how long I'd known him. But still, the idea of having Eleanor as competition had momentarily floored me.

"Evil godmother is much better than ex-girlfriend."
What makes you so different, Luke, that I should give a rat's butt either way?

Luke glanced over at me. "Oh yeah?"

I looked away, losing my bravado, and nodded shyly. "Yeah."

I became aware that the speakers from the awards tent had been blaring for quite some time. "Second place in solo performance to Carmen Macy." There was polite clapping from behind us.

We walked silently over to Mom, and stopped when we realized that she was speaking to someone and that Delia had gone quite still.

"—I heard her play this evening, and I just wanted to say that I am quite blown away by her talent. She and her friend are just the sort of people we're looking for. Please, please, take my card and do give us a call."

I looked at the man who was speaking. His pleasant voice belied his image, which was that of a bare-knuckle fighter. Though he was wearing a shirt, the sleeves couldn't hide his enormous biceps and muscled chest. He wasn't like any school representative I'd ever imagined.

"First prize in ensemble goes to Andrew Manx, Tina Chin—" the speaker blared, but Mom's voice seemed louder. "Well, thanks. We'll definitely take a look."

Mr Gigantic Muscles gave me a small nod before looking back to Delia and Mom. "Well, I know you've had a long day, so I'll let you go get a well-deserved rest. They should be announcing the grand prize very soon, shouldn't they? Enjoy the reception."

Mom exchanged a look with me and then stared at Delia after the man had gone.

There was more clapping behind us as awards were read. I was surprised to find that I didn't really care if I won anything. The competition seemed so insignificant – so ordinary – in comparison to the here and now, standing next to Luke and looking at the business card the conservatory representative had left.

"Thornking-Ash," Delia read from the card. She sniffed. "Sounds like a funeral home."

I sniffed, too, but only because I smelled the same herbal smell as before. Was that freak still here?

Luke was at my elbow, saying, "I think I'm going to have to leave early. I think I might have to go *now*."

I was about to protest or beg unabashedly for his number when I realized the clapping had gone quiet. The voice crackled on the speaker. "Ladies and gentlemen, it's six o'clock, and as promised, we're going to announce the winners of the grand prize. Thank you everyone for competing and sharing your talent with us. The judges would like to congratulate the grand prize winners for this year's arts festival – Deirdre Monaghan and Luke Dilling."

Luke whispered into my ear, close enough that his lips brushed my hair. "Tell me you want to see me again."

I smiled.

Three

"Hey psycho, what's up?"

I rolled back on to my bed, cradling the phone on my shoulder. "Nothing much." I caught sight of the clock on my bedstand and groaned. "James, it's not really ten o'clock, is it?" He didn't have to answer. I could tell from the fierceness of the sun coming through the white curtains that it was late.

"I hear," James said, "that introverts have to sleep a lot after stressful encounters with people."

I sat up. "That's true." It was also true that I'd spent way too much time last night unable to sleep. Thinking about winning the whole freakin' grand prize of the competition. Thinking about Luke. Thinking about Thornking-Ash. Mostly thinking about Luke. I didn't mention that part to James.

"So. Today's your birthday." James made a sound like he was chewing something. "Sorry, hangnail. Anyway. Today! The celebration of the first day you screamed."

"*Yesterday* was my birthday," I corrected, getting out of bed. I pulled a T-shirt out of a drawer and found some jeans, cradling the phone on my shoulder. "I'm getting old." I checked my trousers from the day before for any money, and instead found the four-leaf clover that had been stuck to my phone. *Good luck.*

"You were busy yesterday. I'm designating today your birthday. You can't stop me."

"OK, fine. It's my birthday. Want to make something of it?"

"Actually, your mom already did. In typical overbearing fashion, she's invited me and my parents to your house for dinner and cake this evening. Normally, this is the part where I'd complain bitterly about how you let your mom arrange your life for you, but since I really like her food, I'm not going to say anything."

I made a face. Trust Mom to throw me a kiddie party. She'd apparently missed the memo where I officially became an adult, or maybe the memo that said you don't arrange a teenager's birthday like a catering event. Come to think of it, I think she missed most memos.

"Boy, thanks, Mom," I said.

"Well, you could just tell her you wanted to hang out with me unofficially," James suggested. "You're the birthday girl. Snap the fingers. Make it happen."

Ha. Make it happen. It reminded me of Luke yesterday, of what he'd said. *You know how some people can do anything? They want something, they make it happen.*

"I like that idea better," I said slowly, distracted. I set the clover down on my bedside table, studying it – the way the sun cast a perfectly clover-shaped shadow behind it. "But you do like her food." I cupped my hand on the edge of the table, a few centimetres away from the clover.

James moaned. "Oh, it pushes me over the edge, baby."

Some people can do anything. Come here, clover.

The clover fluttered in an invisible wind. Then, leaves billowing out like a miniature ship, it scuttled across the desk into my palm.

Oh crap.

"What, not even a laugh for that? Wow, you're never allowed to sleep late again. You're crankier than a fat guy in stilettos."

James's voice brought me back to reality. It made me realize that the air-conditioning vents in the room were roaring; the central air had just kicked in. The blast from the vent had sent the clover rushing into my hand. Nothing more.

I was oddly relieved.

"Dee?"

"What – yeah – no – sorry." Movement caught my eye from my window. Down below, an unfamiliar car was pulling into the driveway. "I'm really sorry, James, but I'm totally crazy right now. I think I need breakfast or caffeine or something. Can I call you back?"

"Yeah, of course. I've got practice today, but I'll be around this afternoon." His voice was concerned. "Are you OK?"

I bit my lip. I had never kept anything from him before. *Duh, you're not keeping anything from him now, either. There's nothing to keep.* "I'm OK. I'm just like you said: all introverted and worn out."

His tone warmed slightly. "Poor Dee. Go get victuals. I'll be round when you need me." The phone clicked and I went closer to the window, pulling the curtain to the side to see who it was. I jumped slightly as I realized the driver of the car was looking up at *me*, craning his head out the window. Luke. How the hell did he know where I lived? Did I care?

I scurried away from the window and tore off my T-shirt. A quick and untidy dig through my closet netted a better shirt. I'd keep the jeans. They made my butt look awesome. I put the clover back in my pocket and tore down the stairs, where I encountered the first defensive lineman: Delia.

"That flute player is here. Who is he, anyway?"

Good question.

"Luke Dillon," I said. I tried to edge past her into the kitchen but she followed, coffee cup in hand. Caffeine was her secret weapon. To foil Delia was to separate her from her coffee. It wasn't going to happen in time to save me this morning.

"Does he go to your school?"

My lie wouldn't have convinced Mom, but it worked for Delia. "He has friends there."

"He was quite good-looking."

True enough.

Mom's voice sounded from the kitchen – more defenders, not good – and Delia shuttled me in to be finished off for good. "Who's good-looking?" Mom was holding the coffee pot; she refilled Delia's cup, not realizing that she was topping off Delia's head-demoness powers by doing so. I tried to see out, past the yellow-chequered curtains above the sink.

"The flute player who just pulled into the driveway," Delia replied.

Mom spun towards the window. "I didn't see anyone come up! He hasn't knocked, has he?"

I said firmly, "I'm going outside."

Mom pointed to the counter as I was leaving. "Did you want to keep that? Dad found it on your harp case last night when he was bringing it in from the car."

It was a four-leaf clover, sitting on the counter next to the toaster. Like the other two I'd found, it was perfect – all leaves symmetrical – and completely unwilted despite its overnight stay in the car.

"It's not a hard question, Deirdre." Mom pulled her standing mixer out of the cabinet and set it on the counter, no doubt preparing for my birthday cake. "You could press it in a book if you want it to stay nice."

I didn't *know* if I wanted it to stay nice but I took it

anyway, twirling the stem between my fingers. I had a prickling sensation in my stomach but I couldn't tell what it was. Excitement? Fear? Hunger?

"Yeah, maybe." I went outside to meet Luke.

He was crouching by the door of his car, eyes squinted in the white-hot sun, looking at my dog, Rye. Despite Rye's unusual colour – chalky white body and crimson red ears – he's a typical hound dog: loyal, loving, and friendly to everyone in the world.

Which is why his raised hackles stopped me in my tracks. Lying in the front yard, his head so low that it barely cleared the grass, Rye was staring at Luke, his lips raised almost into a snarl. Luke was calling to him in a soft voice, the pattern of it hypnotic and lulling. I guess his words could have been in a lot of different languages – but English wasn't one of them.

Luke saw my approach and straightened. He was wearing the same jeans as before, but his shirt today was a dark V-neck that accentuated the paleness of his hair and eyes. "Hello, lovely. You're pretty as pretty today."

My cheeks warmed. "What are you doing here?"

He shrugged with a smile. "Satisfying my curiosity." His pale blue eyes dropped to the clover still in my fingers and somehow he lost his smile. "Where did you get that?"

"My mom found it. Aren't they supposed to bring good luck?"

"And other things." Luke gestured at Rye. "This beast yours?"

His tone was affectionate, though Rye gave him no reason to be — he was still crouched in the grass, hair spiked stiffly on his shoulders.

"Rye. Yeah. He's ancient. We've had him as long as I can remember, but I don't think I've ever seen him like this."

"He looks like a good dog." Luke's face was turned from me as he said it, but his voice sounded wistful. "Like a clever dog."

"He is."

We both started at the sound of the kitchen door opening. Delia called out, "Why don't you both come inside? It's hot out there!" An interrogation session was clearly in the making.

Before I could reply, Luke shouted, "Back in an hour! We're getting ice cream!"

I looked at him intently.

"You wanted saving, didn't you?" he said.

I didn't know how to reply. I'd never had any real experience with boys in high school and I had a feeling that even if I had, none of it would have applied to Luke Dillon.

Luke took out his keys — no key fob, I noticed, but plenty of keys. Fifteen or twenty of them. My own key ring had two keys and a fob shaped like a fish. I wondered if your key ring said something about you.

"Let me go get my money," I said finally.

Luke opened the passenger side door for me. "I'm buying. Sorry about the car. It looks bad, but the fumes usually stay on the outside."

I hesitated for just a minute before getting into the old Audi. Inside the car it was hot and airless, despite the fact that Luke had only just got out of it, and the seats were of the soft, blue, fuzzy variety that I remembered from all of my grandmother's cars. It smelled like Luke inside; the same smell I remembered when he leaned close yesterday. The memory sent another prickling through my stomach.

Luke climbed into the other side of the car and turned knobs and hit buttons as deftly as he'd played the flute; soon, cool air was wafting from the vents. It reminded me of the four-leaf clover, fluttering into my hand earlier. I shivered.

"Too cold?" He turned it down and, as if reading my thoughts, looked at the four-leaf clover I still held. "You don't need that."

As he backed out of the driveway, I set the clover on the dash and looked at it. "Everyone needs good luck."

"Not you, Dee. You manage it all by yourself. Quite impressively." He paused at the end of the driveway, rolled down the window, and flung the clover into the road. "Where's a good place to get ice cream?"

"You're chucking my luck," I said. "And actually, I work at an ice cream shop."

"Sweet!" Luke paused. "Too cheesy?"

I laughed, too late. "I didn't realize you were trying to be funny."

Luke groaned as he turned right out of the driveway. "You wound me deeply with your careless words: '*Trying to be*'."

I grinned at him. "You'll just have to *try* harder."

"Duly noted. Now, how do I get to this place?"

"You're heading the right way already. It's about a mile up here, on the left. Dave's Ice." *But you knew that already, didn't you?* I looked hard at him, and he looked back at me with an equally intent look before turning his eyes to the road.

"I thought I remembered seeing it when I came in," he said. "I remember thinking it was an ice cream day."

Of course it was an ice cream day. Why shouldn't it be? It struck me that we'd come to a strange unspoken agreement. He pretended to be normal and I pretended I believed him. I *wanted* to believe him. But I couldn't. What brand of abnormal, I wasn't sure yet. I just hoped it didn't involve axes, gags, and the trunk of a car.

Outside, the air looked wavy and greasy as it came up from the tarmac. The heat hung heavy in the tree tops, weighing down the leaves so that the only movement was that of automobiles, roaring slowly past them on the two-lane road. It was a day to do nothing practical, summer at its most stifling.

"Here," I said unnecessarily, and Luke turned into

the car park of Dave's Ice. It felt like I'd pulled in here a million times before. In a lot of ways, I'd learned more here than I had at school.

Luke looked at the squat, concrete-block building and parked in one of the shaded spots at the back of the car park. "Why is it called Dave's Ice?"

"Well, they used to sell just ice to people, way back in the old days, before fridges, I guess. Then, ice, now, ice cream. Makes sense, doesn't it? A sort of logical leap?"

"Do you like it?"

I was taken aback by the question. I didn't remember anyone ever asking me that question about anything before. "I do. This'll sound dumb, but I love making all the scoops perfect. You know, centre the hot fudge, just the right number of swirls to the whipped cream, sprinkles go on in the right order so they stick perfectly. . ." I stopped, because he was laughing. *"What?"*

"So you're saying you've been a perfectionist for quite a while, then."

"Oh, shut up," I told him crossly. "Are we getting ice cream or not?"

He turned off the car, seemingly unfazed by my tone. "I've never seen anyone get angry as quickly as you. Come along, my frosty queen."

"I'm not frosty," I protested, but I got out and followed him across the car park. The heat rose off the tarmac, burning my feet through the soles of my shoes. "I *am* curious, though."

Luke's face was inscrutable. He stepped on to one of the painted lines on the ground, carefully moving along it. I stepped on to it after him, my steps as measured as a gymnast's, as if it were a balance beam and I might fall to my death.

"Curious about four-leaf clovers," I persisted. "About them being good luck. And other things, you said. What other things are they good for?"

"Feeding horses?"

Jerk. He couldn't hint at things and then play hard to get. It wasn't fair. "What *else*?"

His voice was level. "Scaring snakes."

"What else?"

"Curing scorpion bites."

"What else?"

"Seeing faeries," Luke said. He jumped from the painted line up on to the pavement. "Phew. Made it." Then he took my hand and tugged me up after him. "Now stop being so clever and let's get some ice cream."

I wasn't going to let him get away with that. I stopped outside the door. "Clever how?"

He wagged a finger at me. "It's what I like about you. You listen. You watch. It's how you learned to do everything so well, while everyone else talked over the top of everyone else. Now, would you please stop riddling me for half a moment so we can get some ice cream?"

I relented, though my heart thumped as he led me

into the freezing air-conditioning. Not normal. Not ordinary. I knew I should be running back home this second, but I was stuck. Stuck as stuck, Luke would say.

As he looked at the menu board, I said, "I never thought I'd be the sort that went for bad boys."

Luke didn't look at me, but he smiled widely, the biggest smile he'd worn all day. "No more riddling, remember? What's good here?"

I'd eaten enough ice cream in place of meals to answer immediately. "Chocolate Dream."

Sara Madison, a wine-bottle-shaped redhead who occasionally worked with me, was at the counter. She looked at Luke with considerable interest. "Can I help you?"

He politely asked for two Chocolate Dream cones and Sara, with no acknowledgement of my presence, obligingly began to scoop, smiling at him all the while. I leaned on the counter and pretended not to be annoyed. She always flirted with any remotely attractive male who entered the shop and Luke more than qualified. It wasn't a personal attack. And if Luke was worth anything at all, he wouldn't rise to the occasion. Still, I couldn't help but glance over to see what effect the gigantically endowed Sara's attentions were having on him. His face had the same mild expression as usual as he counted out six one-dollar bills, but I saw a glimpse of that private smile right before he took a step to close the gap between us.

"You've got something on your shoulder." While Sara watched, he lightly ran a finger across the skin of my shoulder up to my ear. My stomach dropped so far out from under me that I didn't think I was ever going to get it back.

He said softly, "I think I got it." Then he turned to Sara, taking the cones. "You can keep the change. Let's eat outside, Dee."

Sara's smile had vanished and she turned abruptly to begin cleaning the milkshake machine. I wondered if she'd say anything about it to me later. But I wondered more if Luke would ever touch me again.

Gesturing with his chin towards the door, Luke led me back outside into the unbearable sunshine. The parking space beside his car was empty; we sat down on the concrete barrier at the head of the space. In the dappled shade and holding an ice cream cone, it was almost pleasant.

I said, "Something on my shoulder, huh?"

Luke smiled and licked his cone. "You wanted saving, didn't you?"

"You can't just go and do that to a girl without warning. It's not fair. I could've fallen down or something."

His voice bordered on smug. "You liked it?"

Cheeks hot, I studied the glistening drops of ice cream forming on the edge of my cone. "What a stupid question."

"I'm new to this. I've never tried exercising this particular repertoire of skills. I'm thrilled that I learned something from watching chick flicks."

I *so* wanted to believe him, and I *so* didn't. "You've had girlfriends before."

He shook his head. "No one's ever inspired me to mend my evil ways. May I practise on you?"

It was petty, but I was instantly irritated by the word "practise". I didn't want to be anyone's practice. "No, you may not."

He sighed. "See, you are clever. Very well. Do you mind if I stick around for a while, anyway? You fascinate me and I want to know why."

"'Fascinate' is a very strong term," I said. "Plants fascinate horticulturists. Stars fascinate astronomers. Bugs fascinate – uh – bugologists. I don't know if I want to be studied. I don't know if I'm *worth* being studied."

Luke considered. "Well, of course you're worth being studied. You're extraordinary at everything you do. Without any external influence. You're extraordinary at everything you do just because you *try* to be. No superpowers. Just hard work. It's quite amazing. Oh, I've done it again, haven't I? You're pissed off at me again."

I had tried to keep the look off my face, but I couldn't. He was wrong though; I wasn't angry, I was disappointed. For once I didn't want someone to look at everything I could do and be awed. I wanted someone to just see *me*, what made me *me*, and be fascinated. I was so tired of hearing how great and amazing I was from people who would never know anything about me. I had let myself believe all this time that the real me was what Luke was flirting with, not the me destined for CD covers and exceptional alumni lists.

"God, you're so pissed off that you're not even talking!" Luke moved closer on the barrier to get a better look at my face. "I've really put my foot in it now, haven't I? I don't even know what I said."

My voice was half the strength it was supposed to be, which I hated. How in the world had he reduced me to tears? "I – I'm just so tired of people telling me how talented I am. I'd like to be amazing even if I was the most untalented person in the world. All anybody ever sees when they see me is the stupid harp. They never see who I really am."

Luke reached up a thumb and gently swiped away the single tear that had managed to escape. "Don't cry, pretty girl. Who you really are is why you're so good at everything. You won't let yourself be otherwise. And *that's* what fascinates me."

Part of me wanted his hand to linger on my face, but pride and embarrassment made me knock it away. *Fragile* wasn't an image I liked to wear. "I don't normally cry. I mean, unless I'm frustrated. I feel so—" I struggled for words and for dignity.

He said softly, "Your ice cream's melting."

Relieved, I turned back to my cone. We sat in silence

for long moments, finishing our ice cream. Then I said, without looking at him, "If I still fascinate you, you can study me for a while. But I won't be 'practice'."

"Thank you." He wrestled his keys from his back pocket and laid them on his leg, swallowing the last of his cone.

Without thinking first, I asked, "Is that a key for every secret?" Immediately I feared I'd violated our unspoken agreement and that he would vanish in a poof of smoke.

But he didn't seem concerned by the question. Instead, he smiled vaguely and said, "Possibly. How many keys do you have?"

"Two."

"Is that how many secrets you have?"

I thought about it. One for the clover on the bedside stand. One for the way I felt about Luke. "Yes."

His fingers toyed with his keys. "Would you like another?"

I didn't answer, but I watched him slide a key from his too-full ring. It was a small, heavy, old-fashioned key, with a spot of rust on one side. He glanced around as if someone might care what we were doing, and then pushed the iron key into my hand. Putting his lips right up against my ear, his breath hotter than the summer day, he whispered, "Here is another secret: I have no business being fascinated by you."

His lips almost formed into a kiss. Then he pulled

away quickly and stood up. I was dizzy and had to close my eyes for a moment to reorient myself. I put the key in my pocket.

Holding out a hand, Luke pulled me to my feet and led me to the other side of the car, his eyes distant and his face preoccupied.

Before he shut the passenger door behind me, I briefly smelled a snatch of herbal fragrance in the summer air, quite apart from Luke's odour or the usual tarmac stench of Dave's parking lot. And then I realized I *did* have a third secret to go with my key: there was some sort of danger gathering around me. But I wasn't afraid.

"Oh, Granna's here." I peered over the dashboard as Luke pulled into the driveway. Her white Ford was so bright in the noon sun that I couldn't look directly at it. "Mom must've invited her over for my birthday."

"Birthday?" Luke switched off the car. "Today?"

"Actually yesterday, but I get cake today." I tried to keep the hopeful edge out of my voice. "Want to stay for it?"

"Hmm." Luke got out of the car and came around to open my door. "I shouldn't. It does sound terribly interesting, though. Will your awful aunt be here?"

I frowned. "She's already here. She's doesn't go home until next week. When her concert tour starts."

"Very posh."

I grunted in agreement and then turned as movement caught my eye: Granna getting out of her car. She immediately caught sight of me and smiled. Then she dove back into her car.

Luke looked puzzled. "Handbag?"

"Granna doesn't carry a handbag. She's not that sort of grandmother. Probably presents."

Sure enough, Granna emerged holding an impossibly small, wrapped package in one hand and a gigantic one in the other. "Could you take one of these, Deirdre?"

I jumped out of the car and hurried to take the larger one from her. Hanging back at my elbow, Luke moved restlessly, like a wolf.

"This is Luke, Granna." I stepped to the side. "He played in the competition yesterday."

Luke stilled and held out a hand, formally. "How do you do."

Granna let him take her right hand, and he kissed it – a gesture, oddly enough, that seemed both natural and appropriate.

"Do you see this, young man?" Granna held up her left hand, where a dull, silver-coloured ring and a gold wedding band sat together on her still-strong ring finger.

Luke smiled wanly. "I do, ma'am."

I frowned at them.

Granna thrust the small package into Luke's face, her voice lowered as if I weren't standing right beside him. "What do you think she's getting from me for her birthday present, eh? And what are you doing here again?"

I looked to Luke for his answer, hoping for some clue as to what this conversation was about, but he stayed silent, just looking at Granna.

"Don't you even think of it." Granna took a step closer to him. I had the sense of a small dog barking at a sleeping lion.

"Hey," I started, not even sure what I ought to say to defuse this weirdly combative situation.

Luke spoke as if I hadn't, sounding humble. "I'm just here for a little while, ma'am."

Granna's voice was sharp. "Good. Then go back where you belong."

"I'm not one of Them," he said plaintively.

"I can smell Them on you. You reek of it."

Luke turned from Granna to me, his expression flat. "I don't think I'll be staying for cake."

Furiously, I turned my shoulder towards Granna and crossed my arms. "You don't have to go." *Just because Granna had to stick her nose into it. Ruin everything.* I was so angry with her I was afraid I would say something I'd regret. I could feel her eyes boring into my back.

Luke glanced at Granna again. "I think it's better this way. Thanks for the ice cream."

"*Luke.*" I couldn't even think of what to say. All that was in my head was *damn it, why does everyone else control my life?* "Don't go."

He looked at me with a weird expression I couldn't read, then retreated to his car. In a moment, all evidence that he existed was gone, and I didn't even have his phone number. I also didn't even have a clue why he was gone.

Well, I had *some* clue. I turned back to Granna, caught between anger and loss. "Granna. Why?"

She glared at the road as if Luke's presence lingered, and then she handed me the small present. "You should open this one."

"I don't want to open any presents right now."

She smiled firmly – a humourless smile that was ironically like Luke's – and held the package out. "Open it, please."

Sighing, I set down the large present and took the little one from her. Tearing off the patterned blue paper, I found a little jewellery box, but when I opened it, its white satin centre was empty. I looked up at Granna, quizzical.

She slid the dull ring, the one she'd shown Luke, from her finger and laid it in the box. "It was my mother's, and her grandmother's before. And now it's yours. I suspected you were old enough to need it and now I'm sure."

No, what I *needed* was Luke back in the driveway and Granna to be normal for once. I looked at the ring. I didn't like jewellery anyway, but even if I did, this ring was pretty darn ugly.

I said, my voice icy, "Uh, thanks."

"Put it on," Granna said. "You'll thank me later."

I put it on my right-hand ring finger and Granna's smile became genuine. "Thank *you*. Now, I'm going to get out of the heat and go see my frantic daughter and my scheming daughter." She took the large package and headed indoors.

I stayed outside, staring down at the ring on my finger. I was curiously close to tears, which is how James found me five minutes later when he pulled into the driveway. Where Luke's car had just been.

He came to me and took my arms. "What are you doing?"

"Being pushed around."

"Let's go inside and talk about it."

With Delia and Mom and Granna? "Let's not."

As if to illustrate my point, Delia's voice rose from the kitchen window. James glanced at the window and then back to me. "OK. Into the shade, at least?"

I agreed and we walked into the back garden. Knees pulled up, I sat against one of the massive oaks, its broad trunk shielding me from the view of the house. James sat down in front of me, his knees nearly touching mine. For a long moment he just looked at me, serious. I was so taken aback by this side of him that I almost blurted out everything that had just happened.

But James spoke first. "I have a confession to make."

My heart lurched. I had a horrible idea of what he

was going to say, and I wanted to cover my ears. *Don't, James. You're my best friend.*

He didn't say it. Instead, he said, "I'm a little psychic." He paused. "You may laugh now. But only a little bit. Fifteen seconds is probably appropriate, without being rudely disbelieving."

I didn't laugh. "I believe you."

"Oh. Well, that makes it easier, doesn't it?" James glanced towards the house and pushed his fingers through his auburn hair. "Mind you, I'm not a very good psychic. But I get hunches, and they turn out right. And weird feelings when it's going to be a weird day. Not very often. Peter says it happens to him too." Peter was James's older brother, on pilgrimage in California to find fame and fortune with his rock band. James idolized him, and I thought he was pretty cool, too – maybe the only other non-family member besides James that I could talk to.

James chewed his lip before continuing. "Yesterday was weird. And today was weird, too. I had a hunch I'd find you upset, so I left practice early. What's going on?"

All of a sudden, it seemed stupid not to have told him everything from the beginning. So I told him. I left out the bits where Luke had touched me, and the feeling of Luke's lips on my ear, but the rest I told him, as best as I could remember.

He took the key when I offered it, and the ring from my finger, and studied both. "They're both iron.

Isn't that funny?"

"Funny 'haha' or funny 'strange'?"

James handed them back. "Funny 'occult'."

"Ah. Funny 'strange'."

James looked at me sternly. "Don't start that. I'm supposed to be the humorous one." He watched me put the ring back on and pocket the key again. "Iron's supposed to be a ward against evil supernatural creatures, if you're into that magic druid crap."

I couldn't help goading him. "If it's magic druid crap, why do you know about it?"

"A man should be well educated."

"Well, Granna *is* into that," I pointed out. "She's into all that holistic/natural/spiritual stuff. Cosmic debris. She once told me the colour of my aura."

"Mine's tartan," James said. He took my hand in his written-upon ones and turned the ring on my finger, absently. It reminded me of Luke's hand on mine, earlier. *How can two hands feel so different?* "And the clover? The one that you moved this morning? Do you still have it?"

"*Thought* I moved," I corrected, and shook my head. "Yeah." I shifted my weight so I could pull it from my pocket.

"So move it."

I looked hard at him.

"Well, if you can't move it, like you said, it won't move, and you won't have to worry about it any more, will you? But if it does – well, then you're a freak." James grinned. He plucked the slightly crushed clover from my finger and set it in the sparse grass beneath the tree. "Go, go, magic clover."

"I feel foolish." I did. We were like two kids hunched over a Ouija board, part of us hoping for something strange to happen, proving the world a mysterious place, and the rest of us hoping desperately for nothing to happen, proving the world safe and free of monsters. I cupped my hand, like earlier that morning, making a little goal for the clover to shoot into. "Come on, clover."

A breeze kissed the sweat on my forehead. The clover tumbled end-over-end into my hand.

James closed his eyes. "It makes me cold when you do that."

"It was the breeze." *It was just the breeze.*

He shook his head, and opened his eyes again. "I always get cold when I get one of my weird feelings, and that just about hit glacier-cold on the weirdness chart. Do it again. You'll see. Next to my leg, where there's no breeze."

I picked up the clover and set it down in the shadow of his leg. Cupping my hand, I said faintly, "Come on, clover." The clover and several other leaves rustled, and then skipped across the ground into my hand. A huge, dry collection of leaves, the colour of summer, pressed against my fingers.

"Telekinesis." James's voice was as soft as the rustling of the leaves, and when I looked at him, I could see goosebumps standing out on his tanned legs. "Suddenly the world seems a lot more interesting."

What it seemed was a lot less ordinary.

Four

Tuesday. Wednesday. Two days crawled by. James came round, but he wasn't who I wanted to see. I might be able to move spoons without touching them and make clover sail like tiny ships across my bedstand, but I couldn't bring back what Granna had driven off. Nor could I vanquish the little voice that said he'd been driven off fairly easily.

"Deirdre, you haven't practised for days." Mom pushed open the door of my room and frowned. I was lying on my back, studying the ceiling, and the techno CD James had given me for my birthday was shaking every flat surface in the room in time with the bass line. Mom turned off the stereo. "I didn't know you liked that sort of stuff."

"I do now." It came out sounding recalcitrant, but it was actually true. I'd never listened to techno before, but I was a sucker for good music of any sort. And the pounding monotony of the tracks perfectly matched what was going on in my head. Time passing for absolutely no reason whatsoever.

Mom opened the door wide. "Don't be sour. Go practise. Get out of this room. You make me nervous when you aren't *doing* something."

"Fine, whatever. I'll practise. I'm going outside to do it, though."

"It's almost dark, you know."

I slid off the bed. I didn't want to sit inside and have an ordinary night practising. "Cooler."

She followed me downstairs and watched me gather up my harp, then trailed me to the back door. Abruptly, she bent down and picked something off the kitchen floor. "Deirdre, I told you to press these things in a book if you want to keep them. I'm tired of picking them up." She stuffed a four-leaf clover into my hand.

Good for driving away snakes. Curing scorpion bites. Seeing faeries.

Feeling rebellious, I pulled off Granna's iron ring and set it on the counter before I went outside. Maybe I didn't *want* evil supernatural beings scared away tonight. Maybe the person I wanted to see qualified as one.

Outside, it was all the rich golds and dull blues of twilight, with long shadows cutting across the garden in the shapes of spectral trees. Fireflies glowed in the tall grass on the edge of the garden, and a mourning dove called, low and sad and beautiful. I found a seat on the crook of a tree and leaned my harp against my shoulder. I didn't know what to play, so I just let a little lonesome tune escape from the strings. I really ought to have played an *I'm a Pining Idiot* tune instead.

Mysterious. Extraordinary. That's what I wanted. I began to play a slow reel, "The Maids of Mitchelltown", a tune that promised mystery. The wind lifted the leaves of the trees; it was scented with mown grass, flowers, and thyme.

My fingers stilled and I lifted my head, catching the breeze again. I wondered if I'd imagined the smell. But no, the scent of thyme was undoubtedly there. Not only there, but getting stronger. I squinted at the shadows around me, trying to catch the direction, but it was impossible.

A shadow flicked across one of the bright strips of evening sun and I jerked to look at it. There was nothing there. Then, between two of the oaks at the edge of the yard, I saw a form. The face looked at me and smiled – red-haired, freckled, reeking of thyme.

The kid from the reception. I blinked, and in that second, he was next to a beech tree, three metres closer. My skin crawled.

"Beautiful night."

The voice was right beside me.

In the second it took for my blood to run hot with adrenaline, I swung a hard fist, feeling skin beneath my knuckles.

"God," groaned Luke from next to me. "Remind me never to sneak up on you."

My breath caught in my throat. I suppose I should've felt embarrassed, but I was too overwhelmed that it was *Luke*. I laughed in amazement. "I thought you were that freaky guy from the reception."

He stepped into the light, rubbing his jaw. "No, I'm not. Well, I am *a* guy from the reception." His light hair picked up the gold of the evening and lent him a brilliant halo. He looked at where the four-leaf clover sat on my leg and took it, making a face. "Why do you seem to always have these with you?"

"Why does it always seem to bother you?" I immediately regretted saying it. The last thing I wanted to do was to drive him away again by violating the rules. "I thought you were gone for good."

Luke crouched next to me. He looked over at the beech tree where the ginger-haired boy had been, his eyes intent, then dragged his gaze back to my face. "You sound so sad, pretty girl."

I looked away, pretending to pout to cover up how I'd felt the past two days. "I *was* so sad."

"I thought I was gone for good, as well." He settled down, cross-legged, and set his flute case across his lap. "Unfortunately, I'm still fascinated. May I play with you?"

"Even though I punched you?"

"Despite that. Though you didn't say sorry."

"You partially deserved it, for leaving without any warning." I grinned and put my fingers on the strings.

Luke lifted the flute. "After you."

I began to play "The Maids of Mitchelltown" again, and Luke jumped in immediately, recognizing the common tune. Funny how much difference two instead of one made. With both of us playing, the reel was so beautiful I could have got lost in the threads of melody we wove.

Luke's eyes were far away as we played, staring at the beech tree near the edge of the garden, though there was nothing there. I abruptly remembered the freckled kid again – somehow, Luke's presence made me forget everything but Luke – but there was no sight of him. I didn't want to think about what could have happened if Luke hadn't arrived.

The tune ended. As if sensing my troubled thoughts, Luke lowered his flute and said, "Let's play something a bit happier, shall we? Something that makes you smile?"

You make me smile, I thought, but I obliged him with a crooked grin and began to play "Merrily Kiss the Quaker's Wife" instead. He joined in immediately, and turned his back firmly and deliberately towards the beech.

Five

Thursday found me back at Dave's Ice, wearing the usual white T-shirt bearing the image of Dave the penguin. My co-worker: Sara. We managed to avoid anything but trite conversation during the busy morning, but as the day wore on, the clouds began to threaten rain and customers slowed to a trickle. I tried to fight off further contact by pulling the Thornking-Ash application out of my backpack. Leaning over the icy cold counter with my back to Sara, I began writing my name at the top, very slowly, hoping she'd get the hint.

It didn't work.

"So, you know you've got to dish." Sara's voice was ominously close. I wasn't sure how to respond. This was possibly the first time anyone had ever expressed interest in my personal life, and I wasn't sure if I should answer her or chronicle the event in my scrapbook.

"About this application?"

Sara snorted. "Duh. No. About the hottie you brought in the other day. Are you two going out?"

"Yes," I lied, without even pausing to think about it. I didn't want her getting the idea he might be available. I'd hate to have to punch her like I had Luke last night. Swallowing a laugh at the mental image, I wrote my address on the application.

"Whoa. No offence, but I never thought, like, you'd be the type to get a guy, so. . ."

I turned around. It occurred to me, in a me-looking-at-my-own-life-from-outside-my-body way, that Sara was being condescending. I raised an eyebrow.

She said quickly, "Not that you're ugly or anything. You're just so . . . *ordinary*."

I wasn't ordinary. I was *fascinating*. "I guess he didn't think so," I said.

Sara tapped her shimmery pink nails on the counter and studied them as she did. "It was just a little surprising to see you come in here with this guy who was, like, wow."

I had to turn around again to hide the smile that was forming. "Yeah, he is pretty nice to look at, huh?"

"Are you *kidding*?" Sara burst out. "He is *out-of-this-world* hot!"

I couldn't keep from laughing this time. "Yeah, he is, isn't he?" Which world *was* he from, I wondered?

The bell dinged as the door admitted two men, who ordered from Sara as she smiled encouragingly at them. Shaking my head, I told her, "I'll get one of them."

I took the opportunity to move to the other

end of the counter and make the sundae. I hadn't lied when I told Luke I liked working here. Really, scooping ice cream was quite satisfying. Every flavour was a different colour, and the feeling of the scoop cutting through the perfectly cold ice cream was as appetizing as actually eating the ice cream. I'd tried to explain this to Sara before, but she didn't get it. She just scooped ice cream into bowls and cones. I made ice-cold masterpieces.

"Whoa, that looks so good," said Customer Number One as he watched Customer Number Two take a sundae out of my hands. *Of course it does*, I thought. *Each scoop is perfectly round and I made the syrup and whipped cream perfectly symmetrical. The brownie is square and covered just so by ice cream. The nuts are sprinkled with enough creativity to look random and yet not patchy. It should be on the cover of* Ice Cream Today. *Most gorgeous sundae ever. Created by yours truly.*

Customer Number One accepted a substandard, Sara-made sundae with a slightly disappointed look. His was not symmetrical and would never find its picture on the front of a magazine. Sara had even slimed some chocolate ice cream from the first scoop on to the second scoop, which was vanilla. Quite unsightly.

Customer Number Two smiled warmly at me and stuffed the tip jar in front of my register full of ones. He flashed another smile, and his flirtations rolled gently off my back like water off a duck.

"Better hurry," I said. "The brownie will melt your ice cream."

"Your brownie's warm?" Customer Number One asked with dismay. They made their way out of the shop, with Number Two happily extolling the pleasures of his sundae. I returned to my application and Sara returned to my side.

"So, where did you meet?"

But I was staring at my tip jar. Stuffed in with all the ones and change that I'd acquired throughout the day was a leafy green edge that was out of place. I took the jar and tipped it out on the counter.

Sara jumped back as a few pennies bounced in her direction. "What are you doing? Are you mental?"

Sure enough, among the crumpled bills, half-crushed by a quarter, was a four-leaf clover. I picked it up and Sara stared at it, too.

"Whoa, aren't those really rare?"

I frowned. "I thought they were."

The bell dinged again and both of us looked up. Sara made a soft noise and I grinned, because it was Luke.

He smiled back at me. "Hello, lovely." The smile on his face dimmed when he saw what I was holding. "*Another* one?"

My expression mirrored his. "It was in my tip jar."

Dropping his eyes to the pile of money on the counter, Luke shook his head. "I don't think you need that kind of luck."

"Every girl needs luck," Sara offered. "I'll take it if you don't want it." I looked at Luke, and he shrugged, so I gave it to her.

As I scraped the coins back into the tip jar, Luke said, "Rumour has it you're getting off soon. Can I drive you home?"

"Fifteen minutes. Will you wait?"

Sara sighed. "No one else is going to come in, Deirdre. It's about to rain. Just go. I'll close everything up at five thirty."

I was taken aback by her surprising display of selflessness. "Uh – thanks! Are you sure?"

Sara smiled at me, and then at Luke. "Yeah. Get lost. And take your tips."

"Half are yours," I lied politely.

Sara looked at the tip cup in front of her, filled with nickels and dimes. "Yeah, right."

So I stuffed the bills into my pocket and left the coins – customers tipped better if they saw that there was already money in there – and followed Luke into the oppressive afternoon. From the tightly knit clouds overhead, it was obvious that rain was coming, but until it did, the air would only get more smothering. I was glad of the ride home; when I'd walked here this morning, the day had been bright and clear.

We stood for a moment, staring up at that churning sky, and then my nose caught the now familiar herbal scent. I thought Luke must smell it too, because he was frozen beside me, looking at the edge of the car park.

"Come on, let's go." Tugging my hand, he led me to the car. Inside, he turned on the air-conditioning, but the scent of thyme blasted through the vents – stronger than it should have been from just one freaky guy. I didn't know what was going on, but the smell reminded me of the feeling the freckled guy had given me, circling around me.

"Let's go," I said urgently.

Luke didn't need any more encouragement. He reversed so fast that the tyres scrubbed pavement when he stopped and shoved the car into first gear. With a wail from the engine, we tore out of the car park, clipping down the road at well above the speed limit. A mile away, the thyme began to fade. After two kilometres – past the turn for my house – it was nearly gone. Ten kilometres from Dave's, there was nothing left in the car but the faint clean odour that was Luke's.

I wanted to say something about it, but it would break the unspoken rule of pretending he was normal. Anyway, I knew now that it wasn't just him that was abnormal. There was some big storm, just like the purple tempest above, that was circling around me, waiting to break, and Luke was only one of its elements. The freckled guy was another, and maybe Eleanor from the reception as well. And all the four-leaf clovers.

"Damn!" Luke yelled suddenly, slamming on the brakes. A white hound leapt out of the middle of the road, and I gasped, "Rye?" But then another white hound leapt out from the bushes by the side of the road, and then another, and another, disappearing after the first in the bushes on the opposite bank. There must have been twenty – all copies of Rye, baying and howling.

"They all look like Rye," I said softly. For some reason it was the most supernatural thing I'd seen all week, and it was just a pack of hounds. Just a pack of hounds, all the same colour as Rye. They could have been littermates. A *freaking* lot of littermates. I had gone almost seventeen years without seeing another dog like Rye, and now there were twenty of them?

I became aware that Luke was looking at me. "You saw them?"

"There were twenty of them. Of course I saw them!"

Luke muttered something and made a U-turn to head back to the house. His fingers clutched the steering wheel. I didn't know what had disturbed him, but I knew I didn't like to see him upset. I'd only known him a few days and already I relied on him to be even and understated; this barely hidden anxiety bothered me more than it should have.

I summoned up my nerve and reached over to his hands on the wheel. He let me pull one of them off and I just held it, our hands sitting on the console between us. We rode like that for the few minutes home – my heart pounding, he removing his hand only to shift gears, and then lacing his fingers again with mine.

We got to my parents' driveway too soon. Luke parked on the street and dragged his thumb over the back of my hand. Thoughtfully, he watched a silhouette move past the kitchen window. Whoever it was didn't notice us, lost in dinner preparations maybe.

"Your mom can do just about anything she tries to, can't she?"

It was a weird question. Of all the things I thought he might say, I didn't think that was one of them. "I guess so. She never *thinks* she's good at what she does, but she is."

"So maybe that's all there is to it. Genetics. That's it. You're just from a family of insanely talented people."

I pulled my hand away. "Well, that's vaguely insulting."

Luke's eyes were trained on the kitchen window. "No, it's promising."

Screw the unspoken agreement. "Are you ever going to tell me anything? At all?"

His eyes darted past me to the car windows, and then to the rear-view mirror. He reached over and touched my chin; the lightest of touches could drag away my protests. "Shh, pretty girl." I closed my eyes, letting him draw his finger towards my collarbone.

Mom. The idea that she could look out the kitchen window at any minute instantly forced my eyes open. "Don't think you can seduce me into blind trust."

"Damn," Luke said. "Are you sure? How about shopping? Will you come into the city with me tomorrow?"

"I'm not much of a shopper. You were better off with the seducing."

His pale eyes glanced out the windows again and he leaned in very close, whispering. "The city's more private. Better place to – talk." He leaned back and said more loudly, "You know, to get to know each other."

OK, now wild horses couldn't keep me away. "You're on. When?"

"Pick you up at four?"

I nodded. Luke glanced out the window again, this time at the sky. "We'd better get you in before it rains."

Reluctantly, I climbed out of the car with my backpack and joined him at the end of the driveway. A single cold drop of rain burst on my arm, raising an army of goosebumps around it. Thunder rumbled distantly over the trees.

"It'll be quite a storm." Luke squinted up at the clouds.

I watched another drop hit a leaf on the lawn, momentarily bearing it to the ground. It struck me that there was something not quite right about the way the lawn looked. Maybe it was the half-light of the clouds, but it just seemed darker, more vibrant, greener than I remembered it being this morning. Then I realized what was different.

"Luke," I said flatly, hands dropping to my sides.

He stood beside me and looked at the solid carpet of clover that covered the lawn — every one I could see bearing four leaves. For a long moment, we stood in silence . . . an occasional raindrop penetrating to the scalp or slipping into a collar.

Then Luke said loudly, to no one in particular, "You're wasting your time. She doesn't need them any more." He took my hand tightly and led me towards the house. "Please use your wits until tomorrow. There's a storm coming."

He turned and jogged lightly down the driveway, pausing beside his car. I ducked around the side of the back porch, pretending to go in, and then crept back around, crouching behind an azalea bush.

Luke's voice was faint but unmistakable, with an unusual timbre to it that I couldn't place. "She saw the hounds. She's learning — she'll see the rest of you soon enough. You don't have to waste your time with these silly parlour tricks. She doesn't need them."

He paused, as if someone else was speaking, though I heard nothing but the drip of raindrops and the slow roar of thunder. Luke, again: "I don't need an escort. Do you think I haven't done this before?"

I bit my lip.

"I'm just not sure she's anything that interests you." Pause. "Damn it, I'll get it done. Leave me the hell alone, would you? Just leave me alone." The car door slammed and I heard the engine thrum to life.

I went inside the house, suddenly cold.

I dreamt. It was the dark blue of night and I could see Luke walking slowly away from me. He was on the high school grounds, and he stared at the bench where we had practised. He walked to the edge of the soccer field and I realized it was raining: cold stinging drops in the hot summer night.

He pulled his shirt off – crazy in this weather – and spread his arms out on either side of him like a crucifix, his fingers grasping at the rain. Staring at the sky, the drops biting into his skin with cold fury, his mouth moved as he turned slowly. I couldn't hear him, though, over the rain and the sudden barrage of thunder that shook the ground itself. It seemed like some secret ritual that no one else ever saw: some hidden spell or incantation or some dreadful magic.

Thunder growled again as he dropped to his knees in the sharp gravel, his arms still spread and his head thrown back to the sky.

I was close enough to hear words: "One thousand, three hundred, forty-eight years, two months, and one—"

Thunder cracked like a tree smashing to the ground, and my eyes flew open.

Rain was pelting on the roof and rapping against the window as thunder growled outside. Awake, but not separated from the dream, I was confused as to what was real and what was still the dream. Was the rain real? Did I still sleep?

Light, on. The light switch flicked up as I thought about it, and yellow light partially illuminated my side of the bedroom. On the still, dark side of the room, a figure stood in the corner of the room, black and indistinct.

Blink.

Just a shadow. Though the room was empty, my heart was still pounding. I reached up to my neck, where Luke's secret key now hung on a chain. From next to my bed, Rye lifted his head, sensing my anxiety.

"I thought I saw something," I told him.

Rye looked at the corner of the room. Thunder boomed, and I risked a glance at the corner. Oh. My. God. My eyes watched a figure form again, an indistinct face turned towards me. I squeezed my eyes shut. *Not there.* I opened them again. The figure was still there, very nearly a shadow. Rye's eyes were still trained on it, but he groaned softly and lay his head down on his feet, as if it didn't concern him.

Because maybe it had been there all along.

I grabbed my mobile phone from the bedside table and punched in James's number. The bright numbers on the phone told me it was almost two a.m., but I thought – hoped – that James wouldn't mind.

It rang and rang, while I stared at the unmoving figure. It was going to go to voicemail. No! Then, on the last ring, James's groggy voice answered. "Dee?"

Now that I had him on the phone, I felt a little foolish. "Yeah."

"Is something wrong?"

"Um – no – maybe? This sounds dumb, James. I'm sorry for waking you up."

"Dee. It's two in the morning. Something's bothering you. Cut to the chase."

I told him about the conversation Luke had had with empty air. "And now, I think there's something in my room. I think it was there all along, only I just now can see it. It looks like a shadow. Or a person."

James didn't reply. I stared hard at the shadow. Was it staring back at me?

Blink.

The corner was empty: no figure, no shadow.

"Uh – James – it just *disappeared*." Now I was seriously freaked out; I edged down in my covers, as if that would make a difference against a real bogey man. Natural shadows didn't go away, so it *had* been something. And worse, now I didn't know where it was. I looked around the room, but there was nothing out of the ordinary.

"Real shadows don't disappear." James's voice was flat. "Do you want me to come over?"

Of course I did. "My parents would freak if they knew."

"Like I said, do you want me to come over?"

From the floor, Rye looked up at me, and then settled his head on his paws. With a deep sigh, he closed his eyes. Whatever had been in the room, he wasn't concerned. I vacillated between what I wanted and what I needed, and finally went with the less selfish option. Also the one with fewer possible repercussions.

"I'll be OK. Rye's going back to sleep. He'd let me know if there was something to be worried about, I think."

James sighed, less contentedly than Rye. "You can't call and get me worried and then tell me it's nothing."

"I'm sorry. Can I come over in the morning?"

"You know you always can."

After we'd hung up, I waited long minutes, waiting for the figure to reappear, but it didn't. Finally I let exhaustion pull me into sleep.

Book Two

Now when we're out a-sailing and you are far behind
Fine letters will I write to you with the secrets of my mind,
The secrets of my mind, my girl, you're the girl that I adore,
And still I live in hope to see the Holy Ground once more.
You're the girl that I adore,
And still I live in hope to see the Holy Ground once more.

—"The Holy Ground"

Six

The following day was clear and surprisingly temperate, all humidity and heat scrubbed clean by the storm of the night before. Sitting in the passenger seat of the old Audi, Luke beside me, I couldn't believe the storm last night had been so terrifying. Or that his invisible conversation had been so creepy. Or that freckle-kid had really been in the back garden. It was crazy – every time I was in Luke's presence, I couldn't really be bothered by any of the things that troubled me when I was alone. Was this love?

No, said a cross voice in my head. *It's stupidity. And don't feel bad, it runs in the family.*

For an hour we talked about stupid stuff that I couldn't remember afterwards. Like why "Bill" was a nickname for "William" and why dogs didn't come in stripes. Every time I thought we'd run out of things to talk about, one of us thought of something else.

"Bucephalus." Luke tapped the steering wheel.

"God bless you!"

He laughed. "No, it's the name of my car."

"You named your car?"

He smiled impishly, a little boy.

Looking at my feet, where the carpet was stained two colours and curling away from the edge of the door, I demanded, "After Alexander the Great's horse, no less? Going for a bit of irony, were you?"

"So you know who he was. You know the story." Luke's teeth flashed white in the clear sunlight as he gestured grandly to the dashboard. "That's our story as well."

"You and the car."

"Yes."

I raised an eyebrow. "So, what you're telling me is that nobody else in the world could drive this car. That it threw all comers out and drove over them, leaving tyre marks on their faces, and one day, you as a young boy climbed into it and bent it to your will?"

His eyes smiled more than his mouth did, which was only lifted on one corner. "That's right. And we've been inseparable ever since."

I considered this, and then I looked at the dashboard, faded and scraped. "I dunno. I guess I would've tried to tame a Maserati instead of an Audi."

Now he laughed. "What can I say, destiny chose this one for me." He pointed. "Look."

We were finally getting into Richmond; the car was surrounded by suburbs that gave way to office buildings and stores. Richmond was a very *bright* city. Everywhere, sunlight reflected from white pavements, mirrored buildings, parked cars, and concrete medians between lanes of tarmac. There were trees, but they seemed like an afterthought, almost unnoticeable among all the man-made structures. In my short visits to Richmond, I had never been fond of it, but I could *sense* Luke relaxing as we drove in deeper.

"You like the city." It wasn't a question, though I was surprised.

Luke's eyes glanced off every brilliant surface. "No. I like what the city does. All this – *stuff*. Nobody would live here but a human." He pointed to a huge church spire, distant over rooftops and trees. "And the crosses. Everything makes a cross here. They can't stand it."

"They?" I was chilled by the word *human*. As if "They" might not be.

Luke glanced at me, his expression oddly light. "Shh, pretty girl. Let's enjoy ourselves for a bit before you start riddling again."

He drove the Audi to Carytown, an endless street of shops painted every colour of the rainbow and offering all sorts of odds and ends that couldn't be found elsewhere. After circling a few blocks, he found a parking spot nearly in the shade. "I know where to get an awesome French pastry, if you're hungry."

"Sounds good." I was starving; I hadn't eaten lunch in my excitement. *That's because you're stupid*, the voice in my head reminded me.

We got pastries from a little café, and took them outside to eat at a wrought-iron table that overlooked the street. Luke watched me in amusement as I took my layered pastry apart.

"What are you doing?"

"Seeing what it's made of." I poked a sponge cake layer with a fork and tasted the cream on top of it. "So I could try and make it." Mom had taught me that. She dissected everything, read menus like novels, and then created her own magic in the kitchen.

He shook his head.

"Strange as strange?" I offered.

"I was going to say 'weird as weird'."

I was going to ask him questions – riddle him – but the pastry was so good (the cream was hazelnut) that I finished it before speaking. "Now, you talk."

Luke stood up, correcting me. "Now, we walk. I don't think there's anyone here, but I feel better walking."

I got up and he took my hand, easy and natural. I wondered if my touch gave him the same electric reaction I got from his. We began to walk down the too-bright concrete, cars whirring by us on the right, music beating from one of the clothing shops.

"Let me know if you want to go in anywhere," Luke said. *As if I wanted to freakin' shop.*

"Just talk. Tell me what's going on."

He watched a cyclist slowly pedal down the opposite

side of the street. "Here's my secret. . ." He leaned over to my shoulder and said in a low voice, "I can't tell you my secrets."

It took me a moment to realize what he'd said. When I did, I ripped my hand from his and stopped in my tracks. "You brought me down here to tell me that?" A couple across the street paused in their stroll to look at us, and I lowered my voice. "I really expected better than that. At least lies."

Luke reached out a hand, but I crossed my arms. Sighing, he said, "It's true I can't tell you my secrets. But I don't know *how* much I can't say. You can ask me questions, and I can see how far we get."

I frowned at him. A punk chick and her androgynous punk friend had to push past me. I ignored their snarky comments and instead squinted at Luke. "What do you mean, '*can't* tell me'? Don't know how much you '*can't* tell me'?"

His face begged for understanding; he shrugged helplessly.

I *knew* in my heart what he was dancing around, and even though I could send clover flying across the ground and move light switches, my mind still wouldn't accept it. Funny, because I'd wanted the world to be extraordinary for so long. And now that it was, I couldn't seem to believe it.

I lowered my voice. "Are you asking me to – to believe in *magic*?"

Luke didn't answer. He just kept his light eyes on me, his mouth sad.

"Fine, take my damn hand," I grumbled finally, sticking it out towards him. "Let's walk."

He took it immediately and we began to walk again, past an old record store and an antique shop with a suit of armour by the door, which cast a long shadow.

"Can you tell me why four-leaf clovers keep turning up?"

Luke's grip tightened on mine and he looked around before answering. "They want you to be able to see Them."

"Who's 'Them'?"

He didn't answer.

"Faeries?"

His mouth quirked, humourlessly.

I just stared, searching his face for signs of insincerity, but all I saw was my frowning expression mirrored back at me. My mind formed several questions that never reached my mouth. The one I finally said out loud was the stupidest: "I thought faeries had wings."

"Some do."

"I thought They were little friendly things that liked flowers."

"They do like flowers. They like all pretty things." Luke's eyes took in my face, wordlessly putting me in that category.

I wanted to believe him so badly it hurt. "Why do

They want me to see Them?"

Almost growling, he said, "Same reason They want anyone else to. To torment you. Play with you. Confuse you. Whirl you away."

My mind provided me a perfect image of Freckle Freak. Hey, I liked that. I was calling him that from now on. I seized on other facts I'd learned. "And iron keeps Them away. And crosses. That's why Granna gave me the ring. And why you gave me your key. But – the dogs?"

"Their dogs."

"My dog?"

Luke looked at me.

I blinked. What was he saying – that I'd been watched since I was a baby? That squirrel-chasing Rye was a faerie hound? "But I could see them," I stammered. "The hounds, I mean. I didn't have any clover with me then."

Luke's voice was flat. "You're learning. Some people only need clover for a little while, until they learn from the clover how to see. I guess you're one of those."

So it was only going to get worse? The shadow in the corner of my room? Freckle Freak? No wonder Luke had kept the clover away from me when he could. I remembered something else. "But why did Granna act so strangely around you?"

Luke's mouth worked. Though I looked at him, he didn't look back. Finally he said, "I think she mistook me for someone else."

I wasn't happy with the answer, though I couldn't quite think why. We walked in silence for a long time, until the tarmac gave way to cobblestones and the concrete to brick. Trees grew over the cobblestone road, and lovely old dark buildings crowded against the narrowing road. Overhead, the green canopy completely blocked the late afternoon sun. Every step we took, every word we spoke, took us further into a strange and mysterious world.

"Why would They want me?" I asked, finally.

With surprising abruptness, Luke stopped and pulled me into a little alcove in the bricks – so fast that I didn't feel the thrill of the embrace until several seconds after I was in it.

He said into my ear, almost too softly to hear, "Who wouldn't?" His lips teased a maddeningly slow line down my neck and kissed my shoulder. Though his mouth was as hot as the hidden summer sun, I shivered and closed my eyes. My hands were crushed between us – I wouldn't have known what to do with them anyway. He kissed me again, further up my neck, and I pushed him back against the wall.

My mind searched for logical thought, a rational life raft before I drowned in wanting to kiss him. I managed, "We've only met a few days ago. We don't know each other."

Luke released me. "How long does it take to know someone?"

I didn't know. "A month? A few months?" It sounded stupid to quantify it, especially when I didn't want to believe my own reasoning. But I couldn't just go kissing someone I knew nothing about — it went against everything I'd ever been told. So why was it so hard to say no?

He took my fingers, playing with them in between his own. "I'll wait." He looked so good in the half-light under the trees, his light eyes nearly glowing against his shadowed skin. It was useless.

"I don't want you to." I whispered the words, and before I'd even finished saying them, his mouth was on mine and I was melting under his lips. My hands — I don't know how I could have worried about them — gripped his T-shirt, knuckles pressed against his lanky body, and his were wrapped tightly around my back and neck, as if he had caught me as I fainted.

He finally stepped back, his hands slipping down my arms to hold my fingers. "I don't think anyone could smell as good as you. They can't have you. *I* want you."

I bit my lip. "I think I have to show you something. But I think you'd better take me to a church, to be safe."

In the dim evening light, the church was unoccupied, dark, smelling of incense and mystery. I dipped my fingers into the holy water and crossed myself by habit, then lead Luke down between the pews.

"What do you have to show me?" His voice was sombre and small in the church, muffled by the carpet runner beneath our feet.

I didn't know how to demonstrate it, but I knew he had to know about my telekinesis. Maybe that was why the faeries wanted me. My footsteps inaudible, I led him to the front of the church. Then an idea occurred to me, and I pulled a single yellow rosebud from one of the flower arrangements on the steps to the altar.

I turned back to Luke to find him gazing up at the crucifix hanging at the very front of the church, his eyes sad. He looked back down at me and then at the bud in my hands. He was facing me like it was a lonely wedding ceremony.

"Do you remember what you told me at the competition?" I asked.

His eyes clouded, and his voice was tight. "No."

I pressed on. "About how there are some people who can do anything?"

He spun away from me. "I was just distracting you. I didn't want you to throw up. It worked, didn't it?"

"Don't *lie*," I said fiercely. "You *knew*. I don't know how you did, but you *knew*. You knew I was one of those people, didn't you?"

His back still towards me, he bowed his head and held a fist to his forehead. "No. You're not. Just say you're not." The light from the candles around Mary's feet lit the side of his cheek and left the rest of his face in shadow.

"I can't say I'm not! I am. *Look*." I thrust the bud out towards him, cupping it in both hands. He turned, his face drawn. There was only a second's pause, and then the petals unfolded, one after another, until the bloom had grown large enough to touch each of my fingers. I stared at the velvet yellow petals cupped in my hands, and then back up at him.

Luke hugged his arms around himself. "Impressive," he said in a small voice.

I didn't understand his reaction. "But you knew I could do this already. Why else would you have said it?"

He turned away again, shoulders hunched. "Could you give me a minute?"

I had done something wrong. I shouldn't have shown him. But he had known, hadn't he? What had I done? I retreated quickly down the aisle, pushing my way through the double doors into the porch, where I swiped one of my eyes dry. For a long moment I stood in the dim room, looking blankly at the flyers for bake sales and Bible studies on the noticeboard.

Then I heard him shout, *"Damn you! Why?"*

I looked through the clear glass of the porch doors to see if he spoke to some barely seen faerie. But to my eyes, there was no one there but Luke and God.

★

We didn't talk about the rose on the drive home. For a long time, I stared out the window at the spectre of the moon, hanging above the black silhouettes of the trees, while the stripes on the road whipped by me. Something about the way the moon looked, enigmatic and eternal, reminded me of how I'd felt when I made the rose blossom in my hands.

Abruptly, Luke pulled the car off on to a barely visible dirt lane by the highway. He wrenched the hand brake up and studied the glowing clock face in the dash.

"Are you angry at me?" he asked.

Surprised by the question, I looked at him. His face was green and peaked, illuminated by the lights in the dashboard, and his expression was genuinely concerned.

"Why would I be mad at you?"

"You've gone all quiet. That's the only way I could tell you were mad before, so I assume I've done something to tick you off."

"*You're* the one who went all quiet. I thought *you* were mad at me for—" I stopped short. I didn't know if I was supposed to mention the church or not.

Luke sighed and made a vague gesture. "This is all just unfamiliar territory for me."

"What is?"

"*You*." He shrugged uncomfortably. "I don't know what to do."

"About what?"

"*You.*"

"About what happened in the ch—"

Luke interrupted hastily. "No. Just about you. You, yourself. I keep waiting for you to tell me to leave you alone. To tell me I'm creepy."

I pointed at him. "That's why I haven't told you to leave me alone."

"What – why?"

"Because you keep telling me how weird you are. Truly sketchy people don't tell you how sketchy they are."

"I also forced myself on you, in an alleyway. *That's* sketchy."

So that's what this was about. The kiss. It was sort of charming that he was worried about it. I laughed. "You didn't force yourself on me. And it wasn't even an alley."

"I didn't ask."

I wasn't up on the rules of dating, but I didn't think anyone ever asked permission to kiss a girl. Maybe in the movies. "I kissed back."

He looked at me out of the corner of his eyes. "I don't want to go too far – do the wrong thing – and get myself in trouble."

Crap, that sounded familiar. "Luke, I'm not mad at you. And. . ." I had to look away when I said it, and I blushed, too. "You're not going to get yourself in trouble. Or – maybe I'd like the sort of trouble you'd get yourself into." Afterwards, I thought maybe I shouldn't have said it. Maybe he'd think I was a slut. Maybe he *would* go too far. Maybe he wouldn't know what I meant. Maybe—

Luke gave me a halfway smile, somewhere short of humour, and reached across the car to brush my chin with his hand. I wanted to close my eyes and lean into his touch, to forget about everything that made me Deirdre.

"You're a baby. You don't know how much trouble I can get into."

I bristled, pulling my face away. "What's *that* supposed to mean?"

"I didn't mean it like – aw, see, now you're pissed off at me again."

I regarded him frostily. "No, really? You called me a baby."

Luke thumped back in his seat, voice frustrated. "It was a compliment, really."

"How do you figure that?"

"Because you make me forget how young you are." He struggled to explain, looking away from my glare. "You're just – you're just so like me. You know – you take everything in like you've done it a hundred times before. The way your eyes look when you're playing music – I just forget you're only sixteen."

"Aren't you supposed to add 'incredibly beautiful'

and 'dazzlingly intelligent' while you're pouring on the unreasonable compliments?" It would have been nice to believe him – but my mind couldn't reconcile stunningly invisible with stunningly desirable.

"I'm being serious. You are incredibly beautiful, though." His voice was earnest.

I shook my head. "Eleanor is incredibly beautiful. I know what I am, and beautiful I am not. I'm fine with that, too."

A weird look crossed his face at the mention of Eleanor. "No, Eleanor's something else. *You're* beautiful. Especially when you're staring at me with that *boy he's a condescending asshole* expression – yeah. Beautiful."

I studied my hands; the lights from the radio cast a weird coloured glow over them, like I was lit from within. Softly, I said, "You could say it again."

But he didn't. Instead, he said, "You're different."

His voice sounded like it was the best compliment in the world to be called different – "different" like a brand-new species of butterfly, not like a cardigan-wearing girl in a sea of vest tops.

I heard Luke shift in his seat to gaze out the windshield into the darkness. "You're like me. We're watchers of this world, aren't we? Not players."

But I wasn't a watcher of *this* world, the little planet inside the confines of his car. In this world, scented with Luke's summer-smell, I was an irreplaceable player. I wasn't sure if I wanted to cry or bust out the biggest smile in the universe.

"Dee," Luke said softly. "Where are you?"

I looked at him. "Right here."

He shook his head.

I smiled self-consciously. "I was imagining my life as a little planet all its own."

Luke ran a finger in a circle along the steering wheel: a shape without end. "With very attractive aliens." He reached over and carefully drew the same circle lightly on the back of my hand, raising goosebumps along my arm. His soft, level voice was completely devoid of emotion when he asked, "Are you still pissed off at me?"

I half-closed my eyes as he traced the finger up my arm towards my shoulder, his touch as light as a feather. It tickled in a way that made my gut clench and my breath stop. He leaned across the console and kissed my lips, just as softly. I closed my eyes and let him kiss me again, one of his hands cupping the side of my neck, the other hand braced against the dash. Headlights flashed against my closed eyelids as a solitary car drove by on the highway.

"Do you want me to stop?" Luke whispered.

I shook my head. He kissed me again, biting my lower lip gently. It drove me crazy in ways I hadn't even thought of. Irrationally, I suddenly thought, *So this is making out.* I didn't even know if I was doing it right.

Was I drooling too much? Did he like it? What the hell was I supposed to do with my tongue?

But a part of me was immune to self-doubt, and it was begging me to touch him and be touched. I felt as if I was sitting in the back seat, watching Luke and me kiss. I saw the way the dash light lit up the side of my face as I tipped my chin for his mouth to touch mine. I saw how his tongue carefully traced where my lips parted. From outside of my body, I watched while I leaned into his hand as it pressed down my side, fingers ironing out the wrinkles in my shirt. I heard my breath grow unsteady, saw his eyes close, felt his fingers on my thigh, asking for me to go further, to places I hadn't yet explored.

I froze, and Luke sat back hastily, looking ill, as if his hand had moved of its own volition. His voice was uneven. "I'm sorry."

I wanted to say *I'm not*, but I didn't know if I meant it. I didn't know what I wanted. Lamely, I said, "It's OK," which wasn't what I meant.

"I'm sorry," he said again. "I wasn't trying to—" He closed his eyes for a minute, and then opened them. He released the hand brake.

My leg burned where he had touched it. I could still feel the desire in his touch, and I couldn't stop shivering. I wanted him to kiss me again. I wanted him to start driving so I wouldn't want him to kiss me again.

Luke pulled out on to the highway again, swallowing,

not looking at me. He looked faraway and unfamiliar in the dim glow.

I reached across the console and took his hand, and without looking away from the road, he knotted his fingers tightly in mine.

Seven

I slept on the sofa that night. The idea of sharing a room with some faceless faerie thingy wasn't exactly appealing, and even though I knew it could just as easily be faceless downstairs in the living room, I slept easier on the couch.

I woke up giddy. Last night, I'd been weirded out by the experience in the church and the idea of faeries stalking me, but this morning, fully rested, with early pale light filtering in through the delicate white curtains, I felt on top of the world. All the negatives seemed far away and my mind just kept replaying his kisses over and over again.

Upstairs, I heard movement and thumping in my parents' room. Mom was awake. I'd seen the look on her face last night when Luke dropped me off at eleven and apologized for keeping me out so late. I wasn't keen on having that conversation right now. Or ever, for that matter.

"Rye," I whispered. He looked up from his post at the base of the sofa. "Walk?"

He leapt up, tail whipping, and I followed him to the kitchen, wiping sleep from my eyes and pulling my hair into my usual choppy ponytail. I donned a pair of jeans from the laundry room, folding the bottoms into uneven cuffs so they wouldn't get wet in the grass, and went outside into the morning.

God, the sun was gorgeous today, light trickling through early morning mist. The morning was still cool — dew hanging in spiderwebs, the air smelling of freshly mown grass. Everything was beautiful.

He kissed me. He kissed me.

Rye, oblivious to my inner fireworks, pushed past me, white tail high as he bounded through the still wet grass.

Not that way, faerie dog. We're going this way. Down the road.

He stopped, ears pricked as if I had spoken out loud. Then he wheeled around and trotted towards the road. He paused, waiting for me.

Awesome. Everything was friggin' awesome. I could call Rye in my mind, and *Luke kissed me*. With Rye, I walked out on to the road, sticking mostly to the side, though at this time of the morning I didn't think I'd meet any cars.

My bare feet making no noise on the tarmac, I led Rye to a quieter back road near the house and together we walked down the dead middle of it, watching the mist move and shift slowly over the cow pasture to our right. I slowed, fascinated by a snowy white rabbit that was watching me. Its perfectly colourless ears were pricked, unmoving. Aside from the rabbit, I was alone with Rye and my thoughts.

So Rye was a faerie dog. And faeries wanted to steal me away. It was kind of flattering, actually. Nice to be noticed.

Where did that leave Luke? Why did *he* know about the faeries, anyway? Were they trying to steal him as well? And why had Granna talked to him like she did? It wasn't the malice in her voice that was the most puzzling. It was the *familiarity*. Sort of like how Mr Hill, the band director, had seemed to recognize him at the competition as well. My mind skipped carefully away from the subject. Remembering how little I knew about Luke definitely cut into my morning giddiness. I knew I ought to care who he was and what he was when he wasn't with me, but I didn't want to. I wanted simple.

Deep down, I knew he wasn't a high school student. But was it wrong that that was part of what I liked about him?

By my side, Rye growled and dropped back, and I followed his gaze. Up ahead, backed into an unused dirt driveway, was a familiar beat-up Audi. My heart leapt – *it's Luke!* – and my brain turned over the information a second later – *what's he doing here?*

Padding quietly up to the car, I saw Luke in the

driver's seat. His arms were behind his head, his eyes closed. Sleep erased all care from his narrow features, making him look young and fresh – almost believable as a high school student. His raised right arm exposed a beaten gold band around his biceps, partially eclipsed by the edge of his shirt sleeve. I didn't know why I hadn't seen it before.

I glanced down. His doors were unlocked. When I pulled the passenger side open, Luke jerked to immediate life, his hand flying down to his ankle.

"Shouldn't leave your doors unlocked," I advised. "Never know what kinda weirdos will get into your car."

He blinked at me for a long moment before pulling his hand away from his ankle and thumping his head back on the seat with closed eyes.

I pulled the door shut behind me, watching Rye glare at Luke and then retreat to the side of the road. "I didn't sleep in my own room, either."

He didn't open his eyes. "It's hard to sleep while you're being watched, isn't it?"

I wanted to ask him why They would watch him, but I was afraid he wouldn't answer. I wanted to ask him why he was sleeping in his car a stone's throw from my house, but I was afraid he *would* answer. I thought about his hand darting to his ankle and wondered if there was something hidden beneath his trouser leg, something a bit more deadly than the golden band his shirt sleeve had obscured. Sudden doubts crowded in my mind during his silence, but then he opened his pale blue eyes and smiled at me, and the doubts were swept away like so many cobwebs.

"You're a nice thing to see first thing in the morning."

The giddiness came rushing back as if it had never gone. I grinned. "I know." Why did I become this strange, light creature when I was with him?

Luke laughed. "Well, sing something for me, nice thing."

Entirely shameless, I sang a made-up song about walking without shoes and strange men sleeping in cars, to the tune of "The Handsome Cabin Boy". Seeing his face lighten, I added another verse about the dangers of cow pastures and men who stayed near them. "Lure" and "manure" rhymed nicely.

"You're in a good mood today." He sat up and rubbed his hands through his hair, looking in his rear-view mirror. "I'm self-conscious. You're seeing me without my make-up on."

It was my turn to laugh. "You're hideous. I can't see how you stand yourself in the morning." With careful fingers, I lifted the very edge of his shirt sleeve, revealing the gold band just under it, beaten into a multitude of different facets. "I didn't see this before."

He looked away, out the window, voice oddly dead. "It was always there."

I touched it, rubbing a finger against one of the beaten facets, and noticed that the skin just at the edge was all smoothly calloused and that the muscle of his arm was contoured around the band; the torc had been there a long time. I looked at it for longer than I needed to, wanting the excuse to run my finger along his skin. Staring, I saw something else: pale, shiny marks running perpendicular to the torc. Scars. My mind recreated the dozen slashes running down the length of his upper arm, gashes that sliced his biceps to ribbons of flesh held together only by that torc.

I ran a finger down one of the scars, towards his elbow. "What's this?"

Luke looked back at me and answered with another question. "Do you still have my secret?"

For a moment I didn't know what he meant, and then I gestured to the chain around my neck, lifting it to reveal the key. "One of them. Can I have another one?"

His lips lifted into a smile. "Sure. I'm still fascinated by you."

"That's no secret."

"Maybe not, but it's fairly stunning, all things considered."

I pouted. "I can't consider all things, because I don't know most of them."

"Don't pout. Sing me another song. A *real* one. Something that makes people cry."

I sang him "Fear a' Bhàta" – "The Lonesome Boatman" – and it was sadder and more beautiful than I had ever sung it, because it was for him. I'd never wanted to sing for someone else before – was this how Delia felt every time she walked on stage?

He closed his eyes. "I'm in love with your voice." He sighed. "You're like a siren, leading me into dangerous places. Don't stop. Sing me something else."

I wanted to lead him into dangerous places, if I was included in said dangerous places, so I closed my eyes and sang "Sally Gardens". A car's not the greatest place for acoustics, but I *wanted* it to sound beautiful, so it did. I don't think I've ever sung it better.

I sensed him, close to me, a second before I felt his breath on my neck. I was surprised at the emotion that flashed through me in the instant before his lips pressed against my skin. Fear – only there for a second – but there nonetheless.

My treacherous body had betrayed me with a start, and Luke pulled away as I opened my eyes.

"Do I scare you?" he asked.

Strange way of putting it. Not "*did* I".

I narrowed my eyes, trying to read his face. I felt so strongly that I could see myself mirrored in his eyes: something about my obsession with music and my battle for control of my life. I wasn't sure why, but I just felt in my gut that whatever made me *me* resonated in harmony with whatever made Luke *him*.

I answered with a question. "Should you?"

He smiled mildly. "I knew you were clever." Then the smile vanished; he gazed past me, and I turned.

Sitting outside the car, ears pricked and unmoving, staring at us with unblinking black eyes, was a pure-white rabbit.

My stomach turned over.

Luke stared at it for a long moment before speaking, and when he did, his voice was tight and low. "You'd better go."

Go? "What about—?"

"What about what?" he asked flatly.

I stared out at the rabbit, and when I answered, my voice was cold. "Nothing. You're right. I have a gig today anyway. Mom will have my head if I'm not back soon."

I put my hand on the doorknob, ready to get out, but Luke reached over quickly, below the level of the window, and touched my other hand where it rested on the seat.

I understood. Nothing in view of the rabbit. Climbing out of the car, I shut the door; as I did, the rabbit hopped slowly into the undergrowth, as if that would convince me it was ordinary, not some peeping-tom-supernatural-killer-bunny.

Rye trotted up from the other side of the road and joined me, without a glance towards where the rabbit had gone, and I headed down the road, not looking back. I had gone thirty metres when I swore I heard the car door open and shut. I snuck a look back, shaking my head and pretending to swat gnats away. Sure enough, the car was empty.

Where was he?

Focus. This telekinetic crap has to be good for something useful. I listened hard. Nothing. Just the repetitive twittering of cardinals in the trees overhead. It was hard to concentrate on something abstract like sound; I needed something concrete. I pictured Luke carrying a mobile phone, calling me and forgetting to hang up. I imagined the crackling of bushes as he pushed after the rabbit, the sound of his breath. The sound of his voice, faraway and low.

"Have I ever failed before?"

Another voice, earthy and gravelly. Chillingly plural yet singular. "It's never taken you this long."

"I have my reasons for taking my time."

The single voice that was too many sounded contemptuous. "Have her and be done with it."

There was a pause, a second too long, and then Luke laughed. "Right. That obvious, is it?"

The gravelly voice didn't laugh. "Just screw her. Finish it."

No pause this time. "I can't wait."

I broke into a run, bare feet slapping the pavement. I didn't want to hear any more. My imaginary phone hissed and dropped the call. *He was lying.* He was lying to the gravelly voice. Lying. If I said it three times, it had to be true.

Eight

Mom drove me to the gig. Since she was a caterer, every wedding planner in a two-hour radius knew us, and it hadn't taken long for them to find out that she had given birth to wedding music, as well. It actually wasn't a bad deal. Usually I would arrive on the scene thirty minutes early, spend half that time barfing, and then emerge to play gracefully for a couple of hundred bucks. It was worth the barfing; two hundred bucks would support my CD-buying habit for several more months, until the next gig.

But I didn't want to do it today, and it wasn't because of the puking. I wasn't even thinking about the gig. I was thinking about Luke's laugh. Analysing every angle of it . . . deciding I was overthinking it . . . and then deciding I hadn't been thinking about it enough.

Mom was silent for most of the trip, probably thinking I was nauseated. But I could tell she was cooking something, and I was right. She turned down the radio.

"Last night—" Here it came. Frustration welled inside me like a red, ugly blister and exploded.

"I don't want to talk about Luke," I snapped.

I might as well have slapped her. She even put her fingers to her lips, as if I really had. I was violating another rule, of course. I was supposed to sit and just let her ream me out, and then nod mutely and do whatever she said. Screw that.

Bad choice of words.

Just screw her. I can't wait. Finish it. I angrily tugged down the edge of the fitted blue dress Mom had bought for me. I hated the dress. Made it look like I'd raided an old woman's closet. All I needed was a big gaudy string of pearls and I'd be ready to hit the Moose Lodge.

So what? Luke was in league with the friggin' rabbit? Why even bother to tell me about faeries then? To gain my confidence so he could get in my pants?

Mom jerked the car to a halt and I looked up with surprise, thinking she was preparing for a huge confrontation. But no, that wasn't Mom's way. We were already at the church.

"What are you wearing around your neck, anyway?" Her voice was cold enough for polar bears.

My hand went to the chain that held Luke's key.

"It looks like crap with the dress," Mom said. Wow. Minor swearing. I'd really pissed her off.

"Whatever." Like I felt like wearing it right now anyway. I unclasped it and curled the chain and the key in my palm.

"Put it in your harp case so you don't lose it."

Mom pressed the button to open the boot. "Take your phone."

I took the phone. "You aren't staying?"

Her voice dropped a few more degrees. "Granna can pick you up. I'm going home, I have work to do. Call her when you're done."

"Fine. OK. See you later." I could be just as icy. I pulled my harp from the boot, dropping Luke's secret into the pouch of the case, and headed into the church. Mom was already pulling out of the car park by the time I let the massive oak door close behind me.

Inside, the church lobby was dim and spacious, lushly covered in red carpet. It had that smell that only old churches get, something about lots of people and lots of candles and lots of years. There were already knots of people gathered, all discussing details of flowers and timing and music, and in a rush, my stomach remembered how it was supposed to be feeling.

"You must be the harpist." A woman with blonde hair glued into place popped up by my side like an overwhelmingly perfumed jack-in-the-box, complete with permanent smile. "I'm Maryann, the wedding planner."

I nodded dumbly. If I opened my mouth, I'd toss chunks all over her stiff hair, melting it.

"Your mother explained all about you," Maryann said through her rack of teeth. "The bathroom's right through those doors."

With equal parts gratitude and humiliation, I tore

through the doors and found the tiny, antique bathroom. I shoved aside the fake flower arrangement that was one thousand times too large for the room and promptly puked. Afterwards, my stomach immediately felt better, and all that was left was the faintly sick feeling that I'd had since I'd heard the conversation between Luke and the damn rabbit.

I scrubbed my hands with the potent lavender soap and rinsed them under a blast of water. Something firm and heavy rolled between my fingers, and before I realized what it was, I saw Granna's ring quickly circle the drain and disappear.

I swore and stuck my finger into the drain, but it was an old sink with one of those gaping drains that was just waiting for personal effects to fall in. My ring was unreachable, somewhere in the plumbing. And of *course* Granna was the one picking me up today. She'd go through the roof.

Friggin' ace.

I returned to the lobby, where I found Maryann and worked out the details of when to play during the wedding. And of course, like always, since I'd already puked, I did fine and I found myself a half hour later with a bright shiny check for $175.

Making small talk with people I don't know and will never meet again is not my forte, so I escaped outside and dialled Granna's number. "Granna? Mom said you'd pick me up."

"You're done already?"

"Yes."

"You have a better hourly rate than my doctor." I heard some kind of thump from Granna's end of the phone.

"I guess I do. What are you doing?"

"I'm, uh—" another thump, "painting a piece of furniture that doesn't want to be painted. But it'll wait. It'll be a half hour before I get there, though."

I squinted at the church. It was hot here on the pavement, but it probably wouldn't be too bad if I waited under the birch trees nearby. Of course, I could've waited inside in the air-conditioning, but that would've meant small talk. I told Granna that was fine, and headed over to the trees.

Sure enough, it wasn't terrible. It was hot, but I could stand it. I rested my harp case against one of the trees and walked a little further into them. They had been planted in straight lines, about fifty of them, all beautiful and straight, with canopies so lush that I couldn't tell where one tree ended and another one began. The grass underneath was beautiful and green as well; it looked like something out of a dream.

I couldn't sit, or I'd get grass stains on my old-woman sheath. So I stood next to one of the birches, looking at the way the bark peeled off and left smooth tree-skin beneath it. Beautiful, but smelly.

I sniffed. What *was* that smell, anyway? It was sweet,

fruity – rotten. Like clover cut and left to moulder. And it wasn't the trees.

Three metres away from me, I saw movement blink in and out of focus, like a frame skipped in a movie reel. The rotten smell clipped in and out with it. Black. Big.

I stepped backwards, putting a tree between me and whatever it was. I wasn't dumb enough to think it was my imagination. Not any more. Blink. The movement flickered again. This time it was barely a metre away from me – flashing a negative image on my eyes, as if I had looked into the sun and then closed my eyes. The after-image was of a great, dark animal, taller than my waist, neck pulled back and long, long body crouched. Getting ready to—

The attack came from behind, and the force of it took my breath away. My shoulder hit the ground, but I didn't feel any pain. All I could think about was the crushing weight on my chest, and I wondered if I would ever find my breath again. And that stench. That rotten smell, as if I were already dead and decomposing. A massive feline head, too long and narrow to be a proper wildcat, surged towards my neck.

I threw an arm up; anything to keep those teeth from my neck. The cat's teeth sank into my forearm with no resistance at all. It tossed me up in front of it. I gasped, but there was no one to hear. It was as if this wood were a thousand kilometres away from the church and the wedding goers.

My arm burned in the cat's grip. I used my other hand to jab my fingers into its eye, and with a snarl, it released me. Blink. Flash. It was behind me, paws and claws throwing me to the ground again. Blink. On the other side of me, worrying me like a mouse. Blink. Seizing my arm again.

Fire burned under the massive teeth. I scraped, pummelled, clawed at the cat, but I had no effect on the rock-hard muscles beneath its skin. I was being toyed with and it was going to kill me. Because I'd washed Granna's ring down the drain. I was going to die because I was a *frigging idiot*.

The cat snarled suddenly, spinning, dragging me with it by my arm. I saw a flash of someone else, a person. The person seized my arm as well, gripping the cat's head with his other arm.

"Don't," I gasped. "Not a normal cat – watch out—"

"I *am* watching out," snapped Luke.

Oh God. What was he doing here?

The cat was tearing my arm one way, Luke was tearing it another way, and I saw claws and red. With another raspy snarl, the cat dropped me and sprang towards Luke, probably twice his weight and taller when on its back legs. This was going to be awful.

But in the time it took me to stumble to my feet, Luke had seized the cat by the side of its face and the skin of its neck. As the cat raked a massive paw towards his face, Luke pulled a dagger out of nowhere and slid the blade into the bottom of the cat's jaw. Just like that. His expression was the same vague one he'd wore when he spoke to Eleanor – just as calm – and the motion he used was effortless, practised, efficient.

The cat fell to the ground by his feet, somehow even larger when dead. I stared at it, the limp angle of its neck, the dagger stuck into the bottom of its head. I watched Luke pull the dagger free, wipe it carefully on the grass and replace it in a sheath under his trouser leg. I was frozen in place by the memory of his face as he killed it.

Luke looked at me, questioning. It was the look you'd give a stray dog, holding your hand out, finding out if it would let you approach. I suddenly remembered the question he'd asked earlier: "Do I scare you?"

I swallowed and found out I had a voice after all. "I washed Granna's ring down the drain."

It was all the permission Luke needed. He was by my side in a second, taking my trembling arm in his hands, wiping the blood away with his own T-shirt, examining the four puncture wounds. His fingers touched the bruises blossoming on my shoulder and the scrapes on my neck, and then he crushed me to him. He held me so tightly it hurt, and I felt his breath ragged on my skin.

Then he released me. "Where's the key? Where's the ring?"

I was breathless, though probably for the wrong reasons. "I told you, I accidentally washed the ring down the drain."

"And the key?"

I looked down. "Mom told me to take it off."

"Your mother's an idiot!" Luke circled me, looking for more damage. I noticed the claw marks in his jeans, the red that stained his calf.

"You're bleeding."

Luke stopped in front of me. "So are you. You could've — it could've been a lot worse."

I remembered abruptly. "Granna's supposed to pick me up. What am I going to tell her?"

"The truth."

That was almost laughable. "She'll never believe me. She's pretty out there, but not homicidal-wild-cat out there."

"She'll believe you." Luke pointed to the harp case. "Is the key in there?"

I nodded and watched him retrieve it. I stood quietly as he clasped it around my neck once more, the scrape on my neck stinging slightly as the chain moved over it. He kissed the skin next to where the key hung, sending a chill through my body, and then hugged me again. He spoke into my ear, for me alone. "Please be careful."

That sounded like a goodbye, but I didn't want to be left alone to wait for Granna. "Are you leaving?"

"I'll watch you. But she wouldn't like to see me with you."

I let him get a few steps away, and then I asked the burning question. "Why were you here?"

Luke shrugged. "You wanted saving, didn't you?"

Nine

One of Granna's more positive traits is also one of the most annoying: it's damn near impossible to get her panicked or flustered. Like Mom, she has her extreme emotions packed away in a little box, only to be taken out for special occasions. Seeing me with minor signs of supernatural mauling didn't qualify as a special occasion.

Instead, she just helped me get my harp in the car, got a paint-spattered towel from the back seat, and spread it on the passenger seat so I wouldn't get blood on her fuzzy grey seats that smelled of orange solvents. She put the car in gear without a word.

I poked at my wounds; I was a bit proud of them. They were the best sort of injury – they looked awful but really didn't hurt too much. Their gore was being wasted on Granna, whose pity was in the same box as the rest of her emotions. "Do you have some paper towels or something?"

As she pulled out of the car park, I glanced discreetly in the rear-view mirror, hoping for a glimpse of Luke, but there was only an audience of birches visible. I wondered what would happen to the giant cat's body.

"Alcohol wipes in the glove compartment," Granna said. "We'll clean it up better at my house."

"Your house?" I paused, hand in glove compartment.

Granna really looked at me for the first time, and I blinked, seeing so much of Mom's eyes in hers, hidden with crow's feet. "Do you really want to explain that dress to your mother? I have some of your clothes at my house still."

So maybe Luke was right. She would believe the truth.

"What was it?" Her voice was calm and even; she might as well have been asking, "How did it go?" or "Did you have a nice day today?"

I sighed, a little amazed that I was just going to tell the truth, and then I described the entire attack – from the loss of the ring to Luke's rescue. I took great pleasure in telling that last bit, actually, after the way she'd treated him in the driveway. I waited for her to distil it into some tidy tale devoid of passion and danger, but she said nothing for a moment. The car was silent, except for its tyres whirring on a road dappled with the shapes of summer leaves.

Finally her mouth quirked, and she said, "We should talk about this once you've got cleaned up."

I wasn't sure why the discussion would be any different once I was wearing different clothing, but Granna was as dangerous to poke as Mom. We didn't speak again until we'd got to her old, L-shaped farmhouse in the middle of a cornfield.

"The clothes are upstairs in the guest room. In the wardrobe on the shelf. I'll get you some tea." She headed for the kitchen and I headed up the stairs.

The farmhouse was always draughty, no matter how hot it was outside, and the guest room was the worst. Granna had covered the creaking, splintery wood floor with a colourful woven rag rug and hung bright abstract paintings on the pale-as-ice walls, but it always felt cold to me. Cold like nasty chill-in-your-head cold, not grab-me-a-sweater cold. Dad had told me that this had been Delia's old room, and that as a child she'd nearly died here. Even without the dying part, just knowing that this room had helped form Delia's charming personality made me hate it.

I grabbed my clothing from the wardrobe – so that's where my favourite baggy cords had gone – and changed in the bathroom. As I rinsed the dried blood from my skin, I remembered the feeling of Luke crushing me to him and the smell of him pressed against my nostrils. A fist squeezed my stomach at the memory . . . like nerves, but better.

Where is he now?

I joined Granna down in the kitchen, blinking in the bright sunshine pouring through the windows. She put a glass of iced tea in my hand and gestured for me to sit at the round table.

She studied my arm to see if I'd got it clean. "You know what's happening here, don't you?"

I felt a little stupid. "Faeries?"

She looked up at me abruptly. "Don't say it. Say the word, and They'll listen. There's a reason why They're called 'The Good Neighbours' and 'The Fair Folk'. The other word, it's like an insult. It's coarse."

I drank some tea. Granna never made it sweet enough – something about refined sugars being bad for you, blah blah blah. "So, if you knew about Them all along, why didn't you say anything? Just 'oh here, wear this ugly ring,' with no explanation?"

Granna pursed her lips, but I could tell she was trying not to smile. "So that's why you washed it down the drain?"

"That really was an accident."

"Mmm. They've always been a bit of bother to the female side of the family."

Bit of bother. I'd just been chewed on by a cat that made Jaws look like an irritable guppy. If that was only a bit of bother, I'd hate to see the whole thing.

Granna drummed her fingers on the table. "You're about the right age for Them to start making trouble. Shallow things. I don't think They have much use for anything old or not beautiful. They're only interested in brand new toys." She shrugged, as if she were talking about an ant problem or something equally mundane. "So I gave you the ring."

"You act like They're nothing to be afraid of."

She shrugged again. "If you're wearing iron, They really can't do anything. Why do you think there aren't stories on the news about changelings and stolen children all the time? We have iron everywhere now. They bothered Delia and your mother when they were younger, and then They gave up."

That was a weird thought. My straight-up mother being bothered by faeries? Delia was even weirder. I could picture the scene. Faerie: *Come away, human.* Delia: *Why?* Faerie: *Untold delights and youth for ever.* Delia: *I'm holding out for a better offer. Ta.*

"Why didn't you give me the ring sooner? You know, at birth or something."

"I really thought that They had given up on us. But then I saw him, and I knew They were back."

I didn't have to ask who "him" was. My stomach lurched again, only this time it *was* nerves, and not the good kind. I didn't know what to say. Anything I said would betray my increasing infatuation with him, and I didn't think Granna would respond well to that. And even if I could get a question out with an innocent voice, I didn't want to hear the answer.

I held on fast to the image of him saving me, and clinging to me after the cat was dead; I tied myself to it like a sailor to a mast, with a storm on the horizon.

And the storm came. "He's one of Them, Deirdre."

I shook my head.

"I know he is. I saw him twenty years ago, and he looked just the same as he did the other day."

She had mistaken him for someone else.

"Right before the rest of Them show up, he does. He was there for Delia."

I managed to get a few words out. "He saved me, Granna. Did you forget that part?"

She shrugged, irritatingly nonchalant. I wanted to smack her for casually trampling over my heart. "It's all games, Deirdre. They love games. Cruel sports. Don't you remember the old bedtime stories? Riddles and names and trickery. And why would They want you dead, anyway? They want to steal you away." She mistook the look on my face, and unusual sympathy crept into her voice. "Oh, don't worry! I'll find you another piece of iron jewellery."

I grasped the key at my neck and thrust it towards her. "He can touch iron, Granna. You said They couldn't touch it. Well, he can. He could touch the ring, and he gave me this. He warned me about Them." I pushed my chair back angrily. "I don't think he's one of Them."

Granna pulled the lid off her box of emotions just long enough to let a frown escape. "Are you sure he can touch iron?"

In my head, his fingers touched the skin next to the key, held my fingers, glanced against the ring.

"I'm sure."

She actually let another frown, a deeper one, out of

the box. "He must – he must be some sort of half-breed. Something – did he have eyedrops?"

My heart, which had begun to beat faster at the word "half-breed", stopped when she mentioned the drops. I didn't have to answer; my face told her everything she wanted to know.

"He has to use the drops to see Them." She stood up and pushed her chair in. "I'm going to have to see if I can make something that will work on him."

I couldn't help myself. "Do you have to?"

She looked at me again, hard. "Deirdre, everything he's told you is a lie. They don't have souls. They don't have friends. They don't love. They play. They're big, cruel children and They want shiny new toys. You're shiny and new. He's playing you."

I thought I ought to feel like crying, then, but my eyes weren't even a little wet. Or I should be angry, or something, but I was just nothing. I was so full of nothing that it was *something*.

"Go and relax on the sofa. I'll be in the workshop, and I'll take you home when I'm done."

I didn't answer, because nothing had no voice. I just did what she said and retreated to the living room, reaching for the image of Luke holding me, and finding nothing.

I watched *Cops* reruns until the shadows shifted and lengthened over the edge of the white wicker sofa.

The eight-hundredth cop was slamming the eight-hundredth criminal over the back of their car when my phone rang. I looked at the number and picked it up. "Hi."

"Capital D!" James's voice exclaimed, distantly.

I couldn't work up the same enthusiasm. "Sorry I didn't call you today. I'm at—"

"Granna's. Your mom told me. She sounds pissier than an incontinent water buffalo. Can I come over and hang out?"

I considered. I didn't know what I wanted, but being alone wasn't it. "That would be great."

"I was hoping you'd say that," James said, and I heard a car door shut outside the window. "Because I'm already here and it would suck to drive back home now."

The phone went dead in my hand, and then I heard the screen door slam. James found me in the living room, and I stood up to move a stack of holistic healing books from the other end of the sofa.

He set a large fast-food cup on the end table. "I know Granna doesn't make it sweet enough, so I brought you some of the real stuff from Sticky Pig." He eyed my arm, which was clean but obviously chewed on. "Are you OK?"

He looked so normal and *safe*, standing there with his summer-brown arms and his *Sarcasm: Just Another Service I Offer* T-shirt. He looked like every summer I'd ever known and reminded me of everything I couldn't seem to have right now. I fought valiantly with a strange rush of emotions for about one-third of a second, and then I burst into tears.

"Hey, hey!" James sat down with me on the couch and let me cry on to his sarcasm T-shirt. He didn't ask any questions or try to get me to talk, because that's how awesome a friend he is. Realizing that just made me cry more. And then I thought of how pathetic this whole crying jag was, which made me cry even more.

James bundled me closer as I started to shiver, his arms wrapped tightly around me like a living sweater. My teeth chattered. I finally stuttered, "I think I'm in shock."

He reached up and wiped tears from my cheeks with the side of his writing-scrawled hand. "Does this have anything to do with the chomp marks on your arm? If you had them before, I don't remember them. And I've got, like, a *crazy* eye for detail."

I laughed pitifully. "If I'd had a video camera when I got them, I'd be rich. It was this giant cat-thing." I swallowed a new batch of stupid tears and shuddered again, involuntarily. "When will the shivering stop?"

"When you calm your ass down." He stood up and tugged on my good arm. "C'mon. You need fries, obviously."

I let him haul me up, feeling better already. "What I *need* is a supernatural stun gun."

"Maybe they'll have one of those, too. I didn't look closely at the daily specials."

A thought occurred to me. "I have to tell Granna I'm going. She's doing some sort of voodoo in her workshop."

We headed into the hot day, following the rock stepstone path Granna had made to her workshop. Herbs and gangly flowers intruded into our way, along with their insect retinues, and I laughed when James swung wildly at a bee that came too close.

"Squealing like a little girl," I said.

"Shut up, you!"

Granna's voice came from inside the open door of her shop. "Is that you, James?"

James followed me into the dim blue of the workshop. "Uh-yup." Though the workshop was lit by three exposed light bulbs, and light fell in through the open door, it was no match for the blazing sunlight outside. I blinked until my eyes got used to the change.

"What brings you here?" Granna looked up from her main work table. She'd pushed her paint cans, brushes, and varnish to one side to make room for her latest project; presumably, the faerie equivalent of a bug bomb. Or maybe just the equivalent of insect repellent. Whatever it was smelled sharp and unpleasant, like too much air freshener sprayed in a small room.

"A little bird told me Dee was hungry." James poked around Granna's smaller work tables, looking at the wood plaques painted with complex patterns and prodding at a large rock tumbler. "I rode to the rescue. I know where I can find her some good saturated fats."

Granna laughed. She liked James; but then again, everybody did. "She could use a bit of looking after right now." Then she paused. I think she was waiting to see how much I'd told James before going on.

James picked up a stone with a hole in it and looked at Granna through the hole. "We wouldn't want anything unnatural to carry her away, hmm?"

Granna, satisfied, went back to mercilessly mashing an innocent plant into a green paste. "No, we wouldn't. Have you got anything iron on you?"

"Nope."

Granna offered him the iron band from her wrist; it was smooth and dull, with knobs on the two ends that almost met. "This is the last bit I have. Take it."

"I think you need it more than I do."

She shook her head and gestured to the pile of paste. "This stuff will work a good sight better than iron when it's done. If you're going to be going out and about with her, you'll need it."

James accepted it, reluctantly, and spread the two ends of the band to fit around his wrist. "Thanks."

Granna gestured to me with a green-muck-covered pestle. "Use your head, and remember what I told you. I'll see you later this evening. I'll bring this over. Don't tell your mother I'm coming or she'll feel compelled to make a truffle cake or slaughter a pig."

I laughed. It was too true not to.

James, at my elbow, tugged me towards the door.

"Oh." Granna frowned at me. "And watch what you say around Delia."

How interesting.

Ten

It was always noisy at the Sticky Pig, the only real restaurant in town. It was still too hot to eat outside, though, so we joined the ranks of loud, hungry people waiting to get a table. Smelling the smoky scent of barbecue and standing behind the "Please wait to be seated" sign with the smiling pig on it, I had a momentary sense of déjà vu, or missing time or something. Something about coming here so many times over so many years made me forget how old I really was now, and what I'd been doing before I walked in. James brought me back to the present by elbowing me.

"Come away from the light," he said in a low voice. "Deirdre, come back to the land of the living, come back to us – ah! There she is, folks!"

I gave him a withering look. "I was thinking."

"About outer space, I guess, if your dreamy, distant expression was anything to go by." He smiled charmingly at the hostess, who was dazzled. "Deuce, please. None of that smoking crap."

She was too smitten to respond, so I translated. "Two for non-smoking, please."

The hostess nodded mutely and led us to a booth. We slid in on opposite sides. After she'd gone, I leaned towards James. "She was cute."

James picked up the menu (as if he didn't have it memorized by now) and muttered, "Not interested." He was looking at the back of the menu; the pig on the front smiled at me from beneath its checked apron. "Lucky day. They *do* have supernatural stun guns as a dinner special."

I swatted the menu down from in front of his face. "*And* she was dazzled."

He pulled it back up again, engrossed by the list of side dishes. "Not interested."

"Why *not*?" I was really pushing it too hard, but I felt guilty. I was falling for Luke like a load of books out of a truck, and if I could at least get James to flirt with someone, I wouldn't feel so much like I was betraying our best-friendship.

He lowered the menu and looked at me, eyes narrowed. "I'm interested in somebody else, for your information." He looked away. "I wasn't going to tell you."

Relief washed over me. *Thank you, God; may she be very pretty and all-engrossing and human.*

"You know, you can tell me that sort of stuff." OK, the guilt came back a little bit right there because I hadn't told *him* that sort of stuff. "Do I know her?"

James shrugged. "Maybe." He brightened a bit. "She was in my science section this year." He smiled, but not with his eyes. I looked at them intently, and he seemed to feel the need to elaborate. "Her name's Tara."

Funny thing, that, but as he spoke and I looked at his eyes, I felt like I saw movement shimmer around his head, like oil floating on top of water. I blinked.

"She has red hair," James continued. The oil shimmer became more solid; juxtaposed over James's face was an indistinct female face, hair hanging choppily down on either side of her cheeks. "Wavy. And green eyes." A pair of grey eyes looked back at me, moody and introspective. "You'll laugh," he added, "because she's a goth chick. Black make-up and all. Spiky choker. I dig that." But the girl in front of me, dark-haired, grey-eyed, no make-up, with a blue V-neck, wasn't a goth chick. The girl that was shimmering out of James's consciousness was me.

I looked away from his eyes, at the floor, and the image vanished. "She sounds interesting."

OK. Maybe I was delusional. Maybe I was just imagining myself floating mysteriously in the air on a cosmic television screen. But I didn't think so. I think I read his mind.

Oh man.

This was about one thousand times harder to swallow than being able to move spoons.

The more I thought about it, the more I couldn't seem to wrap my brain around it. I could avoid moving spoons. I couldn't very well avoid looking into someone's eyes for the rest of my life. I didn't want this.

"Deirdre!" I focused on James again. "He asked what you wanted to drink."

The pimply waiter stood by the table, and I tried to look at him without looking at his eyes.

"Sorry," James jumped in. "My friend here was attacked by my mother's ill-tempered Bichon Frise earlier today and I'm afraid she's in a bit of shock. Could you get her some sweet tea? Better bring her some fries, too."

The waiter fled. I stared at the table.

"What is *wrong* with you? You're completely spaced out." James reached across the table and knocked my chin up with his finger. "Is this about the killer cat or the goth chick?"

I sighed miserably. "I didn't want normal until I didn't have it any more."

At that, he smiled. "Dee, you were never normal."

His answer was too easy, like some inspirational poster. "I was never *this* not normal. I'm a total freak and freak-magnet, now."

"Dee, moving clover and being hunted by evil fey doesn't change who you are. It's like learning to play a musical instrument. It's just something you *do*. And the evil fey — well, they're kinda like stalker-groupies.

You're still the same you underneath, no matter how big the spoons are that you learn to move or how wildly the groupies are rocking the van as you drive away. The only thing that can change *you* during all this is *you*."

I frowned at him, careful not to study his eyes too closely. "When did you get so smart?"

He tapped his forehead. "Brain transplant. They put in a whale's. I'm passing all my classes with my eyes closed now, but I just can't get over this craving for krill." He shrugged. "And I feel sorry for the whale that got my brain. Probably swimming around Florida now trying to catch glimpses of girls in bikinis."

I laughed. It was impossible to talk about anything serious with James, but it was impossible to be upset, too. I think I probably took him for granted. "Why do you believe me?"

"Why shouldn't I?"

"Because it's crazy."

James's eyes darkened, and for a second I thought I saw something more to good old safe James. "Maybe I'm crazy as well."

By the time James dropped me off, it was nearly dark. Granna hadn't come by the house yet, or if she had, Mom didn't mention it. I wondered how long Granna's green muck would take to prepare. And where she'd learned to make it.

I escaped from Mom's grip before she could question me too closely and put on a long-sleeved shirt to cover up the chew marks. As I walked back into the twilight kitchen, Mom looked up from one of the bar stools. She pushed a mug of hot cocoa across the island towards me. A white flag. I accepted it without hesitation. For starters, I'd forgotten how she'd left me at the church; also, her made-from-scratch cocoa covered a multitude of sins.

She looked into the steam of her cocoa as it swirled upwards, looking young and pretty in the dim ochre light of the kitchen. Knowing Mom, she probably painted the walls ochre for just that reason. "Did your gig go well?"

So it was to be the cosy approach.

"Very well. Granna and I had a good time together. She—" I stopped, realizing that Granna had asked me not to tell Mom she was coming. "She has my dress at her house. I accidentally got some soda on it and she's going to clean it."

"And James got you some dinner?"

I took a sip of the cocoa. Dark chocolate sludge slid down my throat and for a moment I forgot what the question was. Mom had to repeat it. I took another sip. There was a hint of orange in there. "At the Sticky Pig."

"I'd rather you spend time with James than Luke."

I frowned, but didn't look up. It was one thousand

times easier to cross Mom when you didn't look at her. "Why?"

"For one thing, I know James. I know his family. I know you're all right when you're with him."

"I'm all right when I'm with Luke." I thought of him sliding the dagger silently into the cat's jaw, sticking a blade through its brain without a second's hesitation.

"He's too old for you. And he doesn't go to your school." The last sentence was a bit indecisive. She was guessing.

I looked up, right at her. Her weakness lay in her indecision. I wondered how many times I'd had an opening in a discussion like this and missed it because I was too complacent.

"You're right. He's only here for the summer, and he's a senior. I know he's a little old. But I'm not doing anything stupid. And he's a gentleman. Is there anything wrong with that?"

Mom blinked. I don't think she knew what to do. Had I ever rationally contradicted her before? Ever? She drank her cocoa, still young and pretty, but now with a glaring chink in her armour.

I could have waited for her to say something, but I didn't. I pressed home my victory. "And I have my mobile phone with me all the time, so you can always get me. Don't I always answer it? You raised me to know what to do. You're going to have to trust me."

Oh, damn, that was good! I washed my smile down with some cocoa. *That was killer.*

Mom sighed. "I suppose you're right. But I do want to know whenever you're out with him." She stood up and went to the kitchen to rinse out her mug, her head framed by the dark night window above the sink. "What does James think about this?"

"Uh – what do you mean?"

She turned and faced me, expression slightly withering. "Use your brain, Deirdre."

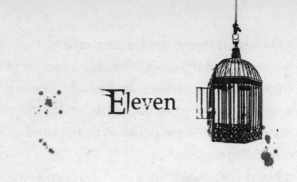

Eleven

In my dream, Luke was sitting in his tired Bucephalus, arms crossed on the steering wheel, forehead resting on them. Barely visible in the moving darkness of the car, the torc on his arm glinted, a dull secret.

I wasn't in the car, but I could see the corner of his face as if I were an invisible, tiny watcher perched on the gear stick. His lips moved, his voice barely audible.

"I am Luke." The pause before his next words stretched into hours, lifetimes. Mist moved outside the car windows, pale, damp fingers leaving marks on the glass. "It's been one thousand, three hundred and forty-eight years, two months, and one week. Please don't forget me."

The mist dragged with it a kind of slow, dangerous music, alluring, like the promise of sleep to a dying man. Luke stretched out his arm to the radio and spun the knob.

Sound blasted out of the speakers and shook me awake. Blinking around my room, I couldn't figure out what time it was; the light in the living room was odd.

Then I realized that it was because mist pressed against the windows, and the moon reflected into every cranny. I groaned and stretched out on the sofa, working out a crick in my neck. Rye looked up at me from his post on the floor. His expression suggested that both of us would sleep better in my bed.

"But there's freaks up there," I whispered to him. I sat up and stretched again, catching a glimpse of the clock on the wall: two a.m. Sleep seemed far away.

Before I had time to wonder what had woken me out of my dream, I heard a dull *tap* on the window. Rye sprang to his feet. I jumped, more startled by Rye's sudden movement than the noise. At the window, a face loomed out of the mist, nose pressed against the glass, leaving a print.

Even as Rye began to growl, I relaxed. It was Luke. He pressed his nose against the window again, making a funny face. I held up my finger to him – *just a second* – and bounded into the kitchen. I paused in front of the laundry room to put on jeans and my long-sleeved T-shirt from earlier, feeling a little stupid that Luke had seen me in my slinky pyjama top and crazy hair. Rye followed me to the back door, still rumbling under his breath.

Only then did I remember what Granna had said. The little voice that always agreed with Mom and Granna and Delia whispered *faerie. Playing with your emotions. Steal you away. Immune from iron. Keep away.*

I don't know why my conscience even bothered. I had known as soon as I saw Luke at the window that nothing would keep me from going out to meet him. I had to. My heart was already pounding at the idea that he was outside, without him having to say a single word. I was pathetic, but knowing I was pathetic didn't help me.

I opened the back door into a silvery, foreign world. The mist hung in the air and the moonlight glanced through it, turning the landscape a shimmery blue. Luke stood just off the back steps, a long-sleeved black shirt covering his torc, his hands in his pockets, everything about him blue and light. This felt more like a dream than the one I'd just had.

"Sorry if I woke you." He didn't sound apologetic.

I shut the door softly behind me and stood on the stairs, acutely aware that Mom and Dad slept inside. I kept my voice low. "I wasn't sleeping very well, anyway."

"I wasn't sleeping at all." He glanced around at the mist and then back at me, smiling vaguely. "In retrospect, it seems awfully selfish to wake you up to entertain me during my insomnia."

I crossed my arms and turned my face into the slight breeze; the night smelled wonderful, all cut grass and faraway flowers. It was a night that made you think the sun was overrated. "How do you want me to entertain you? I can step dance a little, but it looks pretty silly in bare feet."

Luke narrowed his eyes as if he were imagining me step-dancing. "I don't think I need to see that. I'd rather—" For the first time, he looked uncertain, glancing away into the shifting blue light. "I know you said you didn't want to be 'practice'. But you could take a walk with me, and I could pretend I was still only fascinated by you and nothing more."

My stomach flipped. It took more effort than I imagined to force my feet to stay on the steps. "Is it safe for me to go with you?"

His face was unreadable, a mask to me, and he sighed. "Probably not."

I sighed, too, and then I joined him at the base of the steps and held out my hand. Luke looked at my outstretched fingers for a moment, and then up at my face.

"You did hear me say probably *not*, right?"

I nodded. "I don't care. I'll go with you." I was going to stop there, but the words tumbled out. "Isn't that what you do? Tangle me up so I don't know which way I'm going and then steal me away?"

He stared at me.

The silence forced words out of me. "Granna told me what you are."

He stared for another long moment, and when the words came out, they were forced. "What – am – I?"

I almost said "faerie", but I remembered and swallowed the word. "One of Them. She'd seen you before. That's why she hates you. She's making something to keep you away from me." The words were falling out; I couldn't seem to shut up.

Luke's body had gone completely stiff and his voice was tight. "You think I'm one of Them?"

"I don't *know*. I don't care. That's what I'm trying to tell you. I don't *care* what you are." I stepped back, biting my lip. I'd just tipped every bit of emotion out of the box that I, as a Monaghan woman, was supposed to keep locked away.

Luke's hands were tight fists by his sides. "I'm not one of Them."

"Then what are you?"

"I can't tell you. Or anyone. I could sooner fly."

Inspiration blossomed, sudden and brilliant. "You can," I said.

He shook his head. "I *can't*."

"You don't have to say anything. Let me try and read your mind." It was such a simple, perfect idea. Why hadn't I thought of it before? In my head, I saw the image of me shimmering out of James' mind. If I could see that by focusing for one second on his eyes, how much more could I do if I really tried?

I could see the resistance on his face. If he really was what Granna said, he would never agree. Maybe he wasn't what Granna said, and he would refuse anyway. I wasn't sure I would want my mind read, and I didn't have anything to hide.

Luke looked into the mist again, and then closed the distance between us, his voice low. "You can do that?"

"I think so. I sort of did earlier today."

He chewed his lower lip. It was endearing, like a little kid trying to make a decision. "I don't know. It's so—"

"Private?"

"Yeah." He took a deep breath. "OK. OK. Let's do it. But not here. Some place safer."

The mood had changed; suddenly we were on the same side again. I looked out into the slanting blue light, wondering who or what we had to be safe from now. And what counted as a safer place. Surely he didn't mean to drive to the city again. Maybe a church? The nearest church was ten minutes away if we drove.

"There's a cemetery near here, isn't there?" Luke's voice broke into my thoughts. "I thought I saw one."

I nodded. "Do you mean the one just behind our house? The old one with the big monument?"

"It's got an iron fence around it, doesn't it?"

I frowned. "But no gate."

"Doesn't matter. They can't go underneath an iron archway. It's got one of those, hasn't it?" He pressed his fist to his forehead. "God, I can't believe I'm doing this. You don't know how stupid this is for me." He unclenched the fist and held his hand out to me. I took it and he clutched it tightly. "Dumb as dumb."

Together, we walked through the back garden, into

the silvered trees, and down the worn deer trail that led to the cemetery. Around us, the air glowed and moved, changing and swirling, touching us with invisible cold hands, hanging in the trees like gauze, glimmering on the leaves like precious jewels. There was nothing human in this night but me and Luke, holding tightly to each other's hands, surrounded by magic thick enough to touch.

I felt watched.

Luke never let go of my hand, but he never let down his guard, either. Everything in his posture indicated tension; watchful power wound tight enough to snap. After seeing what he'd done to that cat, it was hard to imagine the enemy that would be able to overcome him. Unless he was the enemy.

The iron archway of the old cemetery appeared abruptly among the periwinkle trees, and Luke pushed me through it quickly, jumping in after me as if just barely escaping grasping jaws. I looked back through the archway and blinked as a barely glimpsed shadow passed beyond the arch and disappeared into the mist. Slow goosebumps rose on my arms. I thought about asking Luke what he thought the shadow might have been, but I didn't really want to know. It was easier to be brave without knowing.

"Inside?" I suggested, barely whispering. Luke followed my gaze over to the massive marble monument in the centre of the cemetery and nodded. We picked our way between headstones and tall grey sycamores, the dead listening as our feet walked across them. I had never thought that I would feel safer inside a cemetery than outside.

The monument towered before us; icy white in the mist. It was like a three-sided tomb, and inside was a statue of a man cradling a child. They too were icy white marble, larger than life, frozen solid in a dark blue sea. I scrambled into the monument without pause, feeling safer in its shadows, and Luke followed me.

I sat in the far corner, the marble wall cold against my back, and watched Luke take a handful of nails from his pocket. He laid them carefully in a straight line across the mouth of the monument, all pointing in the same slanted direction, before sitting in the opposite corner from me.

"Why?" I asked.

"The direction of the gate. The nails will move if someone tries to come through by force. If They come through such a narrow hole, their – essence – will push the ends around."

I stared at the nails, unmoving on the marble. "I thought you said They couldn't go under the archway."

Luke's face was pale. "Most of Them."

I didn't want to think about that. I whispered, "Do you still want to do this?"

He jerked his chin in another nod. "What do I have to do?"

I bit my lip, feeling suddenly doubtful. What if I'd been wrong about what happened at the Sticky Pig? Maybe I couldn't really read minds. Maybe it *had* been a delusion. Maybe we'd braved a midnight journey with *something* following us just to sit in a cold marble tomb and stare at each other.

"Dee," Luke said softly. "What do I have to do?"

I looked up; his pale eyes glinted in the chilly darkness. "Let me look at your eyes."

He sighed and pulled his knees up to his chest, linking his arms around them. His voice was small. "Don't think less of me."

Then he fixed his eyes on me. For a moment I could focus on nothing but how nice it was to just be able to unabashedly stare at his face, looking at the straight, narrow line of his nose, the uncertain line of his lips, and the pale eyebrows lowered over his ice-flecked eyes.

A brilliant white bird flapped over his head, startling me. As I jumped, it vanished like smoke in the wind.

Luke was already on his feet. "What?"

I shook my head. "I'm sorry. I saw a bird. It surprised me."

He grinned, a little nervous. "I was thinking of a bird."

We returned to our positions, and I began again. "Try something else."

Even though I knew to expect something, I still

started when the clover dropped to the floor between us.

"Clover?" I asked.

Luke nodded.

But I wanted more. Not twenty questions. I wanted the whole enchilada. "Think of nothing."

He looked uneasy. "Nature abhors a vacuum." But he nodded to show he was ready.

This time, I began to *feel* the sensation of seeing into his mind. My forehead between my eyes felt warm as I began to focus, and as the shimmering medium grew in the space between us, I felt a bit of pressure; hesitation. Luke was letting me in, but only barely.

A low, breathy note sounded, but this time I didn't jump. I could tell now that it was coming from within the shimmer that was Luke's mind. The flute continued, wending a familiar march around the image of a broad green plain studded with boulders the size of men. The image swept away like grains of sand and in its place was a dark bar, musicians packed elbow to elbow, the frenzied music pounding out some sort of eternal heartbeat. Faster than before, that image was gone, replaced with a set of car keys jangling into the door of a car. Just as fast, another image appeared: me, walking into my first day of high school. Another: a young man with a streak of gold in his dark hair, clapping Luke on the shoulder.

I *felt* Luke shiver, leaning against the opposite wall. Images kept flashing before my eyes. Luke curled in a small dark space, shuddering with cold. A fiddler playing a reel, Luke's familiar flute finding counterpoint. A beautiful woman grasping Luke by the back of his neck as he fell to his knees. White lines flying beneath the tyres of a car.

And faster still, a slide show on high speed. A wickedly beautiful knife. A young man, falling on to his face in a wet street, a knife jutting from his side.

Another man, in strange clothing, his neck warm and pulsing life between Luke's hands, gasping and falling. A searing pain in Luke's chest.

A woman, her shrill cry cut off as a blade sliced her white skin. Hands gripping three iron nails until they left red in his palm.

Another young man, his neck stabbed as neatly as the big cat's. A girl my age, life gasping out with each breath, crimson around her.

The savage knife ripping shred after shred in Luke's arm, cutting at the golden band. Lying in a pool of blood and self-destruction. A white bird flapping in blood. Rising out of the blood. Another body. Another. Hands covered with red.

All I could see before my eyes was red, rising with increasing vertigo. I collapsed on to the cold marble, my breaths too slow and far apart. The wounds on my arm stung.

"*Enough.*" Luke's voice, barely audible, came from across the floor. He was slumped against the wall, paler than white. His face, colourless and miserable, turned away, and I saw a single tear made of blood drip down his cheek, leaving a red stain behind it.

I knew then that I had done more than read his mind.

Twelve

I lay on the marble for ever while the gravestones outside marked time, the moon's shadow moving around them, lighting the other side of their worn surfaces and illuminating Christian names that hadn't been used in decades. Cold crept through me, passing from the marble into my veins. Every moment that I lay on the cold stone, hoping and dreading that Luke would pull me from the ground, images of death flew through my head. No. Not just death. Murder.

I didn't know what to think, so my brain just stopped. Then I could sit up. I looked across the dark tomb to where Luke made a light shape on the marble, a strange pale character in an alphabet I didn't know. His cheek lay against the wall as he stared out into the night, eyes dull. There was still a dried blood trail where the single strange tear had traced its way along his cheekbone and found a path along the edge of his jaw. I followed his gaze out to the headstones and watched the mist, ever thickening, creep around their bases.

Graves. How appropriate.

I thought about asking him if he'd really killed all those people. But then I remembered him saying, *Do I scare you?*

He'd really killed them.

So he wasn't a faerie. He was a murderer.

I looked back at him, huddled there so miserable and regretful. Anger boiled in my throat, sudden and hard to swallow. I wondered what twisted logic let him look so torn up over the deaths, now – and then would let him do it again.

"So, that's your secret?" I snapped. Luke's head didn't turn. "You're not a faerie – you're just a serial killer?" I should have said "one of Them" instead, but I didn't care at that point. Supernatural beings seemed the least of my problems.

Luke was perfectly still, just another marble statue in the monument.

Somehow his silence just made me angrier. I found I could get to my feet, and I did, staring down at him from across the ever-widening space between us. "Were you going to kill me, is that what it was? Save me from Them so you could stab me in peace and quiet?"

He still didn't move. But he asked, his voice dead, "Aren't you afraid?"

"No! I'm *pissed off.*"

Finally, he looked at me, and his eyes silently begged for understanding. But how could there be understanding for this? It wasn't wild sex or drugs or a mammoth collection of Britney Spears posters that I'd uncovered in his mind. It was a trail of bodies. Real people, the life cut out of them as quickly as that wild cat's. It was maybe the one thing I couldn't forgive. I'd opened up my tightly sealed armour and let him in — and now it *hurt*.

"So, all those times you asked me if I thought you were sketchy or whatever — it's because you're a killer? A *murderer*?"

His voice was flat. "It's not like that."

I hugged my arms around myself. "Oh, how is it, then? They just accidentally got stuck on your knife? Let me guess. It was self-defence. That girl I saw, she was going to kick your ass."

He shook his head.

He wasn't even *denying* it. "How many? How many have you killed?" As if that mattered. As if it were like a maths test, where the number of wrong answers affected your score. He was a killer, no matter how many bodies he'd left behind.

"Don't make me remember."

"Why? Does it hurt? Don't you think it hurt them more?" Luke looked like my words cut him, but he had no right to mercy. "How many?" I snapped.

"Don't make me remember."

My anger shook my voice, which was wild and out of control. "You asshole. You let me believe you were the good guy. You made me trust you!"

"I'm sorry."

"Sorry doesn't friggin' cut it! You *killed* people. Not soldiers. Innocent people. I saw them. They weren't hurting you! You're just – you're just – a monster." The images were still flashing through my head, the violence perfectly preserved at the moment of death. I wanted to throw up, to somehow get the poison out of my system, but for once, I couldn't. He hadn't just killed them – he'd burdened me with the memories of their deaths. As if *I'd* done it.

I swiped a tear – a real tear, not a weird, bloody one – from my cheek and sank back down on to the floor. My anger was gone as quickly as it had come. I didn't want to feel anything at all.

"Can you forgive me?" Luke whispered.

I wiped another tear before it had a chance to fall. I wanted him to hurt as badly as I did. I looked at him, shaking my head, wondering how he could even ask.

"How could I?" His eyes held me, begging me to change my mind, pleading for forgiveness. I shook my head again. *"No."*

There was a long silence. Years passed before he spoke again.

His voice was barely there. "I didn't think so." He slowly stood up, and then he reached out a hand to me. "Come on. I'll take you home."

I stared at his hand. Did he really think I was going to take it? Those fingers, that strangled a man? That gripped a knife and carved a fine deadly line across a girl's throat? He must have seen my thoughts in my face, because he dropped his hand. The miserable line of his mouth would have broken my heart if I'd let myself forget all the blood he'd spilled.

I stood up without his hand and lifted my chin. If I'd learned anything from my mother, it was how to look like you were all right when you weren't. When *nothing* would be all right again. I turned my expression on him, emotions carefully packed away under ice, and said, "OK, let's go."

I should have been afraid; I knew from his memories that he could kill me before I even knew to run. I even knew where he still kept that wicked dagger, in a scabbard underneath the leg of his jeans. But my fear was locked away with everything else, and I didn't think I was going to open that box for a long time. Maybe not ever.

Luke sighed and retrieved his three nails from the entrance of the monument. "For what it's worth – I'm not going to hurt you. I can't."

I eyed him frostily. "The same way you 'can't' tell me anything about yourself?"

He shook his head, not looking at me. His eyes scanned the graveyard, though nothing was visible through the cloying mist. "Not that way at all. Come on. Before They come out."

A tiny chill escaped from my locked-away emotions.

Just when he said "They" – then, it was gone. It was probably stupid to be afraid of Them and not him, but I believed They wanted to hurt me. I couldn't believe that of Luke. I followed him from the monument, moving between the graves. We were as silent as ghosts. The mist fooled my eyes, but I was pretty sure we weren't going back the way we came.

"Why this way?" I whispered.

Luke's eyes darted past me. "We're climbing over the fence. They'll be expecting us to come out the gate." He looked back at me, his eyes finding the key that was still hanging against my skin, and kept moving. The mist shifted and shimmered, hiding even the massive trees until we were upon them. I didn't see the iron fence until I was close enough to touch it. The waist-high iron was solid and black, in a way that nothing else in the cloud around us was.

Luke gripped it and was over in half-a-breath's time. He held out a hand to me again.

Without touching him, I stepped on to the bottom rail of the fence and clambered over it. He lowered his hand again and led the way. It only took me a few moments to realize where we were – on the end of the road where I'd found his car parked. We were only a few minutes away from my house.

Then I smelled it. A familiar, sharp, sweet smell, hovering on the edge of the cut-grass smell. And I heard it, too: a sound almost like music, forming snatches of tune somewhere in the part of my brain I didn't think I used.

I *felt* Luke start to move a second before he moved, and then he grabbed me, pulling me towards the side of the road, his fingers tight on my arm. *Is this when I should start being afraid of him?*

He hadn't pulled me more than a few metres when a pleasant voice, halfway to a song, said, "I thought I was the only one who couldn't sleep."

For a moment I didn't recognize the voice, but then Luke stiffened and turned. I saw a tall, snowy figure step out of the mist towards us. She was all the more frightening because I knew her from far more ordinary circumstances — and she *shouldn't be here*. Eleanor was walking dead-centre down the road towards us, solidifying as she did. I couldn't tell if it was the effect of the mist or if she really was materializing right there on the road. Luke tightened his grip on me, shifting me subtly so that he stood between myself and Eleanor.

He looked at her, voice casual, as if he wasn't obviously shielding me from her. "What do you want?"

Eleanor smiled, so beautifully my head hurt. "Couldn't this be just a chance meeting?" She reached into the folds of her fine white dress and withdrew a long, pearly blade with a round, unadorned grip.

"It could be," Luke snarled. "What the hell do you want?"

The words sounded wrong in his mouth; desperate.

Eleanor laughed, a delicate sound that made the trees shake on either side of us. "Temper looks so bad on you, dear." She held out the polished bone knife towards him. "I brought this for you, since you seem to have lost yours."

"I didn't lose it."

She circled us. Luke held me so tightly it ached.

"Yes," she said finally. "I see that." She reached out as if she were going to touch my hair, her elegant fingers stretching towards my face, and then jerked back. Eleanor looked down at her fingers as if surprised at what they'd done, and then looked at Luke's secret, hanging around my neck.

Luke stepped back, pulling me with him. "Don't touch her. Keep your filthy hands away from her."

Eleanor studied her fingernails. "Hmm. I don't know why you're being so rude, sweetheart. We've been so forgiving of your schedule these past few days. Everyone's been so nice to you. I really expected to find you in a good mood. It's been quite long enough for you to be all rested up." She extended the knife towards him again. "And now you can just finish everything up and we'll all go back to our lives." She laughed, and this time the trees shuddered up and down the road. "Well, most of us."

I imagined its pearlescent surface lying gently across my neck, leaving a red trail behind it. He'd killed so many people before; I didn't know him at all. In my head, I saw his dagger slip into the cat's jaw. But I still couldn't be afraid, no matter how much my logical mind warned me to be. I couldn't seem to think of him as anything but my protector.

Next to me, Luke shook his head wordlessly.

Eleanor circled us again, her eyes on me this time, appraising. "Ah, Luke. You've made some poor choices over the years, we both know that, don't we? But I think this one is possibly *the worst choice you've ever made.*" The words oozed out, studded with poison. "So, are you sure you really won't do it? Just real quick? It would only take a moment. I would do it for you — but, you know."

"No." His voice was hard, but I felt him shaking against me.

Eleanor pouted gently, so beautiful that angels wept and flowers shrivelled. "Whatever shall I tell *her*, then?"

"Tell her—" Luke paused, and when he spoke again, his voice had a desperate edge. "Tell her I throw myself on her mercy. Tell her I can't do it and I beg for her mercy."

Eleanor looked puzzled. "You *can't* do it? Kill this girl? Why?"

"I love her." Luke's voice was flat and matter-of-fact, just as if he'd said, *the sky's blue.*

I felt my knees go weak; if he hadn't held me so tightly, I would have stumbled.

The smile on Eleanor's face was so radiant, I couldn't bear to look. She glowed with fearsome joy. "Oh, I shall tell her. Shall I tell her that last part as well?" She clasped her hands together, pressing her fingers to her lips as if she would burst with the tremendous gift he had given her.

Luke was about to answer, but the road was empty.

The mist moved slowly over the surface of the tarmac. After a long minute, Luke released me and took a step back, his eyes fixed on where Eleanor had been. He linked his hands behind his head and squeezed his eyes shut. "God, what have I done?"

It was a good question. I had no friggin' idea what had just gone on. Except I remembered the words, "I love her." Those stuck in my mind, playing over and over with the images of his murders providing a horrible counterpoint. Everything else seemed difficult to hold on to, sliding away as soon as I thought about it. I watched Luke pace, his fingers still laced behind his hair, and images began to flash through my head again. Mindless memories – Luke as a child, reaching up into an adult's hand. His hair glowing in a city sunset. His fingers typing on a keyboard.

My head swirled. Looking away, I tried to focus on my own life and my own memories, but Luke's kept flashing through my head in dreamlike spurts. My eyes were suddenly heavy, as if the sleepless night had caught up with me all in a rush. I wanted to lie down on the street and give in to sleep, but a part of me knew my exhaustion couldn't be natural.

"What's wrong with me?" I asked, my eyes half-lidded.

Luke glanced over to me and sighed. "You're tired?"

I nodded slowly.

He held a hand out towards me for the third time since the tomb. I shouldn't have taken it. But screw it. I was too tired to process my doubts and the still-flashing images of his past and I *wanted* to take his hand so badly it hurt. I reached my hand out and he took it firmly, leading me down the road towards home like a small child.

"Have you ever heard of psychic vampires? People who take energy from other people to fuel themselves?"

"Uh-huh."

"Those people only *wish* they could be Eleanor when they grow up. She must've used a lot of energy to do that vanishing trick of hers. I was wondering who she got it from."

I stumbled and pulled myself back up. "Why aren't you like this? Why only me?"

"Because you were easy. Because she wanted to hurt you."

He said something else too, but I wasn't paying attention. I was falling asleep on my feet. Luke released my hand and I immediately sank down on to the road, relieved just to stop.

"No, pretty girl. Come on." He leaned over and lifted

me as if I were only the slightest of packages. The tiny bit of me that was awake whispered, *Can't trust him. Tell him to put you down.* I just rolled my face next to his soft black shirt, his familiar smell lulling me to sleep, wishing life was just this simple.

I woke up a little bit when cold air-conditioning bit my skin. He'd carried me right into the house, past a grumbling Rye on the kitchen floor and up the narrow stairs, turning me so I didn't kick the wall. It was proof of how much Eleanor had drained me that the idea that Mom might discover us didn't make me leap from his arms. Somehow it didn't surprise me that Luke knew right where my room was, making his way silently across the floor, quieter than fallen snow at night.

Carefully, he set me down on the bed and tugged the blankets up around me. My bed felt amazing after two nights of sleeping on the couch – cool and soft. Luke knelt so he was eye level with me. I looked at him through slitted eyes as he gazed back at me, his expression pensive, the dried, red tear stain untouched on his cheek.

"Is everything ruined now?"

I blinked slowly, an image of him laughing and playing with a dog very like Rye flicking behind my eyelids like a slide in a projector. I wasn't sure if I answered out loud. "I don't know." I couldn't think of a way to answer that question without knowing why he'd killed those people. Blink. An image of his fingers hooked around the edge of the torc, tearing at it. Blink. The present-day Luke again, fingers close enough to touch me, but not.

"Do you still see my memories?"

I forced my eyes open and nodded against the pillow.

His voice was barely a whisper. "I see yours, too."

I mumbled, "I really screwed up, didn't I?"

He touched the bloodstain on his cheek – *my* blood – and rested his forehead on the edge of the bed. "Oh, Dee. What am I going to do?" Time passed, unnoticed. Was I sleeping? Blink. An image of him kissing my cheek softly, or maybe it really happened. Then a hollow feeling in my gut, when I realized he was gone.

And then just sleep.

Book Three

I sat within a valley green
Sat there with my true love
And my fond heart strove to choose between
The old love and the new love. . .
While soft the wind blew down the glade
And shook the golden barley.

—"The Wind That Shakes the Barley"

Thirteen

I woke up to a beeping mobile phone and loud voices downstairs. Mom and Delia. No surprise there. They argued like other people breathed; it was instinctive and unavoidable. I buried my face away from the too-bright sun; I must have really slept in.

Rolling on to my stomach, I extricated the phone from my back pocket (good thing I'd rescued these jeans from the laundry when I went out to meet Luke, or else the phone would've been washed). I sat up and wiped the sleep out of my eyes. I felt like I'd been dead for the past few hours. I'd been lost in a dreamless sleep so heavy I'd slept through my phone ringing.

Luke.

I was instantly awake, the events of the melodrama that was now my life running through my head. I flipped open the phone: fourteen missed calls, three new texts. Every call was from James. They started at about six a.m., with the last one just a few minutes ago. I opened the text messages.

First: *wakey wakey.*

Next one: *i need 2 talk 2 u.*

Last one: *call granna.*

I didn't call Granna, of course. I called James. He picked up before the first ring had even finished.

"What are you, sleeping in a coffin these days? I've been trying to get you for hours."

"What's wrong?"

"Did you call Granna?"

I climbed out of bed, stiff from sleeping in my jeans. "No, I called you. You called me fourteen times, so I figured it was important."

"It *is* important. I think something's happened to your grandmother."

"Huh?"

"Call it my spidey sense. Did she bring you that stuff she was making?"

Come to think of it, she hadn't. I felt a little guilty for forgetting about it. "No. She didn't call, either. Is this your crystal ball spidey sense we're talking about, or just common sense?"

"Crystal ball. Would you please just call her and find out if I'm right? I mean, I hope I'm not, but I've had the most awful feeling about it since early this morning. I couldn't sleep. I even did a Deirdre."

"You *threw up*?"

"Yeah. Please call?"

"OK, OK. I'll let you know."

I hung up, but before I had a chance to call Granna's

number, Mom shouted my name from downstairs. She had that barely-in-control sound to her voice that meant someone was going to fry.

Oh. What if she knew about last night? She would torture me, kill me, and then perform a black rite to resurrect me to kill me again if she found out. Mom had never bothered to have the sex talk with me – that might have actually required finding out how I felt about something – but she'd made it quite clear what she thought of girls that did more than hold hands with their boyfriends. I still remembered the time she dropped me off at Dave's Ice when I first started, and Sara was kissing her boyfriend in the parking lot. I remembered wondering why I would want someone's tongue in my ear, and then Mom saying, "Girls like that have no self-respect. Why buy the cow when you get the milk for free?"

I kinda wondered what Luke's tongue would feel like in my ear.

"Deirdre!" Mom shouted again. I stalled, scrubbing off the bottoms of my feet so it didn't look so much like I'd been wandering around the neighborhood all night. "Don't make me come up there!"

I steeled myself and headed down to the kitchen. Mom, Delia, and Dad were posted at various points in the room, all holding coffee cups, all looking tired and strained in the strong late-morning light coming in the windows. So it was to be three on one. Hardly seemed fair.

"Good morning," I said. Admit nothing, that was my plan.

Mom barely looked at me; she gulped her coffee before speaking. "You're supposed to be at work this afternoon, right?"

The question was so far from what I'd expected that my voice was a bit incredulous. "Yeah, at one."

"Dad can drop you off, but James will have to pick you up, or if he can't, you'll have to call in and take time off. I can't get you." She drained her coffee cup and set it in the sink. Dad looked hangdog, and I bet a fight had preceded my arrival.

Mom continued. "Delia and I have to go to the hospital."

With a faint prickle of dread, I echoed her. "The hospital?"

Delia withdrew an enormous set of keys from her handbag and took my mother's arm firmly. "Granna fell down or something. The paramedics aren't sure. It's probably nothing serious."

"Fell down?" I repeated again. Other people's grandmothers fell down. Granna wasn't the frail, falling-down type. She was the hauling-and-painting-furniture type. She was the beating-herbs-into-green-pulp-to-drive-off-the-faeries type. For some reason, I thought of Eleanor's fearsome smile right before she'd left.

"Or something," Delia said loudly, louder, if possible, than her usual voice. "We're just going to see if she's all right. I'm sure she'll be released shortly. It's just precautions."

Mom glared at Delia, and I wondered what *that* argument had been.

Impervious to the slings and arrows of her sister, Delia looked regally down at me. "You saw her yesterday, Deirdre. Did anything seem unusual to you?"

I had probably been too self-absorbed yesterday to notice anything out of place. The only unusual thing there yesterday had been me. I shook my head. "She seemed fine."

Mom shot a triumphant look at Delia. "Let's go."

The two of them pushed through the door, leaving Dad and me alone. As usual, he was quiet, all the words he might have said already used up by Delia and Mom. Finally, he scratched his chin and looked at me. "You're seeing that flute player from the competition?"

Talking with Mom was difficult: you had to follow rules and play her games. Dad was easy. I nodded.

"Do you like him?"

I didn't *feel* embarrassed, but my cheeks reddened anyway as I admitted the truth. "A lot."

"He like you?"

"A lot."

Dad nodded and got his car keys from the hook by the door. "I'm glad. I'm going to go get the AC running in the car. Meet me out there when you're ready to go, OK?" He let himself softly out the back door, as quiet as Mom and Delia were loud, and I went back upstairs to get changed into something that didn't smell quite so strongly of wet grass and staying out all night.

Upstairs, as I was transferring my phone to the back pocket of a nice pair of jeans for work, it rang. I looked at the number, but didn't recognize it.

"Hello?"

"Hi."

I recognized Luke's voice at once, and despite everything, I shivered. In a good way. "You have a phone?"

"I do now. I never had anybody I wanted to talk to before." He paused. "Do you want to talk to me?"

"I shouldn't." I remembered Dad waiting in the car and began to hunt for a clean pair of socks. "But I do. I just keep thinking you're going to bust out an explanation for what I saw in your head last night."

There was silence.

"Is this the phone version of that sad face you do where you say you can't tell me anything?"

"Yeah, I guess it is. I guess I was hoping that you'd see something that would counteract all those – the – that stuff – when you read my mind."

"*Is* there something that would counteract all that?"

Luke sighed. "Better count this as another phone version of the sad face."

I had more important things to ask him, but curiosity

pushed me forward. "What happens when you can't tell me something? Does your tongue freeze, or what?"

He paused. "It's painful. My throat seizes up, sort of. I never know exactly what's going to set it off, so I try to avoid it."

"What about writing it down?"

"That would hurt. A lot."

"So . . . telling me who is keeping you from talking would definitely cause you problems."

"Just thinking about telling you that makes my tonsils go cold," Luke said, and I could hear the smile in his voice. "Can I see you today?"

I contemplated just how idiotic that would be. Then I remembered. "Luke, Granna's in the hospital. My mom just left with Delia. They said she fell down or something. But—"

"Granna doesn't fall down," Luke finished.

I hesitated. "Do you think that it could be—"

"Maybe. Do you want me to visit her? I'd be able to tell."

"She hates you."

"She's not the only one. What about us? Can I see you again? You can say no. You'd crush all my hopes and dreams, but it's an option."

I pulled on my shoes while I thought. I could probably blame my hormones for all this. For my complete lack of ethics. A friggin' pile of dead bodies and here I was allowing myself cold chills at the idea of seeing him again. Oh man, and if he kissed me again, I'd probably explode. *Earth-to-Deirdre. Snap out of it. We're talking killer here, remember?* But maybe there was a reason for the bodies. Or maybe I was just being pitifully hopeful. Out loud, I reasoned, "So, there just *might* be something to counteract what I saw in your head."

"I think I am allowed to say a definite maybe."

"And you aren't going to kill me."

The smile vanished from his voice. "I promise you that. If nothing else, I promise you that. I won't ever hurt you."

I wondered what it was like to have a normal relationship, where you didn't have to ask these sorts of questions. Would I feel the same about him if he just had a normal life and a normal past? I made my decision. "Then I'll see you later."

"You've made my day, pretty girl. I'm off to visit your granny. Keep my secret with you." The phone went dead in my hand.

Dave's Ice was officially dead. The hazy blue-grey sky of earlier had traded in its stifling heat for growing knots of storm clouds, and no one was in the mood to get ice cream. I leaned against the counter, staring out the large pane-glass windows at the gathering clouds and playing with the iron key, sliding it back and forth on its chain. I could think of one thousand places I'd rather be.

I didn't want to look at the clock, because it would

just remind me how much longer I had to stay here. I didn't want to read old text messages from James, because that would just remind me how nobody had called and updated me on Granna yet.

"He gave you that, didn't he?" Sara interrupted my boredom. She leaned against the other side of the counter, revealing a lot more of her cleavage than I'd ever wanted to see. Even though she was wearing the same chaste Dave's apron I was, she'd managed to find a shirt that made it look like *all* she was wearing was the chaste Dave's apron.

I glanced up at her. "Yeah."

"I saw you guys on that first day, sitting out by the car. He really is cute."

"Yeah."

Sara leaned towards me, conspiratorial. "And *older*. He's a senior, isn't he?"

"Yeah."

She poked a finger in her ear and squinted out of the window as if trying to see what I was looking at. "I know I said it before, but I just can't get over, like, that someone like you ended up with someone like him. No offence. Seriously, no offence."

Previously, on *Deirdre's Life:* in the last instalment of our show, Deirdre receives casual put-down from Sara, and because Deirdre's socially paralysed, she takes it without a squeak.

This week on *Deirdre's Life:* Deirdre fights back.

I rolled my eyes towards her. "I think older guys go for a more subtle look, don't you?"

Sara followed my gaze down into the cavern between her breasts. "I – uh – never noticed. Do they?"

"Yes," I said firmly, warming to my theory. "You know, younger guys want arm candy. Older guys want *depth*." I swallowed a smile and went in for the kill. "It's why I wouldn't date any of the guys from school." I couldn't believe I was having this conversation with her – like we were friends. I wondered if this was how the other girls in high school were, the ones that babbled in front of their lockers about their boyfriends and the music they liked. Maybe they were all just pretending to be buddy-buddy, when really they knew nothing about each other.

Sara's eyes opened wide. "*That's* why you didn't date? I totally thought it was because you were some kind of freak."

On a scale of one to ten, Sara definitely scored an eleven on the Tact-O-Meter. I don't know how I could have been intimidated by her before. I shrugged. "That's what a lot of people say who don't know me. Their loss."

The awed look on Sara's face was worth a million bucks. The feeling I had pulsing through my veins was worth a million more.

And then Freckle Freak came into the shop, and my two million bucks went down the toilet. Again, he was perfect and preppy, the collar turned up on his layered polo shirt and fingers linked in the pockets of his perfectly tailored khaki shorts, revealing half a dozen leather bands knotted around his wrist.

There was one big difference from when I'd seen him before, though – this time, I could tell he was a faerie. It wasn't the sharp herbal scent that accompanied him into the store. Rather, he had the same kind of mind-bending perfection as Eleanor, which I was beginning to think was the mark of a faerie. It wasn't that he was beautiful, though he was – it was the way the beauty *hurt* to look at. Also, he glowed from within, healthy and warm, though the fluorescent lights of the shop and the storm-light outside washed all the colour out of my face and Sara's. How could I have ever mistaken him for human?

When he put his hands up on the counter and smiled at us, I saw the dull glint of a torc under his left sleeve. Sara discreetly tugged up her apron and slid down the counter towards him. "What can I get for you?"

Freckle Freak looked from Sara to me and back again. "I don't know. Everything looks so *delicious*." Sara's mouth quirked; I stayed where I was, my skin crawling. Just beneath the surface of my own perceptions, I could sense Luke's memories of Freckle Freak churning, threatening to break through.

"Well, you can take a minute to decide," Sara said, gesturing to the empty store. "No hurry."

He pushed off the counter, running his fingers on the edge of the display glass, ceaselessly moving as he had the last time I encountered him. I watched his fingers jerk back from a metal strip on the display, and then return to their lazy path along the glass as if nothing had happened. In my head, Luke's memories flickered dimly: Freak driving a herd of yearling cattle into a river, laughing as their wide eyes disappeared into the unexpectedly deep water. Freak circling Luke as Luke held three iron nails in a white, knuckled hand. Freak running his hand over the bloody skin of a terrified-looking girl, the knots of the leather bands on his wrist dragging tracks across her. I gritted my teeth, wanting to forget what I'd seen.

"So hard to choose," he said softly, smiling slowly at Sara. "Can I get more than one if I can't decide?"

Sara glanced at me and laughed. "Are we still talking about ice cream here?"

"Were we ever?" Freckle Freak leaned towards Sara, his tongue flicking on the edge of perfect lips. I had my necklace, but there was nothing to keep him from Sara.

I couldn't believe I was going to have to protect the skank from him. I joined her, my arm pressed against hers, and said firmly, "I think you ought to pick a flavour – of ice cream – or get lost."

To my surprise, Sara didn't protest, but moved subtly backwards, away from him. Maybe even she had her limits. Maybe even the most innocent of sheep could smell a wolf if it stank enough.

Freckle Freak made a startlingly high leap on to the counter with surprising grace, and behind me, Sara made a soft noise. He swung his legs over and dangled them on our side of the counter. I stepped out of reach of his legs, and he clucked. "Oh, don't be like that. I just thought Luke might share his playthings." He grinned at me, hungrily, and pointed to the key around my neck. "Maybe I can help you out of that later." He looked over his shoulder, at the sun blazing in the sky. "Very soon, I think."

"Creep," muttered Sara. "Get out or I'll call the cops on your ass."

He seemed unfazed by the threat. From an empty palm, he dropped a line of clover on to the counter. They flapped their butterfly wings, taking flight as beautiful swallowtails before crumbling to the floor – wilted clovers after all. His smile rose goosebumps on my skin. "I can show you some things Luke can't, lovely," he murmured.

"I can show you some things he can't, as well." James let the shop door close behind him. *"Lovely."* James's attire was a bit strange – he had accessorized a T-shirt that read *You: Off My Planet* with an iron fireplace ash scoop, which he held over his shoulder like a rifle. The combination was oddly appropriate.

Freckle Freak smiled, all teeth, and slid off the counter, flicking his tongue at James. "Maybe you'll play as well?" He leaned back towards me and sniffed. "Although she smells better. Good enough to swallow whole."

James lowered the shovel and matter-of-factly approached Freak. "Get. Out."

Freckle Freak let himself be guided by the iron until he was by the door, then looked back at me and made a rude gesture.

James growled and swung the shovel at Freak's head. The shovel never made contact with his scalp – Freak jerked violently away from the iron, slamming his skull into the door with enough force to rattle the glass. Then he smacked down on to the floor, hard.

James spat on him. The faerie opened his eyes when the saliva landed on his cheek, and smiled. "So this is how we're playing the game."

I had a sudden, vivid image of Luke, holding the Freak against a wall, his dagger nearly touching his neck, and Freak grinning and saying, "So, it will be a good game."

Then I looked back to the door, where James stood over empty floor. Outside the door, a white rabbit hopped across the pavement.

James and I watched the rabbit until it disappeared in the scrubby brush beyond the car park, and then exchanged a glance. "Rodent problem?" he asked.

"Weasel, I think." I let out a deep breath I'd been holding without realizing it. "Why are you here?"

James shouldered the shovel, glancing out the window as thunder boomed, but Sara interrupted from her spot beside the milkshake machine. "What the hell just happened?"

I wasn't sure how to answer. James shrugged. "Homicidal faeries."

Sara stared out the window into the car park where the rabbit had been. The girl who could never shut up when there was nothing to talk about had nothing to say when there was.

I looked at the clock. "I'm going to lock the back door. I think it's time to get out of here." Sara still hadn't moved. She was chewing her lip, lost in thought, her face transformed by the introspection.

"Good idea," James said. "I'll take you to see Granna after you're done. And I'll walk Sara to her car."

I went through my closing routine, locking the back door and closing up containers of sprinkles and cookie crumbs. Sara went through hers, mechanically wiping down the milkshake machine and the counter. Her silence made me uncomfortable, like I ought to say something just to make her speak. I suddenly wondered if that was why she normally babbled all the time – maybe she'd been trying to get me to break my pensive quiet.

We emerged from our uncomfortable female bonding session to find James stacking the last of the chairs on the tables. He retrieved his shovel from beside the door. "We should go before it rains."

My phone rang in my pocket, and I pulled it out. This time I knew who the number belonged to, and I opened it halfway through the ring. "Luke?"

I could barely hear him say, "I saw Granna. It was Them."

Fourteen

Lightning glowed inside the towering thunderheads as they crowded out the last of the blue sky. A second later, the boom of thunder was loud enough to shake the windows on James's old Pontiac. I slouched down inside the car, turning my head into the familiar camel-coloured leather of the seat. The smell of this car, old leather and carpet, would for ever be associated in my head with James. In a way, this car *was* James. He'd spent so many hours rebuilding it from the chassis up, it might as well have been a part of him.

He turned down the Audioslave album we'd been listening to and seemed about to say something before thinking better of it. The quiet built between us, strange only in contrast to our usual banter, and for a moment I couldn't think of anything to say. Then: "How did you know Granna was in trouble? What was it like?"

James drummed his fingers on the steering wheel, making himself busy staring at the road. "She told me. Your grandmother. I started to feel sick, and for some reason I thought about her in her workshop. So I called you, and somewhere in between all those calls I was making to you, she told me." He let out a noisy breath. "Man, Dee. I'm almost as big of a freak as you. Soon you'll see me on TV with my crystal ball and my 900 number."

I frowned at him as lightning flashed one side of his face pale and featureless. "You'd have to change your name to something more foreign sounding, I think. No one would believe a *domestic* psychic."

"Esmeralda is pretty," James mused.

Thunder cracked, so loudly that my ears hummed afterwards, and shifted my mind to another, more immediate subject. "I just can't believe They did something to her. That's what Luke told me."

"I know." James's eyes flitted over to me. "She told me that, too. She called it 'elf shot'."

It sounded so innocent, like "love sick". Elf shot. I wondered what I was going to find when I got to the hospital; the thought made me shift anxiously in my seat. "It's just so hard to believe. Error. Resubmit. Cannot compute."

"Oh, there's more," James assured me. "I've been doing some research on Thornking-Ash – do you remember them?"

"Duh. They keep calling, trying to get me to send in an application."

"I got a letter from them, too." James slowed at a sign advertising the hospital and turned down a tree-lined road. Even through the lush green canopy overhead, purple-black clouds were still visible. Cars in the hospital car park glinted on the other side of the trees; my stomach squeezed, thinking about Granna inside. "Apparently, they're a freak school."

"I thought they were a conservatory. A what-do-you-call-it? Charter school?"

"Yeah, I did too. But I started looking up some grads and they all seemed sort of peculiar. Then I started *calling* the grads, and they *were* sort of peculiar. Apparently, musical genius, such as we possess, is strongly associated with being freaks, such as we are."

"Do huh?"

James found a parking spot among a sea of cars; they all seemed to be silver, reflecting dull purple back at the sky. He turned the car off and swivelled in his seat to face me. "I finally got hold of the recruiter you talked to, Gregory Normandy — he's the head honcho, did you know? Anyway. I pinned him down. He told me psychic ability was linked to musical ability, and that good musicians frequently had what he called 'gifts'. What you and I call 'freakdom'. He claimed to be able to tell whether or not a musician had freakdom just by listening to them."

"No way!"

"Yes way. He knew I was psychic. Luke was something else — I can't remember what he called it. Astral something? And he said you were freakdom off the charts."

I felt oddly flattered.

"I think that's why They're after you, Dee. Not they, the Thornking-Ash people. They, like capital 'T' They. I mean, it seems like an awfully big coincidence that you should be a major freak *and* They should want you this bad." His red-brown eyebrows furrowed. "Maybe They can hear your freakdom in your music. Didn't this all start at the competition?"

It started with Luke.

I put my hand on the door handle. "So, why do they want people like us at the school? Lower case 'T' they."

James opened his door. A rush of humid air, smelling of rain, flooded into the car. "Apparently a lot of people like us get really messed up in life. Normandy's kid was a concert violinist at age fifteen, and he killed himself. They set up this school to help us deal with it, I guess."

I shook my head. Of all the things I'd heard this week, this turned out to be the one thing that was too big and distant to really comprehend. A freak school for the musically talented.

"I can't process this right now. Let's go before we get soaked."

Together, we hurried across the silver car park into the ugly, flat hospital. It looked like a giant white box that someone had squished down in the centre of an equally ugly concrete car park. A vaguely artistic soul had painted the doors and window frames bright teal, but it didn't make the hospital any less flat or ugly.

Inside, it smelled like antiseptic and old people. The low ceilings and chemical smell seemed to squash all thoughts out of me, making me aware of only the smallest, most inane details. The short squeak of my shoes on the tile. The hum of a fax machine. The whistle of air from the vent overhead. The tinny laugh of an actor on the waiting-room television.

"How can I help you two?" The receptionist behind the counter smiled brightly at us. I stared at the bright pattern on her uniform; it was like one of those hidden picture images where, eventually, if I stared long enough, I ought to see a sphinx or a farmhouse.

James kicked me. "What's your Granna's real name?"

"Uh. We're here to see Jane Reilly."

The receptionist tapped efficiently on the keyboard and puckered her lips as she read the information on the monitor. "She's not allowed to see any visitors but family."

"I'm her granddaughter."

The receptionist eyed James.

"I'm her pool boy," James said. He crossed his fingers and showed them to her. "We're like this. Very close. Like family."

The receptionist laughed and told us the room number. We headed down the hall, trainers still squeaking, vents still whistling, looking for Room 313. We followed the door numbers past motivational photographs plastered along the walls, and then Mom's hissed voice announced Granna's room. I froze in the hall, and James hesitated behind me.

"This is *not* normal." I had to strain to hear her voice, but Delia's voice was clearly audible.

"She fell. What's not normal about that?"

"No. This is all wrong. This is like – like—"

Delia's voice was taunting. "Like what, Terry? Like the dreams you used to have? Back when you wet the bed?"

"I didn't wet the bed," Mom hissed furiously. "That was where their feet were. They always had wet feet."

"Right. I thought you said back then they were dreams."

"*You* said they were dreams. Mom said they were dreams. *I* never said that."

Delia laughed. It wasn't a pleasant sound. "I didn't tell you they were dreams, Terry. I was dying, remember?"

Mom hesitated. "I remember – damn you! Stop smiling! You're part of this, aren't you?"

"Don't be stupid." Louder, Delia said, "You can come in, Deirdre."

James and I exchanged looks, and I followed him in. Mom and Delia stood on opposite sides of the single hospital bed, all colour absent from their faces in the green-white lights of the room.

Mom looked hunted. Her eyes darted to me. "Deirdre. I didn't know you were coming over right now."

"James brought me," I said unnecessarily, pointing to him.

"I'm going to go get something to eat," Delia said musically. She flashed a rack of teeth at Mom. "Unless you need me for anything."

Mom glared at her with an expression that clearly said *drop dead* in three different languages, and Delia vanished. After she'd gone, I peered around Mom to see Granna, and saw only a mass of tubes and machines. My voice came out more accusing than I meant it to. "I thought you said she fell." I pushed my way further into the room, joining Mom by the side of the bed; she slipped away from me like a bubble of oil touching water.

Granna lay perfectly still, blankets pulled up tidily, hands laid stiffly on either side. There were no visible injuries, nothing to say what the faeries might have done to her or what "elf shot" might be. But she wasn't awake, either, and a heavy sensation of slumber or unconsciousness seemed to ooze from the hospital bed.

I spun to face Mom. Behind her, James hung his head, seeming to analyse Granna's condition faster than I could. "What's wrong with her?"

Mom's voice was efficient, her emotions still carefully locked away. "She's in a coma. Nobody knows why. She didn't fall. She wasn't sick. She's just in a coma, and they don't know when she's going to come out. They've done a bunch of tests like MRIs and stuff and so far everything's coming back normal. But we're still waiting on some of them. They say she could just sit up at any minute."

Or lie like this for another hundred years. I looked down at Granna, quiet as the dead. I couldn't seem to feel upset; it was as if I were watching a TV show starring myself and my family, and the real me sat safely outside the television set. I wondered if it would be like the day the cat attacked: emotion would catch me later, when my guard was down.

The room faded; twilight. I was outside, staring at muddy clothing in a ditch, all crumpled up in angles that made my gut squeeze, the water of the ditch half-covering them. It took me a moment in the faded light to realize that it was a pile of bodies, limbs twined in a macabre puzzle. A tight white hand pulled on my arm, grasping it firmly below the newly glinting torc. Its owner, a tall young man whose brown hair bore a shocking streak of gold, said, "Come on, Luke. Come on. They're dead."

I just stared at the bodies, feeling cold and mercifully empty. In a way, I was relieved that I had no tears for my brothers; if I cried, I'd be blind. I'd have to spend hours making the drops so I could see Them again. Hours wondering what They did while I was oblivious to Their presence.

"Luke. There's nothing you can do."

"If I'd been here—" *Here, instead of doing Her bidding—*

"Then you'd be dead, too." The brown-and-gold-haired man pulled harder on my arm. "Come away. We'll make you forget."

"I'll never forget." Luke closed his eyes, and the broken bodies still burned a painful image behind his eyelids.

"Deirdre, James is talking to you."

It took me a moment to separate reality from Luke's memory; to trade the smell of mud and death for the antiseptic smell of the hospital. Embarrassed, I blinked myself free and turned to face James by the door. "What?"

"I said, 'I'm sorry I can't stay'," James repeated. "I have a gig this evening with the pipe band. I can't get out of it."

Mom's face suddenly clouded. "Deirdre. Gig. The Warshaws' party. That's tonight."

"I thought it was Sunday."

"Today *is* Sunday. I can't believe I forgot about it." She paced, looking apprehensive for the first time. James raised an eyebrow at me behind her back, bewildered, but I understood Mom's consternation. She always had every aspect of everyone's life planned out and categorized in some invisible mental ledger; for her to forget a detail meant that she really was shaken by Granna's condition — and to admit she was shaken wasn't acceptable.

"How are you going to get there? Delia's gone to

do whatever she's doing – Dad was going to pick me up late tonight after work. I don't have a car here."

"I'll take her." James's voice interrupted her pacing.

"No. You have your gig."

I shook my head, imagining going to a party and barfing while Granna lay in the hospital. "Mom, it's not that important. I'll tell them I can't make it. They can just play CDs on the stereo or something. It's just a dumb party, and Granna's here in the hospital."

She stopped pacing and stared at me. "The Warshaws have planned this for months. You can't back out. *This* isn't going to change because you're here." She pointed at Granna, finger shaking slightly. "If only Dad didn't have to work so late—"

Irritation bubbled up in me at how she clung stupidly to her damn schedule. "If you'd let me get my licence, I could drive *myself* places. What a crazy idea, huh? A sixteen-year-old with a driver's licence?"

Mom pursed her lips at me. "Don't be ridiculous, Deirdre. We both know you're not ready to be driving on your own."

James didn't need to be psychic to sense what was about to go down. He edged towards the corner of the room.

"That's crap," I told her. "I can parallel park better than you can! You just want to control every piece of my life. Of course you don't want me to drive! How'd you be able to monitor my every *fricking* waking move?" I was terrified that I'd gone too far, but I couldn't seem to stop. Why was I doing this now? *Shut up, Dee, shut up.* But I didn't listen to myself. "I'm tired of doing everything your way. I'm tired of everything being planned out for me."

Mom's face hardened. "I can't believe how ungrateful you are. Can't you see how lucky you are to have parents who care about your future? I care enough about you to make sure that you do something with your life."

"Because *you* didn't," I snapped back. "Because Delia did everything you wanted to do." *Oh God, I didn't just say that.*

Her face stayed exactly the same. "Do we need to have this conversation right now?"

"We never talk, Mom. You never ask how I feel about anything. You just push me all the time, and it's *stupid.* We should've had this friggin' conversation a long time ago."

"So, what do you want me to say? Delia stole my life? Delia gets everything? You could be everything I couldn't be – I push you too hard – I'm an overbearing mother – there, you happy?" She half-turned away from me and began to dig in her handbag. "I'll call Delia. Maybe she'll come back and take you."

I was still shaking from standing up to her, and shocked at my outburst. I didn't know what was wrong with me, yelling at my Mom over Granna's body. Her fingers hesitated on the mobile phone – I think she was as excited about calling Delia as I was about riding in Delia's car.

"No. I'll call Luke. He can probably give me a ride." I took out my phone and punched in his number, willing him to pick up, needing him to pick up. I just wanted out of this room and away from my family. Even away from James, who was standing in the doorway trying to look as if he hadn't noticed our argument. I wanted away from everything that was my life right now.

"Hello?" The effect of Luke's voice was slightly distilled by the distortion of the phone, but it still made me ache to be near him.

"Luke?"

At Luke's name, James looked away.

But Luke's voice pulled me away from the image. "I've been thinking about you."

I thought about the dead bodies in the ditch. "Me too." I couldn't say much more in front of my unsympathetic audience. "Um. I'm at the hospital. Can I ask a favour?"

Luke agreed immediately and promised to see me soon. James mumbled some sort of goodbye and escaped from the room before I could think of what to say to him. And Mom just stood there, arms crossed, studying me.

I braced myself. "OK, *what*, Mom?"

"Wear your blue cardigan set."

I had been standing by the hospital entrance for twenty minutes when I saw Bucephalus cut through the pouring rain, a dark mass in a grey, formless world. I shivered, part nerves, part anticipation, part sheer relief, and watched the old Audi pull up under the concrete overhang, dripping water on to the slick-dark tarmac.

As I ran to the car, lightning flashed, brilliant and overwhelming, and a second later, thunder beat the air, momentarily deafening me. I slid in and slammed the door on the storm.

As the car started to move, a curious feeling of release overcame me, like a release from pain that I hadn't known I'd had. I couldn't help but let out a huge sigh.

"Sorry it took me so long."

The moment I heard his voice, right there with me, I didn't care how wrong he was for me. I was just so glad to be in the car with him that it was hard to imagine anything else mattered. I knew it was selfish, but I didn't care.

I turned my face towards him. He looked back at me, unsmiling, with dark circles beneath his eyes – his battle scars from the night before. "Hi, pretty girl."

I told the truth. "I'm really glad to see you."

"You don't know how much I needed to hear that." He sighed deep enough to match mine. "Where to?"

"Home for my harp first. And my friggin' blue cardigan set."

"Brought you a present," Luke said. Without looking

away from the road, he reached into his pocket and dropped Granna's ring into my hand.

"You got it out of the sink?!" I slid it back on to my finger; now that I knew how useful it was, it wasn't nearly as ugly. Still running my finger absently along its edge, I looked out at the rain. Wind buffeted the car. Light filled it, brief and brilliant, and I cringed a second before the thunder boomed. "Great night for a party."

Luke glanced in the rear-view mirror, though there was nothing behind us but a wall of grey. "It'll be over in time for the party. All this lightning, though." His face darkened. "Puts a lot of energy in the atmosphere."

I guessed what he was thinking. "Like the sort Eleanor could use to pull another vanishing act?"

"It's not the vanishing I'm worried about," he said ruefully. "It's the appearing."

Was that why he kept glancing in the rear-view mirror? The thought kept me glancing in the passenger-door mirror the entire way to the house, though there was nothing to see but the spray from the tyres.

We pulled into the driveway. "Do you want to wait out here while I get the harp and change?"

Luke peered over my shoulder at the empty house, barely visible through the sheet of rain. "I don't want you to be by yourself. I'll come with."

We jumped out of the car and ran to the back door, where I fumbled with keys, rain pouring over my fingers, and got us inside as quickly as possible. Sliding into the kitchen, I looked over at Luke and groaned.

He looked down at his soaked shirt and said, his voice mild, "Well, you did take three years to unlock the door, so what did you expect? Where's the dryer? I'll throw it in while you get changed."

The idea of him shirtless stuck my tongue to the bottom of my mouth, so I just pointed towards the laundry room and retreated to my room, where I rejected the frumpy blue cardigan Mom would have worn in favour of a fitted white shirt and a khaki skirt. I liked to think it was an outfit that said *professional but sexy*. As opposed to Mom's blue cardigan set, which said something more like *frigid puritan music geek*.

I returned downstairs, picking my way carefully in the rain-grey darkness. It was weird to be home without the rest of my family. Without the hum of the TV, or Delia's loud voice, or the constant whir of Mom's standing mixer, the house seemed very still and empty; the only sound of life was the slow, rhythmic pulsing of the dryer in the kitchen. I thought of Luke standing down there, waiting for me, and the same thrill of nerves I got before playing in public trembled down my arms.

I didn't trust myself with him.

I moved into the dim kitchen and picked out Luke's pale form. He was leaning his hands on the counter, looking out the window. Without his shirt, I could see how his body truly was – how every inch was muscle, a perfectly tuned, deadly machine. Shallow scars traced a mysterious map across his shoulders, leading my eye to the enigmatic gleam of the gold band around his biceps. I knew he heard me come in by the subtle tilt of his head, but he stared out into the rain for a few seconds longer before turning.

"That was fast." When he turned, I saw the largest scar of them all; a huge, white, amorphous shape near his heart. I didn't bother to disguise my curiosity and closed the space between us; my eyes narrowed when I saw just how large the wound must have originally been.

"What's that from?"

He didn't reply, but his eyes wore the same dead expression they'd had after I'd read his mind. I reached out with careful fingers and touched the raised, uneven scar tissue, felt the shiny skin. As I did, I fell into a memory.

It was one I'd seen before, back in the tomb. But this time I got a longer look. His back to an old wooden building, Luke held his wicked dagger point against the skin on his shoulder, lightly tracing a careful line down to the torc, as if trying its strength. Beads of blood raised up in its wake and I shuddered at the expression in his eyes – like there was nothing behind them. The next cut was stronger but still unflinching, slicing into his skin and skipping over the torc. And the next was stronger still. But of course it was madness. If he was trying to rid himself of the torc, it was a fool's errand; the torc itself wasn't affected by the knife. It stayed solidly around his biceps as he tore his arm to ribbons, a viscous blanket of red obscuring each new slash and covering the gold of the armband.

Finally, Luke lowered the knife, hand trembling, and I sighed with relief. But too soon. Fast as a viper strike, he dug the blade into his own chest, twisting it viciously. His hands slid from the grip at last, and his head fell back against the building, his body twisting and arching.

I gasped, pulling myself free of the memory with effort and blinking my wet eyes. "You tried to kill yourself." Saying it out loud made the memory real. I stared at him, repeating, "You tried to kill yourself?"

Luke swallowed, still as a statue beneath my fingers.

Trying to put this piece into his puzzle, I traced the pale lines that coursed over his torc. "Why would you do that to yourself?"

"You saw." He looked into my eyes, unflinching. "Why wouldn't I?"

Sixteen years of Catholic church filled my mouth with answers, but they all tasted like paste and I was silent. Suddenly it occurred to me that I didn't have to have an answer – that I didn't want to speak. Instead, I hugged him, throwing my arms around his lean frame and pressing my cheek against the scar on his shoulder where he'd first traced the blade.

Luke lay his head on top of mine, his breaths

counting the minutes, my heartbeat slowing to fall in step with his. Then I felt his mouth, his breath hot on my cool skin, push against my neck, at once tender and insistent. Part of me urged me to stop him while I still had my senses, but the better part of me wanted it too badly — wanted to feel him lay a path of kisses up my neck, under my ear, along my jaw, until his mouth found mine and stole my breath. I couldn't think, with the musky smell of his skin pressed so close to me and the feel of his fingers tangled in my ponytail. My brain screamed *too far!* but my body moved on its own accord, pressing closer to him.

A sudden, stabbing pain in my heart forced a gasp out of me, and I felt Luke's body stiffen. He pushed away, his hand moving up to his chest, his fingers against his skin, his eyes darkening. As the pain flamed through my chest again, Luke shuddered, squeezing his eyes shut.

"What's happening?" I whispered. But the finger of fire dragged across my heart again, and this time, Luke's body spasmed and he crashed against the counter, sending a pot lid clattering to the floor. He reached a shaking hand towards the counter before collapsing down next to the pot lid on the tile. The torc glowed white hot on his arm, illuminated by some sort of fearsome magic.

It was only then I figured it out. This wasn't my pain — it was his. What I was feeling was only a shadow, some sort of sympathetic pain caused by the weird magic I'd performed on us in the graveyard. I dropped down next to him as he shivered in time with the waves of fire that rolled through my chest.

"Luke." I touched his face, and he focused his eyes on me, biting his lip. "What's happening to you?"

It was worse than I could have imagined, feeling his body shaking underneath my hand and seeing him work so hard not to cry out. His voice was tight. "I'm – being – punished."

I jerked my head up, looking at the windows, trying to see what could have been watching us.

Luke, seeing my gesture, forced out, "For – what I told – Eleanor." He groaned, and curled his body tightly around his clenched fists.

I remembered Eleanor's face then, the puzzlement on her face when she asked Luke why he couldn't kill me, just a girl. Faerie bitch! I wasn't just a girl. I was a girl with freakdom off the charts. I reached into the tangle of limbs and pressed my hand against Luke's chest, feeling the thump of his heart, slow and laboured, each lethargic beat slamming against his ribs.

I closed my eyes, trying to think about the feeling I got when I was moving clovers across tables. In my head, I saw the fire in Luke's chest, burning brightly across the wings of a frantic dove. The flames, reflected orange and white in the dove's black eye, ate one feather after another, curling them black and useless.

"Go out," I whispered. But the fire kept burning, and the dove opened its beak and stared at the sky, eyes frozen and empty with the pain. I had to concentrate, to focus on the problem. What made fire go out? Lack of oxygen, right? I imagined the air sucking away from the flames, fleeing from the heat, leaving nothing but emptiness for the fire to feed on.

The fire flickered and diminished on one of the wings, and the ache in my own heart flickered in response.

"No," gasped Luke, and I opened my eyes to see him shaking his head. "No, don't do it. Just leave me alone."

"Why?"

"She'll *know*." Beneath my hand, his heartbeat crashed convulsively. "She'll – know what you can do. She's – only – guessing – now."

I could see the pain written on every muscle in his body. "I can't just watch you like this."

"I – lied to her. Told her you – weren't – a threat." He turned his face away, bitten lip bleeding. "Please – Dee – don't."

I didn't know what to do. I was so afraid that he would die there on the kitchen floor, lying next to the pot lid on the tile. If he *could* die; after seeing the knife blade stuck in his chest, I wasn't so sure he could. But I knew he could feel pain, and watching him writhing on the floor was harder for me to bear than physical pain of my own.

I lay down on the cold tile beside him and curled my body next to his, wrapping my arms around his shuddering muscles and burying my face in his neck. And lying like that, together, him growing hotter and hotter and me squeezing tighter and tighter, I waited until he stopped shivering and finally lay still, breathing hard. Knowing, the whole time, that I could have stopped it. I think it was the hardest decision I had ever made.

Luke opened his eyes and lay a hand on my cheek, his words barely loud enough to be heard, "Thank you."

Maybe he hadn't even said it out loud.

Fifteen

I didn't want to go to the party. It had seemed pointless to go in light of Granna's condition; now, after watching Luke tortured in the kitchen, it seemed downright idiotic. I had a horrible sense that time was precious and that entertaining a bunch of rich lawyers was a waste of it.

"Life has to go on," Luke said when I told him I wanted to blow the party off. "You can't just stop. What else would you do?"

Spend it with you. Lie on my bed with you and memorize your smell and the sound of your voice so no one could ever take it away from me.

"Dee." He ran a hand down my arm, twining his fingers in mine. "You've got to go on as normal. If you don't – They'll come in to finish my job for me."

So we packed my harp in the car and went on our way to the Warshaws. As Luke had promised earlier, the sky was clear and fresh, the only signs of the storm already disappearing behind the trees. While Luke drove, lost in his thoughts, I slouched in the passenger seat and typed an epic text message to James – confessing all, like we always used to do. For as long as we'd been friends, we'd relied on the written (well, typed) word to convey thoughts that seemed too embarrassing or serious to talk about in person. I remembered getting a long text from James about guardian angels and whether or not everyone had one, and another one about whether I thought being an introvert was a mental illness, and I remembered sending a long one about how I thought I'd never fit in and another about music as a possible time-travelling device – so long that it took an hour to punch in all the letters on the cumbersome keypad. This one was a bit shorter than that:

james, i should've been honest with u from the start, but i was afraid of hurting ur feelings or ruining our friendship. i've been spending a lot of time w luke & i think i'm falling in love w him. i know it's crazy and too soon but i can't help it. somehow he's in this faerie thing, but i don't know how yet. i read his mind that's one of the new freaky things i can do i guess & i found out he'd killed a lot of people. i know this will sound messed up but i think he was forced to do it. he's supposed to kill me too but he won't & now i'm afraid whoever's behind it is going to do something awful to him. i don't know what to do. maybe i'm supposed to save him. plz dont be angry w me i need ur help.

I sighed and deleted the message without sending it. Closing the phone, I turned towards Luke. "What are you thinking about?"

"Whether they'll write my life story as a tragedy or an epic fantasy." He had pulled himself out of his thoughts with effort, and it seemed he'd lightened them a lot for my benefit.

I laughed. "And whether or not they'll get a cute guy to play your part?"

"No, I was wondering if it was going to be a kiss at the end, or sad music and a sweeping camera shot over the fields I once roamed freely." He glanced over and brushed the top of my hand with his fingers before looking back to the road. "I'm hoping for the kiss, but expecting the sweeping camera shot."

I frowned. "Can you tell me who did that to you, back in the kitchen?"

Luke paused, as if trying out the idea. "Someone . . . who started out like you."

"Oh, that's specific."

"I can't *be* specific."

I squinted in the dying evening light and tried to think of what I was like. "Shy? Ruled by an iron-fisted mother? Musical?"

Luke groaned at all of my choices. "Think basic."

"Female? Human?"

"Ding! Give the girl a prize!" Squinting in the evening light, he put on a pair of sunglasses; they made him look almost unbearably cool. It really wasn't fair that he had so many Deirdre-felling weapons in his arsenal. "So theoretically, if she's like you, I can talk about you and you'll learn about her and I won't get in trouble."

"That makes my head hurt, but I think I'm with you."

Luke warmed to the idea. "OK. Let's talk about your gift. It can't change who you are. It's like—" He struggled for the words. "It's like being drunk. Getting sloshed doesn't change who you are – it just takes away all your inhibitions. It makes you *more* you. So if you've got a nasty streak, you're a mean drunk. If you're a nice person, you're one of those amiable drunks. *You're* a crazy talented girl with an amazing force of will, and this gift just takes that and explodes it."

"You've already won me. You don't have to compliment me."

Luke made a vague motion. "It just comes naturally to me. I can't seem to stop. You have an amazingly cute ponytail; it makes me want to touch it. See, that one just slipped out."

"If you make me blush, I *am* going to hit you." I was thrown off-balance by his sudden lightness of mood – this was the Luke who had flirted with me at the competition, not the Luke shedding tears of blood in a tomb or the Luke lost in memories in the kitchen. I'd missed him.

He glanced over at me and rewarded me with a brief, shining smile.

I bit my lip and blushed anyway. "So, go on with the gift bit. I assume that this someone else who might be a lot like me, but isn't, *wasn't* a nice person who became an über-nice person after they found out about their gift." My emphasis on the word "gift" was decidedly sarcastic; the jury was still out on whether or not I agreed with Luke's terminology.

"No. Someone who might be like you and might have something to do with my condition was a nasty, paranoid-schizo girl who loved telling people what to do. And when she grew into her gift, she was a nasty, paranoid-schizo girl who told people what to do and hurt them if they didn't do it. A lot of people."

I contemplated this. "And where do you come into it?"

"I think that might be where the hurting comes into it. If I try and tell you, I mean." His glance towards the torc was almost imperceptible.

"Then where do I come into it?"

"The paranoid part."

"She's afraid of harpists?"

"Your *brain*, Dee. Use it. What were we just talking about?"

It dawned on me. "My telekinesis. That's what you meant back in the kitchen, when you told her I wasn't a threat." I thought further, and burst out, "But that's so *stupid*. If I hadn't been messed with at the competition and had four-leaf clovers hurled at me by perv freaks, I would've never even known faeries existed. The only people I would've been a threat to would've been the ones between me and the bathroom when I got nervous."

Luke grinned at me; I'd never seen him so cheerful. "That's where the paranoid-schizo part comes in."

"But I can't be the only one like me – oh." Suddenly, the pile of bodies in Luke's memory was starting to make sense. "So, that's why – oh." All the overheard conversations were starting to make sense, too. "So, she makes you do it. Why you?"

Luke answered with another question. "Why not Eleanor?"

I saw Eleanor in my mind, her elegant fingers jerking back from me and the key around my neck. "The iron . . . Eleanor can't touch it. But can't the Queen touch it? She's human."

"Not quite, not any more."

I shook my head. "But I saw you – I saw how you felt about all this. How can she make you do it?"

"You know I can't tell you."

I thought of Luke plunging the knife into his heart, trying to destroy himself. And of him sitting in the tomb, plaintively asking me if I would ever forgive him. Whatever it was that compelled him to kill those people must have been pretty awful. A horrible idea occurred to me. "You don't go into a trance, do you? Does she do some sort of voodoo remote mind control?"

Luke shook his head. "I'm afraid I'm utterly conscious for the whole thing. But you came along and fascinated me, and that was the end of it all." He grinned suddenly, surprising me. "I'm so damn giddy. Is this what love is?" Before I could answer, he braked hard. "Is this the place?"

I looked up. "Yep."

The Warshaws' enormous brick house sat well back from the road, its columned façade dominating the massive sloping lawn in front of it. Luke drove Bucephalus up the steep driveway, peering at the immaculate grounds. "I don't see any cars. Are you sure we're here at the right time?"

"It's seven-thirty, isn't it?" A glance at his car's clock confirmed the time. "This should be right. Mrs Warshaw said the party started at eight but to just go around back and set up in the rotunda. I've been here before, for her daughter's reception; they're friends with Mom."

"Your mother has *friends*?"

"Be nice!"

Luke grinned and parked the car near the house. He took my harp, I took his backpack, and then he came closer and clasped my hand tightly. Together, we walked around the back of the huge brick house, past bushes sculpted in spirals and a stone fountain in the shape of a little boy peeing into a puddle. I hoped that if I ever got rich and famous, I wouldn't be so warped by my gobs of money that I thought little peeing boys counted as acceptable lawn ornaments.

The spacious back garden was empty of people, although folded tables leaned up against the wall near the back door and folding chairs leaned in long rows against a screen porch. I led Luke through the orange-green evening to the rotunda, a brick-floored circle of columns covered with a white dome.

"I think we must be very early," Luke remarked. He retrieved a folding chair for me and sat on the edge of the rotunda, watching me set up. After a few minutes of silence, he said, "I know about your brother."

I looked up from tuning my harp. "My brother?"

He reached into his battered canvas backpack and withdrew his flute case. "From one of your memories. How old were you when your mother lost him?"

I could have feigned ignorance, but the truth was that I remembered the exact month, day, and hour that Mom had lost the baby, down to the weather outside and what I'd eaten for breakfast. I wondered what else Luke had dug up from inside my head. "Ten."

His deft fingers assembled the flute pieces while his eyes scanned the edges of the yard, ever on guard. "Does it bother you to talk about it?"

I remembered Mom's huge belly disappearing too soon, and the last time I'd ever seen her cry. But it wasn't my sorrow; I was a step removed, and to me, the pregnancy had always been a bit surreal anyway. "No. Why do you want to know?"

Luke's eyes flitted over the trees closest to the rotunda: three petite thorn trees a few metres away. "Before I decide I don't like someone, I always try and figure out if there's a reason why they are who they are."

"Me?"

He gave me a withering look. "Your mom, stupid."

I chewed my lip, feeling both defensive and relieved that an objective third party thought she was hard to live with. "She's all right."

Luke frowned. "I've had plenty of time to watch the two of you, thanks to your memories, and I don't think she's been all right in a while. And don't get me started on Delia." He shook his head, and added after a moment's pause, "We're going to have to protect your family. If I won't touch you, They're going to try to come at you any way they can."

I imagined trying to coax Mom into wearing iron jewellery. Or trying to have an intelligent conversation with Dad about faeries. And Delia – well, she could fend for herself. Maybe I could use Delia as a decoy.

Luke laughed when he saw my face. "I think we have to find out what Granna was working on before They got to her."

I sobered, remembering that Granna was lying in a hospital while we were laughing. "Will the doctors be able to fix her? Do *you* know how to fix her?"

Luke shrugged and shook his head. "I'm afraid I don't know anything about that. Some of Them might know, but it's not as if I can just call Them up. Even if I could, I don't know if I'd want to. Even the best of Them aren't exactly *safe*."

"They aren't all like Eleanor and Freckle Freak?"

"Freckle Freak?"

"He was at the reception. And again, at Dave's Ice."

Luke frowned, remembering. "Aodhan. That's his name." His eyes narrowed further. "He was at Dave's?"

"James bitch-slapped him with a fireplace shovel." That reminded me of something else I wanted to say. "I think James is jealous of you."

Luke rolled his eyes. *"You think?"* He lifted his flute as if he were going to play it, and then rested it on his knees again. "He's known you for years, Dee. He had plenty of chances and he blew it."

I raised an eyebrow. "You aren't worried about it, then?"

Luke shook his head and blew an "A" before pulling the slide out a bit on his flute. "Nope. I love you more than he does."

I sighed. I wanted to take this moment, wrap it in paper, and give it to myself as a gift every time I felt crummy.

Luke glanced at the silent house. "We're definitely early. Do you want to play some tunes to warm up?"

I *wanted* to hear him say that he loved me again,

but playing tunes with him came in as an OK second. I leaned my harp against my shoulder, the smooth wood fitting perfectly into the crook of my shoulder; it felt like it had been too long since I'd played. "Sure."

Luke seemed to feel the same, because he ran his fingers over his flute and said, "It's been a while. What do you want to play?"

I rattled off a list of common session tunes I thought he might know, and he nodded recognition at all but one. I ripped into a bouncy reel and Luke tore in after me. It felt like we were two pieces of a puzzle: the high, breathy note of the flute filling in everything that the harp lacked, and the rhythmic arpeggios of my low harp strings pulsing beneath the melody of the flute, driving the reel forward with a force that made me forget everything but the music.

At the end of the set, I dampened the strings with my hand; Luke's attention immediately returned to the thorn trees.

I cuffed his arm, pulling his eyes back to me, and demanded, "OK. Enough's enough. What are you looking at? I don't see anything. Is someone there that I can't see?"

Luke shook his head. "I'm pretty sure you can see Them all now, if you try hard enough. But there's nothing to see there. Yet."

"Yet?" That was an ominous way of saying "nothing".

He gestured to the upwards curve of the garden.

"This massive hill, those thorn trees, the storm – I can't imagine a time and place any more perfect for the *Daoine Sidhe* to make an appearance."

The name seemed to whisper recognition in my soul. "What's that?"

"The 'Forever Young'. The faeries who worship Danu. They're –" he seemed to struggle to find the right words, "– *of* music. Music calls them. It's what They live for." He shrugged, giving up. "And if any music would call them, it'd be yours."

My fingers touched the key at my neck. "Should we be worried?"

"I don't think so. They refuse allegiance to her, and in return, she's done everything she can to destroy Them. Of all the fey, They're the weakest in the real world – the human world. They'd need a storm like the one we just had to even think about appearing before the solstice." But I knew from his persistent observation of the thorns that he still regarded them as a possible threat; I raised an eyebrow. He added, "But I did say there's no such thing as a safe faerie, didn't I? There are *Sidhe* that would kill you just for the prize of your voice."

I stared at the thorns, a bit taken aback by this new bit of knowledge.

"I won't let anyone hurt you." Luke spoke softly.

I almost believed it was true; I could have been convinced of his infallibility if I hadn't seen him slain on the kitchen floor by an enemy that wasn't even in the same building. But I lifted my chin and leaned my harp against my shoulder again. "I know. Do you want to play anything else?"

"You make me want to play music until I fall asleep, and then wake up and play some more. Of course I do."

I leaned my harp back and began to play a moody, minor reel, slow and building. Luke recognized the tune immediately, and lifted his flute again.

Together, we twisted the reel into something at once towering and creeping, inspiring and sobering. The melody dropped low on my harp strings and Luke's flute ripped upwards, dragging an aching counter-melody ever higher in the octave. It was almost too raw; both of us laying everything that made us who we were out in plain musical language for anyone who cared to listen.

In the shadow of the three thorns, the darkness stirred.

The tune throbbed, driven by a faint drum from the depths of the trees like a heartbeat. I could *see* the music, pulled tight like a cobweb, stretched into the darkness where it coaxed and lured the shadows into life. Every infatuated note, every hopeful measure, every bit of emotion-charged sound took shape; and, in the shelter of the thorns, the tune became real – music became flesh.

The two faeries that stood there in the trees were slight and sinuous, with pale skin tinged green, either through trick of the light or by birth. One held a fiddle in his long green hands, his young face turned towards us, and the other held a skin drum under her lean arm. Unlike Eleanor and Freckle Freak, there was no chance of mistaking them as human, though they were as beautiful as they were strange.

I let the reel fade away, half expecting them to fade as well. But they remained, watching us from their nearby copse.

Luke whispered in my ear and I started; I hadn't seen him move. "I know them. I call them Brendan and Una."

"'Call them'?"

His voice was still low. "The *Daoine Sidhe* don't tell anyone Their true names; They think it gives others power over Them. Stand up when you talk to Them — it's very rude not to."

He stood, lifting his chin, and addressed the faeries. "Brendan. Una."

Brendan stepped closer, his face curious if not friendly. "Luke Dillon. I thought I heard your particular brand of suffering." He started to move out of the trees, but fell back, holding his hand in front of his face. "And still armed to the teeth."

I thought he might be talking about Luke's hidden dagger, but his eyes were on the key around my neck. Luke nodded. "More than ever."

Brendan held up his fiddle, a beautiful instrument covered in some sort of paint or gild, patterned in woven flowers and vines. "I was going to ask to play with you, but you know I cannot abide that rubbish. Can't you take it off so we can play like old times?"

Luke shook his head and looked at me; his expression was so protective and possessing that warmth stirred inside me. "I'm afraid it's not coming off this time. I'm sorry."

Una – slighter than Brendan, with pale hair piled on her head in a half-dozen fat braids – spoke from the trees, her voice either teasing or mocking. "Look how he glows when he looks at her."

Brendan frowned over his shoulder at her and turned back, assessing me and my harp. "So you're the other voice I heard. You play nearly as well as one of us." Luke looked at me sharply, and I knew it was an incredible compliment.

Standing, I tried to remember what the old faerie tales had mentioned of human–faerie etiquette. All I could remember were random passages about being polite, not eating faerie food, and putting out spare clothing to get rid of brownies, and I wasn't sure any of that applied. I went for complimentary; it always worked with Mom's catering customers. "I'm not sure that's possible, but thank you anyway."

The compliment tugged Brendan's mouth into half a smile, and something inside me sighed in relief at answering correctly.

"I think you'd find a more agreeable existence

playing music with us than in this world," he replied. "Surely you know that Luke Dillon and his music aren't like most of your kind."

Una added, disconcertingly close, "He learned from the best."

I turned my head to see her a few metres away, just as I felt Luke step behind me, wrapping his arms protectively around my body. His voice was amiable, despite his firm grip around me. "Not that I don't trust you, Una."

Una smiled and spun in the grass. "Aw, Brendan, look how he holds her."

Brendan, unsmiling, studied us. "So this is Deirdre, is it? I've heard rumours whispered around *Tir na Nog*, about Luke Dillon and his disobedience. How the man who has no love for anyone now suffers in its grasp."

Luke's voice was pensive. "It's true."

Brendan's face mirrored Luke's. "Defiance is a trait we prize, but I do not think it's one that will serve you. The Queen is a jealous monarch." He looked at me. "Do you know what fate awaits him for sparing your life?"

"She didn't ask me to," Luke snapped.

Una came close, seeming to be less affected by the iron than her companion. Her eyes locked on mine and I felt disconcerted, falling into their ageless green depths. Then wrinkles formed around them as she grinned and asked, "Do you love him?"

Luke went very still behind me. There were a million reasons why I should've said no, but there was only one answer that was true, even though it seemed completely irrational, even to me.

I nodded.

Luke let out a deep breath.

In the thorn trees, face half-lit by the fading sunlight, Brendan's eyebrows knitted. "How interesting. It's very difficult to understand humans – even you, Luke Dillon, and you so like us."

Una swirled back to Brendan, running her hands around his chest and back as she circled him. "Didn't you hear their music, my friend? Have you ever heard humans make music like that before? That must be what love is."

Behind me, Luke's voice was sympathetic. "It's just what it sounds like."

"A symptom," Brendan said, as if love were a disease only humans could catch. But there was something like fondness or respect in his voice. "You're both fools."

I stepped out of Luke's hold. "Tell me why. Please, can you tell me about Luke, since he can't?" I felt three pairs of surprised eyes on me, but I pressed on. "I want to know who controls him and what keeps him from doing whatever he wants to do. I know you must know." I remembered that faeries liked politeness, and added, "Please."

Una looked at Brendan, her face eternally smiling. "Oh, Brendan, do." She said *Brendan* with a bit of sarcasm, mocking the names Luke had given them. "They might stand a chance if she knows. And that would please me."

Brendan frowned petulantly in her direction. "I've not seen anything please you in four hundred years."

"This will. Look at Luke Dillon, how he stands beside her though the Queen—"

"Shut up," Brendan said, so modern that I almost laughed. "Don't give it away for nothing." He regarded me. "What will you give me if I tell you the story?"

Una laughed and spun away from Brendan, dancing in the grass again to get a closer look at us.

I was taken aback. I didn't know what a faerie would be interested in, but I doubted it would be anything I'd be willing to give. Luke's lips brushed my ear as he whispered, "A tune."

"Cheater," Una said reproachfully.

"Shut *up*." Brendan turned towards her, and Una smiled brightly at his annoyance. "Do you never shut up?"

I addressed him. "I'll give you a song. Not just any song. I wrote it myself."

Brendan pretended to consider, but even in his strangeness, I could see that he was sold. "Fair. Begin."

I looked to Luke, and he nodded. I sat at the harp, fingers trembling a bit with nerves that I didn't otherwise feel, and played the most difficult song I had ever written — fast, complex, and beautiful, and I played it perfectly because it had to be. When I was done, I got back to my feet and looked at Brendan, waiting.

"I am envious," he said. His face looked like he really meant it and I remembered Luke saying that some of Them would kill for the prize of a voice. I believed it.

"You're also tall," laughed Una, and she whirled around the rotunda and back to his side. "Neither is likely to change."

Brendan ignored her and spoke to me, though he looked at Luke. "Shall I tell you the entire story?" Without waiting for an answer, he continued. "About a brilliant young man, the only son of a king who refused to kill his father's enemies on the battlefield? Whose soul wandered while he dreamt? Who played music to make the faeries envious? Who had golden hair and a face to tempt the Faerie Queen?"

"Very poetic," Luke growled.

Brendan smiled for the first time. "Very well. How about a young human named Luke Dillon who walked out into the solstice when he shouldn't have, and was stolen by the thing that calls herself the Faerie Queen? 'Come hither,' she told him—"

"'And kiss me!'" shrieked Una. "'Love me! I shrivel in my self-made prison!'"

"Shut *up*," Brendan said. "She demanded he court her, and he denied her as no one ever had." Una swept up her skin drum from the ground and played an ominous drum roll with the palm of her hand. Brendan spoke over her. "And so, inspired by his soul's dreamy wandering, she ripped it from him and caged it far from his body."

In my head, I saw the memory of it; of the hand clutching the back of Luke's neck and him falling to his knees, the breath from his mouth forming a dove.

"And she bade the man who wouldn't kill to be her assassin, because it pleased her to watch him suffer. And kill he would, or she would hand over his caged soul to the minions of hell. And so he killed. All the faeries in creation knew his legend; how she used him to overcome our intolerance of iron; how her enemies fell under his knife."

Luke looked away, face pained.

Brendan continued, taking pleasure in his story-telling. "He begged her to release him, but our vicious Queen has no mercy and no forgiveness, and she remembered his refusal of her as vividly as on the day that it happened, so she denied him. And so he killed for her. He was the Queen's hound; he hunted as no faerie has ever hunted – never dying, but never living, either, until the killing destroyed him and he turned on himself. But would the she-witch let her toy die, especially a death he'd chosen for himself?"

"Never!" cried Una. Luke closed his eyes.

Brendan shot her a look. "There are whispers – that the

Queen used her only daughter in a dark rite to resurrect her favoured assassin. However it was accomplished, he didn't die. And he killed again and again for her, while his soul languished in a faraway cage. Until he was set upon a girl who shared the Queen's name – only *this* Deirdre he loved, and Luke Dillon did not kill her."

Brendan went silent.

"Yet," Una added. She looked at Luke's trouser leg, as if she could see the dagger underneath the fabric.

I didn't know what to say. I wanted to take Luke's hand, but he stood a few metres from me, his arms clasped around himself, looking out towards where the sun lay on the edge of the trees. "You're willing to risk going to hell for me?"

"There's no 'risking' about it," Brendan answered for him. "The Queen will not forgive this betrayal."

Luke's voice was flat. "I don't care."

Una sighed. "Is he not noble?"

Brendan took a step out of the thorns, far enough that his face was again in the light. "You don't care only because you don't know hell. I've—"

Luke turned towards him and snarled, "Don't tell me that. I've *lived* in hell for the past thousand years. I spent a thousand years wishing I'd never been born." He thrust a finger towards me. "*She's* the only thing that's made my life worth living and if that's all I get, a few months with her – a few *days*, it's more than I've ever hoped for. Do you really think God would forgive me for the blood on my hands, even if my soul was free? I'm going to hell no matter what happens. Let me have my pathetic hopeless love while I can. Just – let me pretend it will turn out all right."

I put my hand to my face, covering my tears.

Una, outside the rotunda, watched the tears sliding through my fingers with interest. "May I have one?"

I bit my lip and looked at her. "What will you give me for it?" I managed to say.

"A favour," Una said immediately. "And you need all of those you can get."

I wiped my face and held my arm out of the rotunda. A tear dripped from my fingertip, and Una, only centimetres away, caught it in her outstretched palm. Then she darted away to the thorns, smiling as ever. I looked away from her to Luke, who was watching me with a hollow expression.

"Kiss me," I told him. When he didn't move, I begged, "Please."

He stepped closer and crushed me against him, face buried in my neck. I held him tightly, and we stood motionless for a long minute. Then he lifted his face to mine and kissed me softly on the lips; I tasted blood from where he had bitten his lip earlier.

"Deirdre?"

We broke apart from each other at the voice, and I blinked in the twilight, trying to make out the form. Brendan and Una were nowhere to be seen. Anyway, this newcomer was twice as large as either of them.

"Mrs Warshaw?"

"Yes! What are you doing here?" She peered at us, clearly puzzled.

Feeling oddly disconcerted, pulled so abruptly back into the real world, I gestured feebly towards the harp. "For the party."

Mrs Warshaw put a hand to her mouth. "Have you been here since seven-thirty?! My goodness, Deirdre. The party is next week!"

Oh.

I pulled myself together. "My mother told me it was tonight! The tables—?"

"Oh, dear, no! We had a wedding reception last night. The party's not until next week. My goodness. Were you waiting all this time? With— ?"

"Luke," I said, and immediately added, "My boyfriend." My supernatural, doomed, gorgeous, killer boyfriend.

"Well – come inside and have something to eat, anyway. Dear me, I can't believe you've been waiting all this time. We just got back from D.C. and heard voices out back."

"That's kind of you," I said, "but we really ought to go. My grandmother's in the hospital; that's why my mom got the date wrong—"

And then Mrs Warshaw blustered into sympathy and hurried us both through the opulent house, pressing a bag of cookies made by their private chef *(private chef!)*

into my hands and begging us to have Mom call with news before walking us out to Bucephalus. We climbed into the darkness of the car and sat for a long moment in silence.

Luke sighed deeply.

"Well." I looked at him. "I kinda liked Una."

Luke smiled wryly. "She liked you, too."

As we drove back from the party that wasn't, I stared out of the window at the night and thought about how this night looked like every other summer night I'd ever lived and how it wasn't like any of them. Halos of white-green light, buzzing with insects, surrounded the streetlights on the main drag through town, illuminating the quiet, empty pavements. In this place, life shut down after the sun went down. It felt like Luke and I were the only ones awake in a town of sleepers.

I was starving. Normally after a late gig, my designated driver and I would head to the Sticky Pig to grab some quick fries and a sandwich, paid for with my brand-new bucks. This time there was no gig, and I'd forgotten my money. Stupidly, after everything we'd been through, I didn't want to ask Luke to buy me dinner. And I didn't want to ask him to stop and let me get the private-chef cookies out of the boot, because that would be like a sneaky way of asking him to buy me dinner.

So I just sat in the passenger seat, stomach silently pinching, thinking about how Mom had got the date of the party wrong. The more I thought about it, the more troubling it seemed; Mom, the human computer, failing at an easy sum. Other people's parents messed up on details. Mom lived for them.

Both of us jumped when music sang through the car; I realized after a second that it was my stupid phone. Probably Mom. But the number was unfamiliar. The name above it, however, wasn't: Sara Madison.

I looked over at Luke. "It's Sara." I opened it gingerly and held it to my ear. "Hello?"

"Deirdre? This is Deirdre's phone, right?"

She was really loud. Somehow it was weird hearing her voice without seeing her in person — I felt kind of lost, without the image of her busting out of her shirt to anchor her personality. I held the phone a few centimetres from my ear. "Yeah, this is Dee."

"This is Sara." Without waiting for me to say anything else, she said, "OK. You gotta tell it to me straight. Like, seriously, were you two playing a prank on me at Dave's? You have to tell me, because I've just been — like — *freaking* over it since I got home and I have to know."

I wasn't going to lie to her. Not when Freckle Freak might just try to pull something on her if he couldn't get to me. "No prank, Sara. I wouldn't do that. You know I wouldn't."

"Yeah. Yeah, that's true. I didn't think of that. Duh, right? It's just so hard to, like, wrap my head around it. I mean, he turned into a – God! I'm never going to look at rabbits the same ever again!"

Luke didn't exactly smile, but the side of his mouth tugged up and I laughed in spite of myself. "Look, Sara, you've got to be careful around Them. I don't know what They want. Maybe you won't see any of Them again, but maybe you will. I'd keep something iron around just in case. It keeps Them away."

"Yeah. I got that, with the whole shovel thing. That was, like, seven different kinds of awesome. So what, are They all sketchy-looking guys?"

My stomach growled, and I coughed to cover it up. "Um, no, not all of Them. Some of Them are drop-dead-gorgeous-looking girls."

"Right – they look like me," Sara said.

There was too long of a pause before I realized, *she made a funny*. I laughed, finally, and Sara said, "OK, I was totally joking. But – They're real. I don't need to check myself into the crazy hospital and start taking Prozac and crap, right?"

"Right," I said, shocking myself a bit with my own certainty. "They are real . . . the rest is up to you."

There was another pause, and then Sara laughed. Was it a sign we were on different planets that it took light years for either of us to get the other's jokes? "OK. Right. Thanks. I feel better now."

I glanced at Luke. "Um, call me if you see another one, will you?"

"Yeah. Totally." We hung up and I looked down at the phone for a long moment. Had the world gone mad? Sara Madison calling me and asking about faeries like it was school gossip. I think the Sara calling-me-on-the-phone bit was even more shocking than the faerie bit. I felt like my high school invisibility was wearing off, just as I'd started to find it convenient.

The car slowed and bumped into a car park. I looked up and blinked at the sign, which bore a glowing neon pig with a glowing neon smile. The Sticky Pig.

"This is where you always go, right?"

I looked from the sign to Luke's face, which was pensive. "Uh. Yeah."

He made a face. "I saw it in your memories. I recognized the sign. Are you hungry?"

I nodded and made the understatement of the year. "I could eat."

He looked relieved. "Thank God. I'm starving. C'mon, I'll buy you dinner."

Guilt nagged at me: me eating out, Mom sitting at home getting dates wrong. "Maybe I should call Mom."

Luke paused, his hand on the door. "Why? She thinks you're at the gig still, and if you call her, you'll have to tell her why you're not. Do you want to have *that* conversation right now?"

"That," I said, climbing out of the car, "is a very good point."

He came around the front of the car, his face lit red by the smiling-pig sign, and held out his hand. I took it, wondering if I'd ever get tired of the sensation of his fingers holding mine. We crossed the empty car park and walked into the freezing air-conditioning of the restaurant; the hostess (not the James-bedazzled one) led us to a booth.

Luke slid into one side and I stood at the head of the table for a long moment, tapping my fingers against my legs, torn between bold Deirdre and normal Deirdre.

He raised an eyebrow at me. "What?"

I made my decision and slid into the booth next to him, slamming myself up against him hard and fast enough that his breath escaped in a short puff. "Steamroller!" I said.

He laughed, his face mashed up against the window, and shoved me back. "Weirdo."

"Look who's talking!" We sat arm to arm, staring at the same grubby plastic menu, like we were a normal couple, not a telekinetic freak and a soulless faerie assassin. I let my imagination run wild with the idea of us dating – Luke an ordinary teenage boy, me an ordinary girl. We'd eat the same old barbecue sandwiches we always got, then he'd pull me out of the booth by my hand and we'd go out to his car. He'd let me drive because he knew I liked to, and we'd do things normal couples did when they dated. We'd go to the Smithsonian and try to interpret modern art. We'd go to the movies and watch stupid action flicks and laugh at the melodramatic lines. We'd go hiking at the state park and watch summer disappear over the horizon; I'd lose my virginity while the trees shed their leaves all around us. When winter came, he'd hold my frozen hands and tell me how much he loved me, and that he'd never leave me.

My eyes ran down the same old menu ten times without seeing a single word.

"Is this how it would be?" Luke asked softly, and I knew he was thinking the same thing as me.

I nodded. "This would be our place." I gazed at him, distracted by his proximity and by the darkness outside the window. I could feel that part of me – the part that had escaped into Luke during the mind-reading – all electric and charged.

He shifted so he could look at me properly. "Your ... gift. Is it stronger after dark?"

Was that why I felt so alive right now? "I don't know. Why?"

"Hers is strongest while the sun is setting, so I thought maybe yours was similar." Luke cupped his hand over the top of mine and pulled it towards him. "And I'm getting the most peculiar feeling off you right now. Like someone put fresh batteries in you."

Again, there was that comparison with the distant Queen who had made him her slave – I wasn't sure I liked it. My voice was only a little frosty: "Do you get a 'most peculiar feeling' off *her* when her power is its strongest?"

"Not at all. But I didn't swap brains with her, either. You've infested me."

I looked over to find him grinning, and I finally affirmed it. "I do feel weird. And I haven't been doing much sleeping at night recently. Do you think that has anything to do with it?"

Luke shrugged. "It sounds plausible, doesn't it? It—" He broke off when the waitress arrived to take our orders. Neither of us had read the menu, so I ordered my usual pulled pork sandwich for both of us and she whisked off to the kitchen, probably eager to be rid of the last customers of the night.

Then Luke said, "I want you to work more on your gift."

I swallowed a mouthful of tea in a hurry. "I thought you didn't want her to know what I could do."

He spoke slowly, as if unsure of what he was suggesting. "That was because of what she was doing to me. Nothing's supposed to be able to stop it except her; she'd know it was you if the fire had gone out. If you practise your telekinesis discreetly, she won't know about it until it's too late."

"Too late for what?"

"Too late for her to realize that you've learned to take care of yourself, and that she'd better just leave you alone."

Somehow I didn't think a few extracurricular telekinetic classes would secure my safety. "Do you think that can really happen?"

Luke leaned over and brushed his lips on my cheek; the feeling of his breath on my skin was intoxicating. "It's what I *want* to happen." I closed my eyes and leaned my face towards his. I couldn't help but notice that he hadn't mentioned his own safety. How long did we have together? If the Queen really did send his soul to hell, what happened to the part of me that was tied to him?

"Start my car," Luke whispered in my ear.

My eyes flew open. "Tell me you didn't just whisper 'start my car'."

Luke's smile was crooked. "You want me to lie to you?"

"I don't suppose you're going to give me the keys," I grumbled. "That is, if you meant it literally and not as a dirty innuendo."

Luke's grin widened and he pointed out the window. "Look, it's easy. It's even in direct line of sight."

"This counts as discreet? What's indiscreet? Strangling Eleanor?"

He considered. "That would be indiscreet. Tempting, but definitely indiscreet."

I stared out the pane-glass window at Bucephalus, crouched in a lonely space across the car park, dimly lit in the dull circle of a floodlight, the glowing face of the sticky pig reflected on its windshield. "You do know, the

244

most I've really done is move plant life around."

"You'll never know until you try."

I sighed, feeling stupid as I leaned forward on the table to get a better look at the car. I frowned, trying to remember the warm feeling I'd got between my eyes when I'd screwed up our memories in the cemetery.

The night pressed against the glass, invading my eyes, and I saw a ghost of Bucephalus somewhere inside my head. I was there, in the car. But how was I supposed to start the damn thing? Mentally, my eyes ran over the gear stick and up to the ignition, noticing strange details I'd not noticed before, like the Jethro Tull tape inside the cassette player and the dark, worn prints on the steering wheel where Luke always held it. I tried to imagine a key, but the image slipped away from me, intangible.

If I'd known anything about how car engines started, I could have come at it that way, but all I could remember was something about explosions. I could just imagine that, with my luck, I'd blow up his friggin' car. Maybe I was just being too complicated. *Start*, I willed furiously. *Start*.

This was pointless. Nothing was happening. The image of the car was slipping away, replaced by the red vinyl of the booth seat across from me.

Luke whispered in my ear. "Name it."

Bucephalus, I thought. Instantly, the image of the car strengthened again, forming solid lines around me as if I sat inside it and around it and over it all at once. I could see a line of pistons, the brake line, the gas pedal, the ignition, the seats, all at the same time. *Bucephalus, start.*

Across the car park, headlights flicked on and blinded us both, but not before I saw the car jerk sideways as the engine turned over and roared to life.

The waitress set down two plates in front of us.

"Have a sandwich!" Luke said, glowing brighter than the headlights.

"Can I get you any sauce?"

I blinked at her. "I think I need to *get* sauced."

The waitress blinked back.

"She's fine," Luke said. After the waitress had gone, he looked at me, the corners of his mouth quirking, and said, "Are you just going to leave it running? Now that my salary's not being paid by supernaturals, I have to worry about the price of gas."

I tried to convince the engine to turn off, but it remained running. Eventually, I had to let Luke out of the booth to go switch off the ignition. I watched him out the window, his lanky form trotting to the car and getting in, fumbling behind the wheel for a few minutes, and then popping the hood open and fussing under it. He shut the hood, climbed back into the driver's seat, and in a few seconds the car lurched forward, the lights finally going out.

He returned and slid back in next to me, a little out of breath. "You're a bit of an atom bomb, aren't you? I had to stall the engine to get it to stop."

A smile broke out across my face; I couldn't help it. It was just so crazy. And instead of feeling shaky, like I did whenever I moved stuff in the daytime, I felt great. I felt like that great mass of night pressing in the windows was pulsing through me, huge waves of energy pumping like a wicked bass line. I felt like whooping, but when I found words, it was just an ordinary question. "How did you know I should use the name?"

"*They* think names are very important, remember? And so they are."

I frowned. "Is that why no one can remember your name?"

He nodded, mouth full of barbecue, and mumbled past the food. "Names are a way of keeping someone in your head. Most people don't remember *me* very well, either."

"But *I* do. I can say your name: Luke Dillon. And They can too. At least, Brendan could."

"They see things differently. I guess you do, too. Big shock there." He poked the corner of my mouth where my smile ought to be. "Eat your food."

I remembered my hunger, and we both ate our sandwiches in silence. When we were done, Luke put his arm around my shoulders and pulled me close to him. Resting my head on his chest, listening to oldies music playing overhead, feeling the cold touch of the vinyl booth on the back of my arms, I thought, again – despite the Sticky Pig looking the same as it always did – that this night wasn't like any other night.

Luke leaned over and whispered in my ear, "I wish I could have this with you." Something about his breath against my skin as he spoke, his fingers brushing against my neck, and the unfamiliar, exciting night pressing in against the windows made my stomach turn over. I sat up and grabbed his hand, tugging him out of the booth with a sort of urgency. "Let's go outside."

I waited slow minutes while he looked at the bill and counted out a tip, and then I pulled him out of the restaurant and back into the dull red light of the car park. With every step I took into the night, the pale moon looking down from overhead, I felt like I was shedding a skin; a weighty slab of flesh that peeled away to reveal a brilliant, light creature inside. All around me was a wall I'd spent sixteen years building, and with every thud of my heart, pieces crumbled from it. I was practically shaking by the time we reached the car, and before he could get his keys out, I kissed him. Crazy, out-of-control kissing, my mouth pressed against his, my arms linked around his neck.

Caught off guard, Luke took a moment before he wrapped his arms around me and kissed back, his fingers crumpling my shirt. There was something honest and raw in our kisses; a gasp of fear or impending loss that we couldn't or wouldn't acknowledge in conscious thought. He held me tightly, lifting me off my feet and sitting me on the hood of his car so I wouldn't have to stand on my tiptoes to reach him, and I tasted the skin of his neck and his face and his lips until I had no more breath, and then I linked my legs around him and kissed him some more.

Inside the car, my phone rang, quiet but clearly audible. I didn't want to get it. I didn't want this night to end, because I didn't know what tomorrow would look like. But Luke's hands dropped to his sides and he rested his face against my neck, out of breath. "You have to get that, don't you?"

I wanted to say no. But while I tried to imagine how I could justify ignoring it, Luke lifted me from the hood of the car and got his keys out of his pocket. The phone had stopped ringing by the time he retrieved it from the passenger seat, but my parents' number was still displayed under the words *missed call*.

Standing outside the car, shivering for no reason, I punched the *redial* button and pressed the phone to my ear. Luke stood behind me and crossed his arms over my chest, pressing his cheek against mine while I listened to the phone ringing.

"Deirdre? Where are you?" Mom's voice had a strange edge to it that I didn't recognize.

"At the Sticky Pig. We—"

"You need to come home. Right now."

I hadn't expected that. Maybe her chastity radar had gone off. "We just finished getting dinner. The party—"

"Deirdre, just come home. It's important."

The phone clicked and I stared at it for a few moments before relating the call to Luke. He released me abruptly. "OK. Get in."

I got into the passenger seat, unhappy with the turn of events. "I don't want to go."

"I don't either," Luke said. "But something's happened. We need to go."

We made the short drive from the Sticky Pig to my parents' dark driveway in record time. Every light in the house was on, and I saw silhouettes in the kitchen window. Luke took my hand tightly and we went in together.

Mom was inside the dim yellow kitchen, pacing as restlessly as a caged tiger, her face curiously mottled. Beyond the kitchen door I could see Dad talking on the phone. Mom froze in her steps when she heard the door open, and her eyes fixed on me. "Deirdre." Her eyes travelled down my arm to the hand that Luke held and then stopped, hardening. She took two steps across the room and snatched my hand out of Luke's.

"Mom!" I snapped.

But Mom kept my hand in a pincer grip, lifting it to stare at my fingers. "You're wearing Granna's ring. This is her ring."

The look on her face scared me; I snatched my hand back. "She gave it to me on my birthday."

"*You're* wearing her ring," Mom repeated. "You've

been wearing it all along. Since before the coma."

I shrank back from this wild-eyed creature that had taken the place of my mother. Luke's hand on my back steadied me. "She gave it to me, Mom. In the driveway."

Mom pointed at it wordlessly, her finger shaking, and then made her hand into a fist. Finally, she formed the words and spat them at me. "She's dead."

Strangely, I thought of the emotion I ought to feel without feeling it, as impartial as a National Geographic field researcher, carefully watching the events and chronicling them in a notebook. *Deirdre finds that she is saddened by the news of her grandmother's death, and moreover, suddenly fears for the rest of her family and friends.*

But I didn't actually *feel* those things. I knew that I ought to, but I felt absolutely nothing at all, like I'd just walked into the kitchen and Mom had told me off for being late.

"Did you hear me?" Mom didn't even seem to notice that Luke was there. "She's dead. The hospital called us. Your father's on the phone with them now."

"How?" I finally managed.

Mom's voice shook. "Does it matter?"

"Terry?" Dad's voice, deep and calming, called from the other room. "Could you come here a second?"

Mom whirred to the other room; the kitchen seemed empty and mute without her frenzied presence. I didn't want to look at Luke. I didn't know why. Maybe because he would look at my face and see that there were no tears, that I was a terrible person. In my pocket, my phone beeped a text message; it didn't realize that this wasn't an ordinary night, and that a moment of silence was called for.

Luke reached out and caught my arm, turning me towards him. "You can cry later, Dee. The tears'll come later." He looked at me, eyes narrowed. "I have to go find what she was working on. Something to protect your family. I'll bring it back here."

Fear rose up where grief wouldn't. "Don't go. Please don't go."

"You say that now, but how would you feel if the hospital called and it was your father?" He tipped my chin up with his finger. "That's what I thought."

I felt tears prick my eyes, but for the wrong reasons. I let him kiss my mouth gently and hug me before he let himself out the kitchen door.

In the other room, I heard my parents fighting; Dad talking in his low voice, and Mom screaming at him. I stood alone in the dim yellow kitchen and took my mobile phone from my pocket. One unread text message.

It was from James, and like half of my messages, it had been delivered late – it was sent three hours previously. The subject line was that of all our epic texts – the line we used for things too serious to talk about in person: *deep thoughts.*

I opened it.

d. i love u.

I sank down on to the tiles and put my head in my hands, listening to my mother screaming at my father and wondering when it would all start to hurt.

Finally, I worked up my courage and dialled James's number, trying to plan what to say when he picked up. It rang and rang, until I heard his voice: *You've reached James's mobile phone. By dialling this number you've increased your coolness level by ten points. Add another ten by leaving a message after the beep. Ciao.*

I hung up. I'd never got his voicemail before − no matter how crazy the time was or where he was, he'd always picked up.

I felt alone.

Book Four

The Minstrel Boy to the war is gone—
In the ranks of death you will find him.

—"The Minstrel Boy"

Sixteen

I was having one of those dreams. Where I wasn't sure if I was awake or not. It *felt* like I was awake, lying in my bed. But my head was still fuzzy as if I was sleeping, and the voice that sang to me was vague and dreamy.

The voice went up and down the scale, not unpleasantly, singing in no fixed measure, whispering to me that the name Deirdre meant "sorrow." In the foggy way of dreams, I recognized the story of yet another Deirdre. This third Deirdre was betrothed to the King of Ulster, even though she was in love with someone else. Deirdre eloped with the hot young thing, Naois, who was her true love, thoroughly pissing the king off in the process. The king pursued her, had Naois and his brothers killed, and then stole Deirdre away to be his wife. Deirdre, stricken with grief, threw herself from his carriage and smashed her head on a rock, killing herself. The breathy voice of my dream sang that all Deirdres come to bad ends.

At least Naois's Deirdre was clever enough to kill

herself before it got any worse. All these old Irish legends ended in tragedy; what did I expect now that I was living one? *Come away, human child,* whispered the voice in breathy timbre, *come away from the pain of the world.*

It was like some kind of supernatural version of those "stop smoking" mind-control tapes you listen to while sleeping.

I opened my eyes. I felt like crap – I ached like I'd been lifting trains the night before. My grandmother had been killed by the faeries, my best friend was in love with me, my boyfriend was a soulless assassin for an otherworldly schizophrenic, and my pillow was wet.

Ew. Why is my pillow wet? I sat up hurriedly, looking at my surroundings with distaste. Oh, ten kinds of gross. My sheets were wet. My pillowcase was wet. The bedside table was covered with perfectly round beads of water. Everywhere I looked, I saw a layer of dew, coating every surface with scented condensation. My eyes lifted to the window, which stood wide open, and I lifted my wet fingers to my nose. They reeked of thyme.

What the heck is going on? I looked down at Rye, who still lay on the floor by my bed, morning light from the window reflecting brilliantly in the dew on his coat. "Some friggin' guard dog you are. So, are you on Their side or mine?"

Outside, very close, I heard a laugh, high and light,

halfway to a tune. I leapt out of bed and leaned out of the window so fast that the sill heaved the breath out of me. The morning sun forced my eyes into a squint, but I thought I saw a smudge of darkness blink out of the corner of my vision, far below my window, gone too fast for me to say if it had really been there or not. I lifted my hands from the window sill and looked at them; petals were stuck on my palms. Poppies, maybe.

Friggin' sketchy faeries. I was going to smell like a bag of potpourri left in an Italian restaurant for the rest of the day. Picking petals off my skin, I knocked the rest of the blooms to the ground outside, frowning at the empty garden. I retreated back into my room and retrieved my phone from the bedside table.

James still didn't pick up, and his voicemail was full, so I tried Luke's number. It rang and rang before making a strange static sound and disconnecting.

I stared at the phone in my hand and observed how white my knuckles were, pressing out against my skin. There could be a thousand reasons why neither was picking up, but about nine hundred of them made my stomach roll unpleasantly.

Feeling distinctly unsettled, I turned to go downstairs, and found myself looking directly into a pair of enormous green eyes.

"Holy crap."

It took me a moment to realize that the eyes were Delia's, and that they only appeared enormous because they were so close. Of all Delia's talents, I hadn't thought the ability to be soundless was one of them.

Delia handed me the phone. "Phone for you."

I tried not to look too hopeful as I took it, but she'd turned before I had time to look too pathetic and closed the door behind her. I lifted the phone to my ear. "Hello?"

I didn't immediately recognize the voice, but the fact that it wasn't Luke depressed me hugely. "Hello? Is this Dee?"

Then the voice clicked in my mind; it was one I hadn't heard in a while: Peter, James's older brother. "Peter? Yeah, it's me. I didn't expect *you* to call."

There was a pause. "I didn't call. Your aunt called *me*."

I frowned at the closed bedroom door, wondering if I'd open it to find Delia crouched on the other side. "Ok*aaaay*. That's weird . . . how did she have your number?"

"I'm not in California. I'm at my parents'."

There was something off in the way he said it that made me realize I hadn't been listening properly to his tone until then. "Hey. Is something wrong? When did you get in?"

"I flew in from California last night. God, Dee, you haven't heard? Mom and Dad didn't call you?"

Every so often, I know what someone's going to say before they say it. This was one of those moments, and I sank down on the edge of the bed, gripping the comforter with one hand. I knew I was going to need to sit down to hear what was coming. "Heard what?"

"James—" The word was strangled. Peter paused to regroup, and when he continued, his voice was back in control. "He had an accident on the way back from his gig last night. He – uh – he hit a tree."

I bowed my head down, one hand squeezed into a fist so tight my nails bit into my palm, and the other pressing the phone against my ear. I made myself ask, "How is he?"

"The car is totalled, Dee. The left side's just . . . gone. The police, they had dogs out last night, they're still looking for the – for James."

I knew what he stopped himself from saying – "the body." So it was bad, then. I felt suddenly sick at the idea of James's car, his life, crushed beyond recognition. How many times had we parked in the very-furthest-away spot in a car park so that no one would open their car doors into his paint? All for nothing.

I swallowed. "He wasn't in the car?"

Peter was silent for a long, long minute, and then he said, voice breaking, "Dee, they think he crawled out. They think he crawled out and died somewhere. There's blood everywhere – I saw it. God, Dee!"

My nails dug into my skin. I wanted to say something to comfort him, but it seemed false coming from someone who needed comfort themselves. "Pete – I don't know what to say." It felt horribly inadequate. We both loved James – I should have had something more insightful to say.

Then I thought of what I wanted to ask. "Will you help me look for him?"

Peter hesitated. "Dee – you didn't see how much blood – I – God."

"If he's alive, I can't just sit here."

"Dee." Peter's voice shook, and when he spoke again, it was in simple, clipped sentences, like I was a little kid he was trying to make understand. "He's dead. There was too much blood. They're looking in the river now. They didn't even tell us to keep our hopes up. He's *dead*. They said he was."

No. No, he wasn't dead. He just wasn't. I wouldn't believe it until I saw his body. "Tell me where it was, then. I want to go."

"Dee, you don't. I wish I hadn't gone. I can't get it out of my head."

"*Tell* me where."

I didn't think he was going to, but he did. I wrote it down on the back of the envelope from Thornking-Ash and hung up. Now I had to find some way to get there.

I dialled Luke's number, letting it ring twenty times before I hung up. There was some sort of large gooey lump in the back of my throat that I kept trying to swallow; it wouldn't go away and only seemed to get bigger when Luke didn't pick up. Giving up trying to swallow it, I put on some crappy jeans and my scuffed Doc Martens. I felt the need for busyness, the desire to prepare myself for the search. And all the while I got ready, I was amazed at how cold I felt inside, how calculating. I was watching the entire thing on Dee TV from a million miles away.

I went downstairs, pausing at the sound of raised voices in the living room.

"Terry, you aren't going to cater your own mother's wake. Let Julia or Erica do it." Delia's voice was condescending and loud as usual; she took her coffee black with an extra scoop of superiority.

"Like hell I won't!" Mom's voice was near-scream. "I'm not having my family fly in to eat soggy canapés over my mother's coffin."

"*Our* mother."

Mom laughed, high and wild. "You're a piece of work!"

I didn't really want to walk in on that right now. Maybe I could just steal the car while they were fighting. Maybe Dad would take me. I edged into the kitchen and found Dad swallowing the last of a cup of coffee and stuffing his wallet into his back pocket. He looked hunted.

"Dee, are you OK?"

The stupid lump was still there. I talked around it. "James—"

"Delia told us."

Of course she did. Probably smiling the whole time. I wondered if *she* had a soul. "I want to go look for him."

Dad set down his coffee cup and looked at me. I realized I must look crazy, standing there with my wild eyes and the crumpled Thornking-Ash envelope held tightly in my hand. His voice was gentle as he tapped his mobile phone on the table. "Dee, I talked to his parents while you were upstairs. They said he was dead."

"They haven't found his body." I knew I sounded like a stubborn kid, but I couldn't stop myself. "I want to look for him."

"Dee."

"Please take me. Just let me see the car."

Dad's eyes were full of pity. "Dee, you don't really want to see that. Trust me. Just let the police do their work."

"Peter told me they'd already started looking in the river! They aren't looking for him any more, not really! He's my *best friend*, Dad! I don't *need* protecting!"

Dad just looked at me and shook his head.

I didn't know what to do. I'd never been refused anything before – because I'd never asked. If I'd had my own car, if I'd had my own licence, I could've been gone already. "I hate being treated like a kid! I hate it!"

It felt so weak. Not at all what I needed to scream to make myself feel better, but it was all I could think of. I stormed outside and sat on the back step, picking at a thread at the bottom of my jeans. It seemed wrong for the sky to be so blue, for the summer sun to feel so good on my skin, like I could be fooled into thinking this day was just like any other summer day. It wasn't. They would never be the same.

I couldn't just sit here.

I took out my mobile phone and scrolled down through the calls I'd received until I found Sara's number. I only hesitated a second before I hit *send*.

"Yeah?" That one word, said in Sara's usual voice, pulled me back to the ground.

"This is Dee."

"Ohmygod, Dee, I heard about him. James Morgan, I mean. God, he was on the news! I am *so* sorry."

Weirdly, her emphatic words brought me closer to tears than any I'd heard that day. I swallowed them. "I don't think it was an accident."

"Oh – whoa – what? You think he was drinking?"

"No. I think the faeries did it."

There was a pause, and I was afraid she had decided that Freckle Freak was just a sketchy boy. Then: "No way. Seriously?"

Relief surged through me. "Seriously. They haven't found the body yet, so he could still be alive. I want to go look for him, but my parents are being all—"

"—crappy about it. Yeah. Sure. I can see that. Parents suck."

I gathered courage. "I was wondering if, maybe, since you have your licence, if—"

Sara surprised me and finished my sentence. "Give me, like, two seconds. Where do you live? Yeah. I gotta get out of the house anyway, I'm going crazy. Gimme two seconds. Promise."

Two seconds actually meant twenty minutes, but Sara did come. She stopped at the end of the driveway like I'd told her to, and I ran out to her old Ford Taurus before my parents could realize she was there. We stopped a few kilometres away and consulted a stained map book from the back seat, tracing the crooked back roads we'd have to take to get to the scene of the accident.

"That's the middle of super-nowhere. What the crap was he doing back there?" Sara asked, but I didn't have an answer. In awkward silence we headed out of town and drove down endless identical Virginia back roads: narrow, twisting paths dappled by the hidden sun. What short glimpses of the sky I saw revealed brilliant blue, broken by perfectly white clouds. I couldn't believe anything bad could happen on such a beautiful day.

I hunched in the passenger seat, scrolling through every option on my phone. Received calls, missed calls, dialled calls. Voicemail, text messages. The letters blurred in front of my eyes, meaningless strings of words to my churning mind. Then my fingers stopped and I gazed dully at the message I'd unconsciously surfed to.

d. i love you.

I blinked my eyes dry. I had to keep my cool.

"Thanks for taking me," I said finally, breaking the silence.

Sara seemed relieved that I had spoken. "Oh, yeah, no problem. I mean, seriously, what was your parents' problem anyway?"

I shrugged. "I don't know. I guess . . . my grandmother died last night, too."

"Wow. That's crap timing." Sara stopped at a stop sign and craned her neck to look both ways.

I swallowed, the lump still stuck in my throat. I didn't know what to say.

"I think it's nice that you're sad about her," Sara said.

I looked at her, eyebrow raised, quizzical. I wasn't offended, but it seemed like such a stupid thing to say.

"My grandmother – the one I have left, I mean – she's invisible." Sara shrugged. "It's like she's from another planet. She doesn't watch movies, she doesn't know any of the music I listen to. We talk about the weather and stupid stuff like that, 'cause I can't think of anything else she notices. The other day I thought about her and I realized I couldn't remember a single thing she'd ever worn. How awful is that? I feel bad that I don't feel anything about her, but it's just like she's – like she's already dead. The world changed and left her behind."

It was the most personal exchange we'd ever had, and it was weird. I felt like I ought to say something to clinch the moment, to forever lock us in the bond of friendship. But I couldn't think of anything. Too late, I said, "Makes you afraid to get old, doesn't it?"

"And ugly. Like, when I get too ugly to wear a mini-skirt, just shoot me."

I sort of laughed. She sort of did, too.

Then I saw a sign up ahead and said, "I think this is it." Sara blew past the street and had to make a U-turn to drive down a narrow, dark road marked *Dun Lane*.

We drove out of the dappled sun into complete darkness, the tight-knit tree canopy looming high overhead like a massive green temple. I didn't know where James's gig had been, but I couldn't think of any reason why he would have been on such an out-of-the-way road.

"I guess they'll have towed the car. We'll have to look for the place where the wreck was."

That was the longest minute of my life, scanning the green-brown darkness for a glimpse of destruction, looking for any sign that everything I'd known was gone for ever. And when Sara stopped next to a tree that looked like any other of the massive oaks that lined the road, I couldn't tell what she'd seen to mark the spot.

She turned off the ignition. "Do you mind if I stay in the car? Blood totally makes me pass out."

I nodded. "That's OK."

I got out of the car. Standing out on the crumbling edge of the road, the smell of wet leaves and forest filling my nose, and almost cold in the perpetual shade of the trees, I saw what had made her stop: the bark stripped from the near side of the closest oak tree, and, lying on the leafy ground beside it, a driver's side mirror the tow company had missed when they took the car. And then I saw the dark stain on the road, the sort of stain you see after a deer has been hit and taken away by the state crews. Only this wasn't from a deer.

It was a horrible shape, too; the smudged line of blood spelled struggle.

I closed my eyes and shut out the blood. I wasn't going to think about James. I was just going to do the job.

I went to the base of the tree. I thought about picking up the driver's side mirror and taking it with me, but stopped myself just before I picked it up. It wasn't important. James was important. Leaving the tree behind, I slowly made my way through the ferns and leaves. Everything became formless in this still, everlasting dimness. The only sound was the muffled calls of birds in the canopy overhead. My progress was painstakingly slow – I wouldn't miss a clue beneath the ferns.

About thirty metres from the crash site, my Doc Martens scuffed against something hard in the soft undergrowth. I knelt down, squinting, and saw a white object glowing in the darkness.

I gingerly picked it up, and my stomach squeezed. It was an unmarked bottle of eyedrops. When I opened it, the sweet smell of clover drifted out. A thousand new memories, all run together – of Luke putting the drops in his eyes, Luke laboriously making the drops, Luke shoving the bottle into his pocket – clicked through my mind like a slide projector.

I bit my lip and took out my mobile phone, hesitated a long moment, then dialled Luke's number.

In my ear, quiet and thin, it began to ring. And then – a few metres away – it rang as well, a weird, modern sound in this ancient quiet.

I wanted to slap my phone shut and pretend I hadn't heard it, but it was too late for that. I followed the sound and, sure enough, a dirty mobile phone lay half-buried in a tangle of trampled thorns. I reached down to pick it up. And saw the red spatter on the leaves around it.

My breath somehow got stuck in my lungs and my legs gently refused to hold me. I pressed a hand to my mouth, holding my tears in, willing myself strong, willing myself not to jump to conclusions, but the tears escaped anyway. First two at a time, silently sliding down my cheeks, and then three and four and five until they all ran together and gasped out of me. Folded in the ferns, thorns caught into my jeans, I stared at the single drop of red on the mobile phone and sobbed for Granna, James, and Luke.

As the tears subsided, I slowly became aware that my limbs were trembling, like they did when I tried to move something with telekinesis during the daytime. Energy was funnelling out of me. I remembered that feeling from before – and I looked up quickly, bracing myself for Eleanor or worse.

But it was Una I saw, crouching on a log a few metres away from me, bent into an impossible shape as she licked her fingers like a cat that has just finished a meal. In the green light of the forest, her pale skin looked less green than it had before, though she still couldn't pass as human. Her bizarre outfit immediately drew my attention: some sort of overcoat that looked like an eighteenth-century military jacket with more than a dozen buttons leading up to its high collar, and beneath it, a frilly white skirt. The weird combination was sort of ultra-chic thrift-store, equal parts masculine and feminine.

She wrinkled her nose at me, observing my tears. "You're doing that *again*?"

I smudged my palm across my cheek, and, remembering what Luke told me, stood before answering. "I've just finished."

Una smiled brilliantly at me. "Behold my cleverness, human." Her delicate features puckered into a frown, eyebrows drawn together into instant sorrow, and as her lips trembled into a pout, a single tear – *my* single tear – ran down her chalk-white cheek. The teardrop glistened on her jaw and, just as it fell, Una's hand darted out and caught it, folding it away for later. Her smile returned as quickly as it had gone, and she laughed, high and wild. "Isn't it *perfect*?"

I sniffed, my nose stuffed up from crying. "Better than a human." I was sure *her* nose wasn't stuffed up.

She leapt from her perch with alarming suddenness, fluttering around me like a bird, so close that I caught a whiff of her scent: musky and sweet at once, the smell of a wild thing. She whispered in my ear, "I know what you're looking for."

I carefully avoided looking at the blood-spattered mobile phone, and swallowed. "And do you know where 'it' is?"

She laughed and jumped back on to the fallen log, skimming along it before twirling back the way she'd come. "It's all dreadfully poetic. I cannot wait to sing it. A minor key, I think."

I wanted to strangle her; couldn't she just out and *tell* me? With great force of will, I managed to stuff my impatience away some place and sound gracious. "Will you sing it for me now?"

Una smiled a secret smile at the ground. "Will you

come live with me for ever?"

It was too easy to forget that she was as dangerous as Freckle Freak. Politely, I declined. "That sounds lovely, but I don't think so. Is it the only way you'll sing it for me?"

She looked at me and then said in a fond voice, "No, stupid human. I'll give it to you for free, because it will vex Brendan when he finds out." Two long steps brought her back to my side, and she half-sang, half-whispered in my ear:

Away into the oaks, away beneath the earth
the piper's blood spills
the gallowglass' blood falls
in pools that tell their futures

She bids the gallowglass to
kill his lover;
She bids the piper,
"kill thy love."

The melody and her voice caught me where I stood, cradling me tightly in that moment. I could not think to speak.

Una clucked disapprovingly and snapped her fingers in front of my face. "The slightest tune dazzles thee, lovely. How do you expect to recover your lovers if you don't guard your senses? You *are* going to disappoint me, aren't you?"

I blinked, still slightly dazed by the spell of her voice. "They're not both my lovers. I mean, *neither* are my lovers. I mean—" Her song slowly ceased to be magic and began instead to form meaning in my head. "Do you mean they're not dead?"

Una shrugged and leapt away from me, long ballet-leaps over the bracken, and then turned back, bowing as if she'd done something very impressive. "Not yet!"

I could breathe again. In some way, I felt like I hadn't filled my lungs since I'd seen Luke's phone and the drops of blood. Now, for the first time in many minutes, I took a deep breath and let it out. Inside me, a little voice sang, *they're alive, they're alive.*

"She has them, then. The Queen, I mean."

Una danced over to me, slow and prancing, and stopped a bare centimetre in front of me. Her fingers stretched out and hovered over my iron key, closer, closer, until they were as close as they could get without touching it. She leaned forward and spoke into my ear, so near that her face touched my hair; her voice was balanced between glee and seriousness. "Solstice draws near; see how strong we grow? Soon the Hunter will be able to touch you himself; soon Aodhan, foulest of the foul, will be able to defile you as he defiles everything his fingers reach. They could take your songs and keep them so deep inside themselves you'd never know you lost them. They will play with you until you smile and welcome Death into you."

I froze, profoundly aware of how dangerous she was, this wild, inhuman creature who was close enough to see the dried tears on my cheeks.

Out of the corner of my eye, I saw her lips curl into a beautiful smile, and she whispered, "*Now* would be a wonderful time to ask for that favour I promised you. For your tear."

She drew back, leaving me quivering from her strangeness, and studied me – standing there with my chin raised up in something like courage.

I looked back at those depthless green eyes, trying to read any sort of emotion in them, any clues as to a right answer, but saw nothing but deeper and deeper. So I nodded and said, as if it had been my idea, "I'll take that favour now, please."

"I thought," Una drew a circle in front of her with a finger, "you'd never ask."

She beckoned me, and I edged closer, warily.

"You humans like humans, right?"

I wasn't exactly sure how to answer that.

She drew the circle again, and this time it seemed to stay there after her finger had dropped. "Do you see him?"

I looked at the glowing edge of the circle, but all I saw within it was the gnarled oak tree on the other side. "No?"

Una made an exasperated noise. "Try using your eyes." She drew the circle again, and this time the glow of the edge made me blink in pain; it was like the searing light of the sun, and it shimmered in a way that was *wrong*, that bent the edges of the forest within and the forest without.

And this time, I did see him. It was a man in his late thirties or early forties, his head covered in long, loose brown curls, reading a book in the middle of field. "Who is it?"

"Thomas Rhymer. One of Hers. A human. A man. Shall I get more specific?"

"I think that covers it." I hoped she was going to explain the significance of the bouncy-haired man, because I had no idea how showing me a strange man reading a book was supposed to count as a favour.

"Look how human he is," Una mused as the man turned a page. I wasn't sure if this was a commentary on his appearance or on his page-turning ability. "I think you ought to have a little chat with him."

"Where is he?"

"There."

I once again fought against the desire to bitch-slap a faerie, and rephrased. "How do I *get* to there?" I hoped to God she didn't say "walk", because I really didn't think I'd be able to stop my fist if she did.

"I forget how stupid you all are," Una said brightly. She tugged the edge of the circle larger, so I could see that the man sat in the middle of the cow pasture near my house, the one where I'd seen the white rabbit. Then she popped her finger into her mouth as if the glow had burnt her, and turned to me. "Truly, the magnanimous nature of my favour surprises even me."

Uh. "Thank you," I said.

She spat through the circle and it vanished like smoke. "And here's another suggestion, for nothing. *Gratis*. Drown the hound of the Hunter's you've been keeping. You'll have to hold it under for quite a few minutes." She made a motion as if she were holding one of her hands under water. "Until the bubbles stop."

I blinked at her.

She seemed oblivious to my horror, and instead said kindly, with obvious effort, "Would you like your tear back? You'll need it."

"No thanks. I think it looks better on you."

Una grinned at me.

Sara was so clueless trying to get us home that she finally pulled over and let me drive instead. Even though I rarely get to practise driving, I was much better at finding our way back down the back roads. I was almost giddy. Being stolen away by the Faerie Queen and tortured was bad, but it was so much better than being *dead*. Dead was irreversible. Suddenly I was noticing details that I had missed before: just how gorgeous the day was, how loud the cicadas were, how the leaves of the trees were flipping up to reveal their pale undersides, promising a storm later on despite the brilliant blue sky. With my change of mood, I saw something on the way back that I hadn't noticed before: Luke's car.

I slammed on the brakes.

Sara screamed. "Holy crap! What are you doing?"

I backed her car up to the little dirt road where I'd seen Luke's car.

"Sorry. I saw something. I'm just going to check it out, OK? Just – two seconds."

She squinted out of the windows and then reached into the back seat for a magazine. Apparently, she thought that my "two seconds" meant the same as hers. I left her reading and made my way over to where Luke's car sat, pulled back into the mouth of an overgrown dirt road that was used to access the cornfield behind it. The angle of the car implied a certain haste, and in my head I imagined that Luke had somehow come riding to James's rescue, pulling him from the car where James was pinned. It was a much better image than a bloodied James dragging himself out of his Pontiac on to the tarmac.

The Audi was unlocked, and though I felt a little foolish, I climbed into the driver's seat and shut the door behind me. Leaning back in Luke's seat, I closed my eyes and let his smell trick me into thinking he was there in the car with me. Even though I'd only seen him the night before, I missed him unimaginably; the part of me that was in him felt as if it were a million miles away, in a place too distant to ever visit. When I was with him I felt loved, wanted, protected; now I felt like a little boat adrift in a strange dark sea.

I opened my eyes and it was dark; night surrounded the car like a close blanket. It took me a moment to realize that I was in a memory. I was Luke, sitting in the driver's seat, my heart pounding with adrenaline. Urgency pumped through me – I had to get to the scene of the crash before They did. I swivelled in the seat, looking at a mason jar full of yellow-green paste lying on the passenger-side floor, and thinking I ought to put some of it on my shoes as protection. But no, there had to be enough for Dee and her parents, and I didn't want to risk wasting it. Anyway, it wasn't me They wanted; not until Dee was dead, anyway. Crap. I left it lying on the floor and jumped out of the car, hoping the kid was still alive.

The memory snapped to an end with the sound of the door opening. In real life, *my* life, the door was still closed, and I was still sitting firmly in the driver's seat. I looked over to the passenger-side floor, and sure enough – sitting in the stark shadows cast by the noon sun shining through the windshield – a mason jar full of Granna's concoction lay on its side. It looked like cat vomit.

So he had found it. I sighed, picked the jar up – oh *nasty*, it was a little warm, like it was living – and got out of the car. I wished I could think of an excuse, something to tell Sara so that I could take Bucephalus back home. Selfishly, I wanted the reminder of Luke close to me.

Movement caught my eye, something blocking the light in the sparse trees that bordered the cornfield. Before me, five or ten metres in front of the car, walked a tall man with skin as brown as the dust of the road. Due to his height, he had to move slowly through the tree branches. He was absolutely naked, his muscles long and sinewy like a deer or a racehorse, and though my attention should have been drawn to his indecent exposure, all I could focus on was his tail. Long and whip-like, it ended in a tuft of hair like a goat's. The faerie – because that's what he had to be – paused, and turned his head slowly to look at me. His eyes were too close together, and his nose was too long and thin over his wide mouth to be human. It was the gaze of a feral thing, a creature that knew what I was and was both unafraid and uninterested. I waited long moments until he was out of sight, and then I bolted to Sara's car and got in, cradling the jar carefully.

"What's that?" Sara put her magazine down.

"It's some sort of anti-faerie juice that my Granna made."

"Whoa. Oh. Where'd you get it?"

I pointed. "Luke's car."

"Luke is that cute guy? Where is he?"

"I don't know."

Sara frowned. "I'm getting creeped out. This is totally starting to sound like a horror flick, and everybody knows the hot chick dies first. Let's get out of here."

We did, leaving the only evidence of Luke's existence on the dusty road behind us.

Seventeen

"Why are you looking up 'solstice'?"

Hunched over my father's laptop computer, manically tapping in things like "solstice", "gallowglass", and "Thomas Rhymer" into search engines, I hadn't even heard Delia approach.

"Holy crap!" I swallowed my racing heartbeat. This sneaking-up thing of hers was getting really annoying. I turned to look at her and found her next to my shoulder, holding a cup of coffee, staring down at me with her green eyes. God, she looked *alive*. It was as if she'd been a black and white photo, and now suddenly colour was blooming into her. It scared the crap out of me. Suddenly I didn't feel so bad for putting the Granna concoction on my parents' shoes and leaving hers unprotected.

Delia leaned over my shoulder and read the screen. It was a frilly website called "The Fairy Patch", with lists of plants that would attract faeries to your garden. The part I was reading was talking about how the midsummer solstice thinned the veil between the human world and the faerie world. The site recommended putting out saucers of milk and burning thyme to encourage optimal faerie visitation. Without success, I had tried to imagine the goat-faerie – or better yet, Aodhan – lapping up milk like a tame kitten. Where did they come up with this crap?

Delia laughed. "What else have you got there?"

I contemplated making a run for it with the laptop, but instead I flinched away and let her reach over the top of my hand to click through the other open windows. Her eyes scanned the ballad of Thomas the Rhymer – stolen away by the Faerie Queen and given a tongue that could not lie – and then moved to the website with the definition of "gallowglass": a hired mercenary in ancient Irish history. Her eyes reflected the square of the monitor as she read. When she'd finished, she stepped back.

"I suppose you're going to tell me it's for a school project."

I don't know why that scared me so badly, but it did. It somehow stepped over the line of hinted-at strangeness to out-and-out malevolence. I considered my words carefully. "I think that would be like you telling me that you hadn't met Luke before the music competition."

Delia paused; it was her turn in this verbal chess match. "I think I have a promising search for your school project." She leaned over me again, placed the cursor in the search engine box, and typed "how to free hostages". She hit *enter* with a manicured nail.

I stared at the list of news articles and blog postings and remembered Delia handing me the phone earlier that day. She'd known what had happened to James, hadn't she? And then she'd called his house to make sure *I* found out.

"He must be very badly hurt," Delia said to the room in general. "I heard there was a tremendous amount of blood. If he's still alive, he must not have much time."

I wanted to close my eyes and ears, shut out her voice, pretend that in my increasingly weird life at least the diva aunt stayed the same. "What are you saying?"

Delia held out her hand. "Why don't you give me Granna's ring?"

I blinked up at her, jolted out of my bewilderment by the request. "No, I don't think so. Granna wanted me to have it."

"And it belongs with her now."

"I said *no*."

Delia's hand snaked out and grabbed my wrist with surprising force; I gasped with pain as she gripped the ring with her other hand and ripped it off, tugging the skin up with it. She threw my wrist away from her and shoved the ring in her pocket. I stared up at her, the presence of Luke's key burning against my skin, hidden by the collar of the light sweater I wore, afraid that she would somehow divine its existence and rip it from me as well.

"Now, you're going for a walk," she said, gesturing to the door that lead outside.

"Are you out of your mind?" I jumped up and retreated towards the living room, regretting that I'd chosen Dad's study for my research. I guess I should have run faster, but I couldn't shake the image of her as just my bossy aunt. "Mom!"

Delia grabbed my arm again, her fingers iron clamps. "She can't hear you."

I twisted and writhed, my skin burning under her grasp. "What do you get out of this?"

"Oh, don't tell me you're that stupid." Delia dragged me unceremoniously towards the French doors. I should have been able to escape from her grasp, but her body was wiry and unyielding beneath her pink velour armour. It reminded me of the endless *Cops* episodes I'd watched at Granna's, where they'd said people on highs had inhuman strength. "You've put everything else together, haven't you?"

And just like that, everything snapped neatly into place. The room in Granna's house where Delia had nearly died. The wet feet on Mom's bed. Rye, the faerie hound, who had been in the family before I was born. This had started a long, long time before me. "Your life. They saved your life."

"Don't forget the best part," Delia said, and she sang

a perfect scale in the pristine voice that had netted her a record deal. "Do you think this voice was mine?"

I whispered, "It was Mom's, wasn't it?"

She shoved me hard, reaching for the door handle, and I moved to brace myself against the glass. Too late, I saw that the glass door was already open, and that she'd been reaching for the screen door handle instead. She'd shoved me so hard that I felt the screen give way and tear beneath my weight. I crashed down on to the brick patio, my head striking the ground. My vision throbbed and I gasped, "What do you want from me?"

Delia stared down at me, her eyes hard and glittering. "I just want you gone."

She slammed the glass door; I heard the lock *snick* shut. I groaned, sitting up slowly, pulling my bare feet close to my body. As I did, I saw a little metal plate by the door. A twisted bit of black lay on it, still smoking. *Thyme!* She'd burnt thyme and then she'd thrown me outside.

I barely had time to think *my friggin' aunt betrayed me* when I saw a brown-and-gold-haired faerie striding up through the back garden. A hundred Rye-dogs milled about his ankles – some lean as greyhounds, some huge as mastiffs, but all the same colour as Rye.

Casting no shadow in the afternoon sun, the faerie was curiously difficult to see with the trees as a backdrop. He wore odd, tight-fitting clothing in varying colours of green and brown. The body of the jerkin and his leggings were made of leather, and the sleeves were made of something like suede or moss. Dried braids of grass were tied on the outside of each leg and hung in loose bunches at the cuff of each sleeve, like the frills on a Victorian costume or stuffing hanging from a scarecrow. He looked as if he had been made from the earth and could return to it just as easily, but his features had the same fearful symmetry as Freckle Freak and Eleanor, lending him otherworldly beauty.

His head was turning from side to side – he hadn't seen me yet. I could have tried the door to the house, but I saw Delia on the other side, a massive malevolent presence. I hesitated a bare moment, and then leapt up and began to run. As I bolted across the garden, legs pumping, I was reminded of something Granna had once said: *dogs only chase cats that run*. But it was a little late to change my mind now.

When I cut across our garden into our neighbours', darting around the maze of terracotta pots that dotted their garden, I heard a long, thin wail. It was a terrible sound even without knowing that it meant the hounds had begun their chase. A second later, white bodies burst through the bushes, and I heard the shattering of pots. By then I was already into the hayfield beyond our neighbours' garden, cool blades of grass crushing beneath my feet, the sight of the tree-lined road beyond the field giving me newfound speed.

The sun burned me as I scrambled through the waist-high grass, casting a shadow that was pursued by one hundred bodies with none. That high-pitched wail came again, long and reedy, more bird-like than hound-like, and the bigger mastiff hounds began to cry low and melodic behind it. I tore my sweater off as I ran, feeling faster because of it.

But the hounds were gaining on me. There was no way I was going to make it to the road, much less to the cow pasture, before they caught me. I heard hay being crushed to the ground, close behind me.

I'm faster, I thought fiercely. *Hounds are fast, but I'm faster.*

And I was. I cleared the tangled bushes in the ditch by the field and leapt on to the dappled road on the other side. The hounds were still behind me, not on top of me. My breath was beginning to tear at my lungs, and my knees were aching. My feet slapped hard against the tarmac, and I stole glances over at the cow pasture on my right, looking for anything I'd recognize from Una's glowing vision of Thomas Rhymer. Up ahead was where I'd found Luke in his car that day; it had to be somewhere along here.

I glanced behind me and wished I hadn't; a wall of white dogs filled the width of the road like an oncoming wave, and behind them, walking calmly, was that green-clad Hunter with the two-toned hair.

Please be there. Thomas Rhymer, be there. There was

nothing saying that things would be all right once I found him in the cow pasture, but they *would* be. They had to be. Because I'd seen how close Una could get to the key, and I didn't want to think of what one hundred hounds could do with their newfound midsummer power.

Gasping, I ran to the edge of the cow pasture, hoping at least for some iron barbed wire that would slow the hounds down, but there was only a board fence. Damn our county codes for not allowing ugly fences. I clambered over the fence, more slowly than I would have liked, and suddenly, I saw the gentle slope of the cow pasture – the top of the hill from Una's vision.

Behind me, hounds hit boards and some of the lighter ones cleared it in a single leap. In my head, I repeated again, firmly: *I'm faster. I'm going to find Thomas. I'll be safe then.*

Up the hill I went, muscles groaning, and the hounds streamed after me. I just had time to see that there was a lumpy ring of mushrooms growing at the top of the hill before paws brushed against my leg. *This is it.*

I jumped into the ring, and there was silence.

No, not quite silence. It was as if I had just stuck a pair of earplugs in; the frustrated howl of the hounds had not gone away, it had just grown muffled and distant. I looked behind me, beyond the circle of mushrooms, and saw nothing but the broad field sloping gently down towards the road. If I squinted towards where I knew the hounds ought to be, I thought I could see vague smears of light and dark, imperfections in my vision.

"You certainly know how to make an entrance, don't you? *She* has quite a retinue as well, though they're a good deal less hairy than yours."

I knew who I'd see before I turned. As in Una's vision, Thomas the Rhymer had long, curly hair and eyes surrounded by laugh lines. He was long and skinny and wore a multicoloured tunic, with dozens of buttons up the front, over a pair of close-fitting leather leggings. He looked up at me from his cross-legged perch on the ground, casting a long, long afternoon shadow that fell outside the mushroom circle.

I panted, relieved. "You're *here*."

He smiled at me, puzzled. "Of course I am. *You* are."

"You know who I am?"

"Deirdre Monaghan. We all know your name now." It was hard to imagine any harm coming from him. His words formed around broad Scottish vowels. "Even if I didn't know your face, your ability to do *that*—" he gestured to the nearly invisible hounds circling the mushroom ring, "tells me who you are."

I didn't want to look stupid by asking him to clarify. I think he meant the fact that the hounds couldn't pass into the circle. Or maybe he just meant the fact that I was being chased by a hundred of them. That was probably it.

"Is it true you can't lie?"

"Yes. But, you know I'd say that if I *could* lie." He shrugged and watched my long shadow; its edges shimmered as invisible bodies passed over the top of it, outside the circle. "Of course, I'll let you look in my head if you like."

It was tempting, but I didn't feel like potentially adding the memories of a curly-haired prophet with a Scottish brogue to the ones I already had juggling around in my head. "I'll take your word for it. Una — one of the *Daoine Sidhe* — told me I should talk to you, and showed me this place."

"The *Daoine Sidhe* are not generally friendly with humans." Thomas gestured to the ring of mushrooms. Aching with the effort of keeping the hounds out, I remembered the surge of power — the invincibility — I'd felt when I started Bucephalus' engine, the darkness strong around me. If only the hounds had chosen to hunt me at night.

"But this was a good place to expect me to appear," Thomas was saying as I dragged my attention back to him. "And it's widely known that the Queen and I have had a falling out. Why do you think this faerie wanted you to talk to me?"

Inside, I felt a little prickle of dismay. "I was hoping it would be obvious."

Thomas looked up at me, his fingers plucking absently at the grass by his legs. "So . . . what do you want to know?"

There were a thousand different possible answers to this question, but I went with the one that bothered me the most. "I want to know why she wants me dead. If she'd never messed with me, I would've never known what I could do."

Thomas's thin face was startled. "You think she wants you dead because you can do this?" He pointed to the hounds' barely visible paws digging at the edge of the ring; my control of the circle was waning. "Child, your telekinesis is only a symptom of why she wants you dead. There are plenty of people out there who can move objects with their minds or set fire to a field without a match."

I didn't like the word *symptom*. Diseases had symptoms. "Symptom of what?"

"Didn't you ever wonder at the coincidence, that you and the Faerie Queen should be in such proximity? That a host of faeries should suddenly be on your doorstep?"

I felt foolish. "I – uh – guess I just thought there were a lot of faeries."

"They're here because of you. Faeries aren't like humans; Their realm and Their bodies don't really have fixed locations, like humans."

I seized the chance to look like I wasn't clueless. "You mean how some of Them use the energy of a storm, or a person, to appear."

Thomas nodded his approval; it made his curls

bounce. I fought the urge to reach out and *sproing* one of them. "Exactly. Faeries are drawn to a certain sort of energy, and They move like satellites around that energy. The realm of Faerie centres around one person, the monarch – usually a human – who radiates that energy."

It was starting to make sense, so I finished the thought. "So she kills anyone else who pulls Them like she does."

He nodded. "And your telekinesis is just a side effect of that energy."

"So, is she *here*? I mean, close to here? Or is she back in Ireland? I mean, she's human, right? So *she* shouldn't be pulled by my – what did you call it – my energy?"

"They call humans like you 'cloverhands'. You know, because clover draws faeries as well." Thomas shook his head. "And no, she's drawn to you, just as I am – the more time we spend in Faerie, the more we become like Them, and that means we're attracted to the cloverhands. And yes, she's close, and getting closer all the time, as you get stronger and as Solstice gets closer. She won't be able to avoid manifesting in your presence as soon as the veil is at its thinnest."

It was a terrifying thought; I pushed it to the back of my head for later contemplation. "Does that mean that Luke Dillon was drawn to me, too? You know who he is, don't you?"

Thomas's eyes were grim, incongruous with the laugh lines around them. "The Queen's gallowglass? Everyone knows who he is. And no, he doesn't live in Faerie, so he's not corrupted like the other humans in Faerie are. We live with the faeries to keep from dying, but doing so gives us their weaknesses as well. Luke Dillon doesn't need to live among Them to stay young like I do – he cannot grow old." His face was troubled. "There is rumour that he loves you."

I swallowed.

"And that you love him. That's a fool's game, child."

"I didn't *choose* to." My voice was unintentionally frosty. "I didn't choose to be this – cloverhand – either. It's friggin' unfair, if you ask me. I'm not keen on dying, so she steals my best friend and Luke? How is that fair?"

Thomas lay down on the grass, eye to eye with one of the hounds staring into the circle; they were far more visible than they had been before. "Don't blame me. I'm just a scholar; I've already had my hand slapped for disagreeing with her over matters of life and death. There's a reason I'm sitting in a ring of mushrooms, talking with her latest enemy, instead of fawning on her arm."

Frustration welled up in me and overflowed. "What about my best friend? Will she only let him go if I die?"

Thomas tapped his finger against the empty air of the mushroom ring; it rang back at him as if it were glass. On the other side, the hound whined and pawed at his finger. "The piper? He's too good for this world, you know. A piper that good can attract the wrong sort of attention. Worse than faeries. I've heard more than one faerie mutter he'd be better off dead, anyway."

"He would *not* be better off dead," I snapped. My fingers were beginning to tremble; the subconscious effort of keeping the faerie ring closed to the hounds was draining me too fast. I wasn't sure how long I could keep them out.

Thomas's face was sympathetic. "I'm sorry, child, but she will never let you exist while she does. You challenge her very existence, and you have a leg up with your humanity as well. One of you has to die to end this."

I stared at him, taking it in, hugging my shivering arms around me with the effort of keeping the ring secure. It sounded so cheesy: *one of you has to die. This town ain't big enough for the both of us.*

I couldn't keep the hounds out any more. I just wasn't strong enough without the moon above me.

"And as long as we're telling the truth," Thomas added earnestly, "I'd prefer it to be she."

I only had a moment to realize what he meant

before the invisible walls of the faerie ring burst open and a wave of hounds poured in, instantly blanketing Thomas's body and pressing close to me.

The stench of thyme was overwhelming.

Eighteen

It wasn't just the press of the hounds that made the collapse of the circle unbearable. It was the frost of their fur against my skin, the suffocating scent of herbs and clover, and, above all, the howls of the mastiffs and the screams of the lithe sighthounds: *our prey, our quarry, we have captured our kill.*

The Hunter strode in among them, their bodies making way for him, parting like water. His progress towards me was made silent by the cacophony. I barely heard him speak: "Quiet."

Instantly, the hounds fell silent. The hill was so quiet I could hear the roar of a car's tyres on the road below. I could have cried out, but for what purpose? To the car's driver, I was the only one on the hill.

The Hunter stopped an arm's length away from me. From this close, his strangeness took my breath away. His deep-set eyes were as fathomless as a hawk's, and I could see that the gold streak in his hair was *literally* gold, each strand gleaming as it sat stiffly within his regular brown hair. There were strange brown marks up and down his neck – like tattooed characters, only they looked as if he had been born with them.

"Deirdre Monaghan."

At the sound of his voice, I was immediately thrust through countless memories: Luke, looking at the bodies of his brothers in the ditch, and the Hunter bidding him to come away. The Hunter pinning Luke to the ground, face impassive, as the torc was forced on to his arm by a chanting faerie. Luke dragged from a well by the Hunter, who viewed him with no malice: "Time to work." Playing the flute while the Hunter listened, head cocked and eyes closed. The Hunter dragging Luke's bloodied body into a massive room, a scarlet trail leading out the door behind him.

Thomas whispered into my ear, "Only Luke can kill you with that iron on you. Be brave, child."

The Hunter gazed at him. "Thomas Rhymer, be silent, if you can."

He felt *old*. I sensed when I looked at him that I was looking at thousands of years of pursuit. I was more afraid of his strangeness than I was of Eleanor's vicious pleasure. I was afraid to speak; there must be some sort of protocol I ought to be following so as to not offend him.

"What do you want from me, Hunter? Shouldn't you be pursuing more challenging quarry with a pack like this?"

A strange expression flickered through the faerie's

eyes. "Indeed." He studied me through slit lids. "Indeed, they are wasted chasing such an easy trail."

"You cannot kill her," Thomas said. "So why chase her at all?"

"I bid thee be silent, Rhymer." He turned back to me and the pause dragged out for centuries. At the end of it, he reached to his hip and pulled out a long, bone dagger, the hilt all carved with the heads of animals. "Deirdre Monaghan, you are a cloverhand, and thus you must die."

Yeah. He was scary, but not scary enough that I was just going to sit back and let him stick me with a dagger. I took a step back, stumbling a bit over one of the hounds. "I know you're not thinking of stabbing me with that."

Thomas winced beside me, no doubt imagining how painful getting the dagger plunged into my body would be, even if it didn't kill me.

"Take off your iron," the Hunter said. "I can smell it on you."

"Like hell I will," I told him. "Keep back."

The Hunter's face bore no frown; I was a little rabbit darting away from his knife, and that was to be expected. He stepped forward, lifted the dagger slightly, and said again, "Take off your iron."

I glanced to the edge of the field. Afternoon had dragged into evening, and I could feel the looming darkness over the horizon even if I couldn't see it. It wasn't very close, but it was going to have to be close enough. Something in me seized that darkness, and I let it swell into me.

I held up my hand, and as neatly as if tugged by a string, the bone dagger flew into my palm. The hilt slapped my hand, and a bit of the blade as well; it parted my skin as easily as butter and I flinched, nearly dropping the knife. But I couldn't afford to drop it, so I didn't. I gripped it, a thin trail of blood dripping down the ivory surface, and I raised it towards the Hunter.

My voice shook. "Go back to her and tell her I want my friend back. And I want Luke."

The Hunter's eyes were fixed on me as if they would will the knife from my hand. "I will not leave my quarry."

"You will," I said, holding the knife steady with sheer force of will. "Go tell her what I said." I held out my other hand, the palm towards him, and imagined it was a huge giant's hand pressing into the Hunter's chest, gripping the strange surface of his clothing. And I shoved the giant's hand as hard as I could, pulling what force I could find in the darkness-that-was-not-yet-darkness.

The Hunter stumbled backwards, pressed down the hill. I shoved some more.

"Go, or I'll crush you," I lied. I barely had the strength to hold the dagger, much less to threaten him. It took all that was in me to squeeze the giant hand on his chest a bit, to hopefully convince him I had the strength to do what I said.

He gave me a long look and then he lifted a hand. "Hounds, come."

They streamed after him, coats glittering in the long evening light. I waited, my hand outstretched and shaking, until they had been gone two long minutes.

"Is he gone?" I finally whispered.

Thomas nodded, disbelieving. "Yes."

"Good," I said, and collapsed.

In my dream, I lay on a hill in a ring of mushrooms that glowed dusky white in the light of a million stars. There was no place in the world closer to the night sky than was that hill where I lay, the darkness pressing all around me, holding me to it. Every breath I took, the night filled me.

In this dream, I lay on my back, staring at the multitude of stars above me and at the chalk-white surface of the moon. I knew I was dreaming because as I looked at the moon, I could see curled birds trembling on its surface, white wings folded over one another in an impossible puzzle. There was something so beautiful and vast about their presence that I wanted to cry. Had they always quivered there in the light of the moon, only I'd never seen them until now?

It took me longer than I would have thought to realize I wasn't alone. It wasn't until I heard him sigh. I turned my head to look into his face. "I thought you were dead."

Luke looked tired; there was dried blood on his face and an odd longing in his voice. "I'm afraid not."

I swallowed tears; they got stuck in my throat. "I wish you were really here."

Sitting next to me, he cradled my cold bare feet in his warm hands; the flight from the hounds had left them filthy. "Oh, me too, lovely. But I'm glad enough for a dream; it was clever of you to think of it."

I didn't remember thinking of anything before I dreamt. I only remembered falling into the grass and wishing that the darkness had come sooner.

I pushed myself up, sitting closer to him, taking comfort in the memory of his smell. He wrapped his arms around me and spoke in my ear. "Don't let Them take my secret from you. It's all I have to give you."

He sounded miserable, his head resting on my shoulder, so I said earnestly, "All I want from you is *you*."

Luke's breath escaped in a long sigh. "Oh, Dee, I never wanted to be free as badly as I do now. I didn't think it would hurt like this."

"I'm coming to save you," I said.

He pushed back from me, holding me by my shoulders, staring into my face. "No matter what I say later, remember that I'll never hurt you. I could never hurt you." I didn't know if he was promising me or convincing himself.

"Tell me what to do," I pleaded.

Luke frowned, and I thought he would say that he didn't know what I should do. But he took my chin in his hand. "Trust yourself."

It wasn't what I wanted to hear. I couldn't trust myself; every time I did, I swapped memories with someone, made a car run continuously, or fell down in a useless faint. I didn't know what I was doing. I was a little kid waving a gun, playing with a toy of unimaginable power. I stared away from him at those milling white birds on the surface of the moon, thinking how they represented just how much I didn't know.

"Stop," he said. "I know what you're doing. You're a smart girl, Dee. The smartest I've ever met."

"Smart doesn't have anything to do with it," I snapped, jerking my chin away. "I can teach myself stuff from books or from watching someone else do it. How am I supposed to learn anything about *this*? There aren't any books on being a freak, as far as I know."

"I'm always pissing you off." Luke shook his head. "Even in your dreams, I'm managing to piss you off."

I looked back at him, at his tired, pale face watching me with his pale blue eyes reflecting the light of the moon-birds. He looked so vulnerable and *human* in this darkness. I shuddered. "I'm afraid I'll screw up and lose both of you."

"You have to trust yourself. You don't need someone else to tell you what to do."

Maybe I did. Maybe I wasn't ready for the

independence I'd wanted so badly. I buried my face in my hand, shutting out the light.

He took my wrist, and his voice was soft. "You can do anything you want to do, remember? Now come here and say goodbye to me because I don't know if I'll see you again."

My chin jerked up at his words and I saw that a wet streak glittered on his face before he kissed me, lips rough on mine. Wrapping my arms around his neck, I held on to him as he kissed me again and again, another gleaming trail joining the first on his cheek and mixing with my tears.

I thought the dream would end there, but it didn't end until after he'd pulled me down into the grass with him, lean body wrapped around me, and whispered, "Goodbye, pretty girl."

Above, the birds in the moon began to wail an eerie, lonely song, dozens of voices keening in a strange melody, and I woke up.

Nineteen

"Wake up, girl, it's nearly Solstice."

I opened my eyes and stared at the sky overhead; the moon had shifted from where it had been in my dream, but otherwise the sky was unchanged. My skin was clammy and my stomach was growling, but though there was no sign of Thomas, I wasn't alone.

Three faeries, the size of toddlers, sat at my feet watching me, naked except for flower chains that hung on their shoulders like swordless scabbards. They had plucked the grass from around me and scattered it all over my legs, and they laughed as I sat up and brushed off my jeans.

Their pinched faces were so charming as they giggled that I grinned, too. "Very tricky," I told them.

They squealed with delight and leapt up, pulling at my hands with theirs. "Get up, get up, and dance with us."

I wasn't sure of a polite way to decline, but I *was* sure I'd heard about humans losing themselves in faerie dancing before. Hiding my wariness, I said, "You dance. I'll watch."

"You're so bright and pretty," one of the faeries said, touching my hair reverently. "We want you to dance with us. We want to see you dance."

They really did remind me of children: small, amoral children. I held out my hand. "Let me have some flowers."

They shrilled with pleasure and draped a circle of flowers around my neck, tripping around me within the faerie ring. "Now we dance?"

I shook my head. "Now *I* dance, and you watch me. When I'm done, I'll watch you dance for a little. Does that sound fair?"

They laughed like children on a playground, their smiling faces illuminated by the stars above and the dully glowing mushrooms buried in the grass below. "Very clever, girl! Fair as fair!"

Fair as fair reminded me of Luke, and I wondered if he'd picked up the weird phrasing from the faeries. Ignoring the pang in my stomach from thinking of his name, I stood up and straightened the flowers around my neck. I looked down at the three little faeries, who stood with their arms linked around each other's necks and waists, looking back up at me. "Well, do I get any music?"

"Music! Yes! She wants music!" One of the faeries began to clap its hands and stomp its foot, hard and rhythmic, and another began to make a low, melodic sound halfway between humming and babbling. The third began to sing, voice brash and suggestive, in a language I didn't understand. But I knew the language of their music: it was a double jig. I began to step dance in the middle of the faerie ring, careful not to crush their mushrooms with my dirty bare feet. I like to think I gave them a good show, too; I clapped my hands and spun and step danced, crazy like Una would step dance. I was a bit out of breath when I stopped.

"You outshine the moon," one of them said. "Will you live with us?"

I shook my head. "No. I'll sing you a tune, though. A short one. Would you like me to?"

"Yes! Yes! She sings for us!" They clapped, delighted, and took their places near me in the circle. I didn't know any songs quite as rowdy as theirs, but I sang them "Brian Boru's March," which was fast, driving, and minor. They hooted as they recognized the tune, and then they began to dance together. Their steps were tightly wound and practised, and they moved as one entity, spinning around each other and clapping each other's hands at the end of each twirl. I didn't think I'd ever seen anybody so happy to be dancing. When I'd finished, the faeries clapped and hugged each other delightedly. They were still half-dancing, even though the music had stopped.

"I would like to give you something," said one.

"Is it something I want?" I asked suspiciously. They all laughed at my voice, and I laughed too – I think they liked me.

"Let me whisper it in your ear."

I frowned, unsure if I should trust them. Finally I crouched, letting the faerie step up to my ear. I smelled a sweet, flowery scent, as pleasant as a summer day, and then the faerie whispered, "O'Brien."

The other faeries shrieked, covering their mouths with their hands as if the faerie had said something really scandalous. "Oh ho ho, thou shalt burn for that!"

The whispering faerie giggled at my puzzled expression. "She doesn't know what it is."

I raised an eyebrow. "It's a name."

They shrieked again and clasped their arms around each other, spinning. The faerie who had whispered it to me looked at me, biting its lip. Its eyes gleamed with a wickedly mischievous smile. "You won't forget it, will you, girl?"

"No more than you will, imp," I told it.

They all fell down, chortling in the mushroom circle, helpless with laughter. They reminded me of the pack of junior high kids I'd found smoking dope behind the gym once. I smiled tolerantly at them. "I have to go now. I have to save my friend." They were still giggling, but I tried asking anyway. "Do you know where he is?"

"The bloody one?" asked one of the faeries. "Or your lover?" It pointed at its privates, and I rolled my eyes. Definitely like the junior high kids.

"Either."

"At the beginning," said the one who'd whispered "O'Brien". "It finishes at the beginning."

"Very cryptic. Thanks."

They just laughed. "Will you dance with us again, girl?"

"If I live, I'll pencil it in," I promised.

The summer night was alive with music. I heard strains of a hundred different songs from a hundred different directions as I made the hurried walk back to my parents' house. All around me, I saw glowing beacons of light in the darkness, faeries illuminating the night by means mysterious. Though I was certain I was being watched, I wasn't approached by any other faeries before I padded up the driveway.

Ouch, dammit. My bare feet were killing me. The run from the hounds had really done a number on them, and walking back to the house hadn't helped. Then I froze, in the shadows. Delia's car was still parked on the road in front of the house, and my parents' bedroom light was on. I wondered what poison she'd poured into my parents' ears about my absence.

I momentarily battled between my desire to get my shoes from the house and my fear of encountering Delia. I thought back to what the little faerie had told me about finishing at the beginning. There were countless ways I could interpret the statement, but I knew what *I* thought of as the beginning. The high school, where I'd met Luke. And if I was to walk there some time tonight, I had to have shoes. End of story.

I crept up to the kitchen door and tried the knob; unlocked. I felt a pang of guilt. My mom had probably left it open in case I came back without a key. But there was no way I could tell them I was all right and still be able to search for Luke and James.

Inside the dark kitchen, I waited by the door until my eyes adjusted to the dim green light from the glowing clock numbers on the microwave. My shoes were in the same jumble I'd left them in when I'd returned from searching with Sara; I pulled them on over my bare feet as I scanned the room. I had half an idea that Delia might be sitting in one of the kitchen chairs, ready to pounce. I squinted over at the breakfast table, making sure it was unoccupied.

Delia wasn't there, but her handbag was. A wicked idea popped into my head. It only took me a few minutes to rummage through for her keys. I clutched them so that they wouldn't jingle, grabbed a handful of Mom's apple mini-muffins, and stole back into the night, my heart pounding with daring.

I glanced back at the house to make sure I wasn't being watched, and then let myself into Delia's car. It stank of her perfume, which was as obnoxious as she was. And then I saw the mostly empty jar of Granna's concoction, sitting on her passenger seat.

Bitch. I ought to wreck this car when I was done with it.

I stuck the key in the ignition and imagined a heavy blanket covering the car, muffling the outside world. "Quiet, now," I mumbled, and turned the key. Soft as a whisper, the engine came to life. With another quick glance at the house to make sure they hadn't heard the car start, I pulled away from the kerb.

This is ten different kinds of illegal.

I stuffed a muffin in my mouth to give me some courage.

Once I was away from the house, I flicked on the headlights and headed towards the school. Delia had left one of her own albums in the CD player, so I hit buttons and whirled knobs until I found a rock station. I needed the pounding bass and growling guitar to give me courage. Cramming another muffin in my mouth, I started to focus a little better; I hadn't realized how hungry I was. What I needed to do was prioritize. If you took out the supernatural homicide bits, this was just a problem like any other I'd faced: a super-hard school project, a tune that refused to be tamed, a musical technique that twisted my fingers. I'd tackled all those before by breaking them down into little bits.

OK. So I knew I had to confront the Queen. What did I know about her? Nothing — except that she was both like me and like a faerie from living among them for so long. So I could pretty much abandon any idea of appealing to her emotions. Maybe I could appeal to her human nature, if she had any left. Hell if I knew how to do that. I jammed another muffin into my mouth.

As I pulled into the short access road that led to the empty high school car park, I saw a fire twisting high and wild at the base of one of the streetlights. In the flickering orange light, a massive black animal bellowed and charged as tall, whip-like men with horns tormented it, tossing glowing hot embers at its sides and face with their bare hands. I could almost feel the thinness of the veil between my world and Faerie — in my head, I could imagine it crackling, paper-thin and fragile.

I slowed the car. The whole stupid thing was right in front of me; I was going to have to get out and do something about it in order to get to the high school. I addressed a silent prayer to the skies: *I'm an idiot. Please don't let me die for the sake of a black cow-thing.*

I jumped. A glowing ember had smacked the windshield of my car, burning a black spot on the bonnet before sliding out of sight. I almost swore again, before remembering it was Delia's car. Outside, the whip men laughed before turning back to their torture; they thought they were playing a prank on someone who couldn't see them.

I grabbed the jar from the passenger seat, opened the door and got out to face them. *I'm brave.* I remembered an episode that happened when I was thirteen or so, when I found one of the neighbourhood boys piling dirt on an injured bird and watching it struggle beneath the dust. I had just stood for a long moment, trying to think what to say to stop him, frustrated by my shyness and by the boy's cruelty. Then James had appeared at my shoulder and said to the boy, "Do you think that's the best way to be spending your admittedly miserable life?"

I took strength from the memory and adopted my Ice Queen posture. My voice oozed contempt. "Having a nice Solstice?"

The whip men's heads turned to look at me. Their narrow bodies were black as tar and seemed to absorb the firelight instead of reflecting it. The giant bull, on the other hand, was pale dun beneath the ash that covered his coat, and I saw panic and rage in his liquid eyes.

"The cloverhand," hissed one. The voice was the same I'd overhead talking to Luke; many voices all rolled into one. "She is the cloverhand."

"That's me," I agreed, still standing next to the car. I was scared snotless, but I stood perfectly straight. "I'd think there'd be better things for you to do, on this night of all nights."

One of the whip men turned to me, his mouth curving into a smile. With a jolt, I realized he had no eyes beneath his brow — just empty hollows, with smooth skin in the shadows. The others looked at him, also without eyes, as he spoke. "Truth, cloverhand. I can tell the truth when I hear it. Can we do *you* on this night of all nights?"

"Go to hell."

After I said it, I thought it might be a bit redundant, since they looked like devils already. But the whip man said, his voice grating in a thousand whispers, "Hell is for those with souls."

Another, equally tall and with too many joints in his spine, said, "Come to our fire, tell us what you want of us. Make us a trade: the *tarbh uisge's* body" – he gestured to the massive dun bull – "for yours?"

I unscrewed the lid of the jar. "I have a better idea. How about, the bull goes free or all your fun stops for the night?"

The whip man who had suggested "doing" me approached; his walk was all wrong, and it sent a shiver through my body. "That does not sound like a truth to me, cloverhand."

I scooped out a warm handful of the green muck in the jar, trying not to think about just how nasty it felt (exactly like picking up a handful of fresh dog crap), and hurled it on to the faerie.

For a moment there was nothing, and I thought *Granna, you let me down*. But then he began to sigh. His breath went out and out and out, and then he just fell to the car park, still breathing out, until he was empty.

I'd thought I might feel bad, but I just felt intense relief.

I held the jar out towards the others. "Not much left, but probably enough for each of you. Let it go."

One of them hissed, "I don't think you want to see the *tarbh uisge* freed. He will bear you down into the water and your salve will not help you there."

I looked at the wide eye of the bull as its massive body trembled, lit both by the bonfire and the green-grey light of the streetlight overhead. It didn't belong here; it was a remnant of another time and another place, and I saw its fear of the present weeping from every pore.

"I'm not afraid." I took a step forward, forcing myself to step over the body of the one I'd killed, though part of me imagined it grabbing me as I did. "Leave this place."

With angry buzzing, like distant bees, the whip men backed away, towards the fire, their posture deferential. They backed directly into the fire and their bodies incinerated instantly; I would have thought they'd died if I hadn't still seen hints of their eyeless faces in the coals and wood of the bonfire.

The bull lowered its head and stamped a hoof at me, its eyes enormous and sentient. Something about it was so ancient and pure that I ached for an intangible past I had never known.

I gave a little bow. "You're welcome."

It blew its red-lined nostrils at me and plunged into the night.

My skin prickled. Faerie pressed in around me. I had to go back to the beginning before it was too late.

Book Five

My love, fond and true,
What else could I do—
But shield you from wind and from weather?
When the shots fall like hail,
They us both shall assail—
And mayhap we shall die together.

—"Ned of the Hill"

Twenty

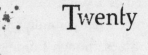

The high school doors were locked, but with the moon behind me I wasn't worried. It only took a moment to mentally click the doors open, and then carefully lock them behind me. Inside, the halls were lit sickly blue-green by the fluorescent lights, and the windows to the classrooms were black squares in the doors lining the walls. The familiar smell of hundreds of students and books and cafeteria food turned my stomach with anxiety. It was as if I'd never left. It took me a long moment to gather my nerve and remind myself just how strong I could be now.

Still, I hesitated in the main hallway, uncertain of where to go. *It ends at the beginning*, the dancing faerie had said. But where was the beginning? The bathroom where Luke had found me throwing up? The picnic bench out back where we'd flirted?

No, of course not. It had all started when we played onstage and silenced an auditorium full of people. *That* was the beginning: the first time I'd ever used my powers, though I hadn't known it then. It was painfully obvious – what James called a "major duh moment."

My shoes squeaked as I walked down the hallway towards the auditorium. I felt painfully conspicuous. I listened for other footsteps, though I didn't know if I'd even hear them over my stupid squeaky shoes. I glanced at every dark classroom window to make sure I wouldn't be ambushed by some strange faerie creature.

But the high school seemed abandoned, chilling in its emptiness. In my head, Luke's voice said, *trust yourself.*

The memory of his voice gave me courage, and I squared my shoulders. *I'm strong.* I pushed open the doors to the auditorium.

The bulk of the auditorium was in darkness. Rows of invisible folding chairs stretched out before me, but the stage was lit as if a production were in progress. Pieces of half-erected set lay in the corners of the stage, remnants or beginnings of *A Midsummer Night's Dream.* In the middle of the clutter, there was a bare circle. And I saw a little dark pile in the middle of it, with a spotlight trained on it.

It could have been a pile of anything, but I knew exactly what it was. I wanted to bolt down the aisle and vault on to the stage, but logic told me it was a trap. Why else would They have put James under a spotlight, if not to encourage me to bolt up there?

So I made my way cautiously down the dark aisle,

spinning, surveying every seat, listening for rustling and smelling for thyme. But it seemed empty like the rest of the school. I made it all the way to the stage stairs, up the stage stairs, on to the slick pale wood of the stage; and still I was alone.

Feeling exposed under the bright, hot lights, I crept over to the pile and recognized the colour of James's favourite Audioslave T-shirt. I couldn't see his face, but after seeing the crash site, I knew I wasn't going to like what I saw. I swallowed; I wasn't ready for this. *Please be alive.*

I crouched, hovering a hand over his shoulder, hesitating. "Please be alive."

The head turned towards me, and Freckle Freak grinned up at me. "I am."

I scrambled backwards, shoes slipping on the floor, and Aodhan stood up, wearing James' bloodstained shirt, his torc glinting at the edge of the sleeve, his smile widening at my shock. His nostrils flared as if he were taking in my scent, and he ran his tongue across his lips.

"Where *is* he?" I snarled, putting more space between the two of us. As repugnant as the thought of Aodhan touching me was, for some reason I was stuck on the idea of him wearing James's shirt. He'd taken it while James lay bleeding; I just couldn't stop thinking of that. "What have you done with him?"

"Very little. The car really did most of the work."

I had nowhere left to back up to; my next step would take me down the stairs, into the darkness. Breathtakingly fast, Aodhan was beside me, his herbal scent so strong it made my head spin. "Soon," he whispered into my ear, thyme infecting every bit of me, "I'll be able to touch you." He spread his fingers out and pushed his palm towards my collarbone. It hovered, millimetres from my skin, so close that I could see every nick and stain on the leather bands around his wrist. Again I saw Luke's memory of him tormenting the girl, saw the red-stained leather at his wrists.

Do something. Do something. Instinct kicked in. My knee jerked up, missing his family jewels but slamming him in the thigh. I struck at his face, thinking of how nice it would be to smash out a few of his grinning teeth. He took a step back, easily dodging me, and watched with an easy smile, his head cocked charmingly. For all the world, he looked like an extremely evil model who had escaped from the pages of an Abercrombie & Fitch catalogue.

I scrambled away from him, back towards the centre of the stage, thinking only that I needed more room to manoeuvre. Aodhan followed my progress with a mild smile on his freckled face. "I asked Luke if he'd share you after She had punished him for his disobedience. I'm pretty sure what he said was 'yes'."

"Asshole."

Aodhan chewed his thumbnail and then jerked his

hand towards the stage behind me. "Watch your step, lovely."

I jerked to look behind me. *Oh crap oh crap oh crap.* There, lying in a pile of broken lumber jutted with nails and set debris painted an ugly green, was a shirtless body. Though I didn't want to see more, I took a closer look at the dark, stained jeans, the smeared chest, James's bruised face under a mop of hair. I swallowed vomit.

"I think he punctured a lung, poor thing," said a bright, clear voice above me. "He stopped breathing just as I brought him in here."

I looked up at Eleanor's beautiful features. She gazed down benevolently at me. Blood was smeared all over her elegant white dress, and she examined a spattered nail before licking her finger clean. My world swayed.

"Oh," she said, voice so lovely I wanted to cry, looking down at the pile of James. "There he goes again. He *is* a fighter, don't you think, Aodhan?"

Beside me, James took a shuddering breath, and then, too far apart, another one.

"Bitch!" I burst out. I wished I knew a worse word.

Eleanor gave a lovely, perturbed frown and exchanged a look with Aodhan. "I always forget how angry they get."

Rage boiled inside me, swelling and mixing with the night already in my heart. I felt as if my skin would burst with the enormousness of my anger. Freckle Freak reached to touch me again, and I exploded upwards, striking out with my hand and everything inside me. He literally blew across the stage and into the orchestra pit; I didn't hear him moving, but I was sure he wasn't dead.

Eleanor covered her mouth with her hand. "Oh. Ah ha. That was *not* very nice." She shook her head at me. "Oh dear, that won't please her at all. She's going to stop *all* our fun early if you provoke her."

Fun. I couldn't even begin to speak. How could I reason with creatures who thought this was *fun*?

"Deirdre Monaghan," Eleanor tried the words out; they sounded elegant in her mouth. "I'm sorry that you don't seem to be enjoying this."

"I'm not here to enjoy myself," I muttered.

"Oh, right," Eleanor laughed delicately and the fine hairs on my arm stood up, very slowly. "You're here to rescue your friend from our clutches. And free Luke Dillon from Her clutches." Her smile was winning. "I knew right when I saw you that you were a very ambitious girl."

She stepped closer and ran a finger through the air next to my cheek, so close that I could almost feel her. "But I don't think you've quite thought it through. Would you like me to help you wrap your mind around your — your *conundrum*?"

"Not really."

Eleanor laughed as if I were very funny, and then she stepped into the spotlight. Holding her arms out, looking like a crucified beauty queen with the red stain on her dress, she said grandly, "All the world's a stage. It seems a shame to waste this one, doesn't it? Let's put on a little production. Aodhan, get up, we need you."

Aodhan, however, needed no prompting – he was already climbing the stairs to the stage. My explosive attack on him didn't seem to have misplaced even one of his fashionably spiked hairs.

"Look now," Eleanor said. "We even have props. Lights, please!" She clapped her hands. The sound resonated through the room, and small, twinkling lights like fireflies dropped from between her palms. She breathed on them, sending them whirling to the back corner of the stage.

My harp. I was unexpectedly floored by the appearance of it. They'd been in my house. They'd taken my harp. I imagined Delia smiling and opening the door for them.

"No play is complete without good props." Eleanor held a hand out to me, gesturing for me to sit at the harp. "Will you play, Deirdre?"

I spoke through gritted teeth. "I'd rather watch."

"Very well. I'll be Deirdre." She put her palm to her chest and I felt a gasp of energy pulled from me. And before me stood another Deirdre, but with Eleanor's voice coming from it. "Aodhan, will you play the unfortunate and doomed Luke Dillon?"

"I'm too handsome for the part. But—" and he looked at me – "being Luke Dillon has its uses." I knew enough to steel myself against the energy drain this time, but as Aodhan's features melted into Luke's, I saw James jerk on his pile of rubble.

Eleanor frowned, her pout achingly pretty even on my face. "Oh, now, that was selfish. You could spare it far more than him." She cast her eyes around the stage. "And as you won't play, and everyone else is out enjoying Solstice, I suppose we'll just have the corpse play the piper." She gestured casually towards James. "He's doing a good job, anyway."

She clapped her hands again. "Music, I think!" My harp began to play, of its own accord, my arrangement of "The Faerie Girl's Lament". Eleanor sang,

> *The sun shines through the window*
> *And the sun shines through your hair*
> *It seems like you're beside me*
> *But I know you're not there.*
> *You would sit beside this window*
> *Run your fingers through my hair*
> *You were always there beside me*
> *But I know that you're not there.*

She paused on the stage and held her fingers to her chest. "Oh, dearest Luke, I love you so."

Aodhan laughed derisively. It was so bizarre on Luke's face that I looked away. "And I you, my lovely."

"I would free you from your chains."

Aodhan stepped closer to Eleanor. "And I would free you from your clothes."

Eleanor smiled. "Truly, it is destiny, is it not? We will run away together."

"We'll do *something* together." Aodhan reached for Eleanor's hand, but she pulled it away and held it under her chin in a mockery of deep thought.

"But what of my rejected lover? The piper lies dying." Eleanor wandered over to James's body and looked down upon it, her sorrow almost convincing. "Ah, but I know. I'll take him to a doctor for repair."

"What God has made, let not Fey eviscerate," Aodhan noted.

Eleanor reached towards James and began to lift one of his arms; the horrible gasp he made had me halfway across the stage towards him before Eleanor held up her hand to stop me. She dropped his arm back on to the rubble and turned sadly to Aodhan. "It's no use, Luke, my love. The piper is beyond human help. Let's leave him and run away."

She rubbed her palms together as if working hand cream into them, and then worked them slowly apart. In between her fingers was now a specter of a dirty pigeon. "I have found your soul. I will free you."

Aodhan stepped forward dramatically and thrust his chest forward. "Let's get it on."

Eleanor pressed the ghostly pigeon into Aodhan's chest and began to sing again.

To the haunting tune of the harp
For the price I paid when you died that day
I paid that day with my heart
Fro and to in my dreams to you
With the breaking of my heart
Ne'er more again will I sing this song
Ne'er more will I hear the harp.

Under her fingers, Aodhan smiled large, and then his face turned to ash. With a crash, he hit the stage and closed his eyes. Eleanor pretended to wipe a tear away as she faced an imaginary audience. "Dear audience, you may find this turn of events . . . *shocking*. Why should my love lie dead when I have freed him? Oh, but you forget how old the gallowglass is. And how can a thousand-year-old boy live once he is whole again?"

She turned to me, and as she did, her face melted once more into her own. "Do you see what a fool's errand you've come on now? He cannot be freed, no matter how noble your intentions. Either tonight or a thousand nights from now, his soul *is* going to hell. I have seen his life, and believe me, he has earned it."

I stared, frozen, at Aodhan-turned-Luke lying on the stage. I couldn't move until Aodhan stripped himself of Luke's form and stood up again, watching my reaction with evident pleasure.

And it was then, when I thought I couldn't get any lower, that I felt all sound and light sucked from my eyes and ears. The curtains dropped behind me, cascading to the ground in velvety piles. Then sound came roaring back into my ears and the light returned. The curtains trembled, rising.

The Queen stepped out from the velvet and thrust the curtains behind her, chin lifted high. There was no doubt as to her identity; she reeked of power and age, though her face was as young as mine. Delicate blonde hair shone on either side of her cheeks, held flat on her head by a beaten gold circlet that bore an eerie resemblance to Luke's torc. She was one of those beautiful girls that made you despise looking in a mirror, no matter how pleased you'd been with yourself before you'd met her. Then her eyelids flicked open and two ancient eyes stared back at me. I was repulsed; it was as if I'd peeked in a pram and found a snake looking back at me.

Eleanor and Aodhan bowed low, their cheeks touching the stage.

The Queen's eyes drifted over the scene: my harp, James in the rubble, me standing mere metres away from her.

"Why isn't she dead yet?" To my surprise, her voice sounded weary, a bit reminiscent of Luke's – maybe that was how a human body became after one thousand years.

Aodhan grinned at me. "We were just having a bit of sport."

"There will be more sport when she is dead." The Queen looked at me and said, disbelieving, "And you are Deirdre? I thought, when I saw you, I would understand why Luke Dillon wouldn't do as he was told. But you're—" she shrugged, obviously bemused. "You're so *ordinary*."

The words were so human that they at least gave me the courage to speak. "You were ordinary once yourself."

The Queen looked at me incredulously. "You compare the value of your life to mine? You're nothing. And I am everything. Is *that* why you won't die? You thought you were worth something? Your story has been written a thousand times, and in every version, you and your lover die."

She stepped towards me, power seeping from her, and I stumbled back from the sheer drowning force of it. Was it true? Was I living "The Faerie Girl's Lament"?

Suddenly I felt a tug on my ankle, and a second later my leg was pulled out from under me, so fast that my breath abandoned me. In a blink, I was hanging upside down by an ankle, my iron key hanging precariously below my face. I jerked my hands upwards towards the rope, but I was snared securely in the most obvious trap ever.

Aodhan's laugh carried across the stage and he clapped his hands, ignoring the Queen's dark expression. He strode over and stood face-to-face with me, his face right side up and mine upside down, the key hanging between us. "I thought you would *never* step into that."

He reached up behind my neck, his fingers too hot on my skin, and untied the cloth string that held the key.

No. Crap, no.

I summoned the dark outside, gathering it into me, intending to push it into his face. Anything to keep him away from Luke's secret.

"No, Deirdre Monaghan," the Queen said flatly. "I don't think so."

And just like that, as soon as she said my name, I went empty inside, like a balloon deflated in an instant.

The key clattered on the floor at Aodhan's feet. And I just felt limp, drained, captive. So, this was why the faeries kept their names secret.

"May I play with her now?" Aodhan's words were directed at the Queen, but his eyes never left my face.

"He's worked quite hard enough for it," Eleanor suggested.

The Queen made a vague gesture – like a teen's *whatever* – and instantly Aodhan was clambering up the side of the stage to cut the snare. My mind raced through possible plans, but my thoughts seemed to slip away like water, pumped out of my brain by my pounding heart.

And then I was falling. I barely had time to wheel my arms out when pain seared through me – the back of my head first, then my left hand. I gasped for breath and consciousness, lying in the same rubble as James. I couldn't move. I couldn't breathe. And my hand was killing me.

Oh, God. My eyes drifted to my hand and my stomach turned. Driven through the back of my hand was a long nail. The point protruded several centimetres from my palm, with almost no blood around its base.

"Did you hurt yourself?" Aodhan leapt on top of me, pinning my other arm to the ground, not worrying with the one nailed to the stubby board. He grinned down at me, his eyes bright. His body was too hot, burning me, and his thyme-scented breath invaded my nostrils. I should have been afraid, but all I could think of was how glad I was that Luke wasn't here to see me, pinned beneath Freckle Freak. The thought pricked tears of shame at the corners of my eyes. "I think I'll enjoy you quite a bit."

At his words, James shifted on the rubble near me. His teeth gritted, and his voice was barely audible. "Get off her."

Aodhan told me, "You'll have to wait a minute, lovely." He reached to his waist and unsheathed his knife. "I have to take care of this first."

OK. This was enough. As Aodhan lifted his knife, I summoned every bit of physical strength I had and swung my left hand – nail, board, and all – at Freckle Freak's pretty face. There was no time for him to jerk away, and the nail stabbed into his cheek.

The knife dropped from his hand.

Aodhan wrenched his cheek from the nail and stumbled off of me. Staring at me, he touched the wound with his fingers. It was no worse than the wound on my hand, certainly not enough to kill him, but his eyes told me otherwise.

And then, bursting from the hole the iron had made, a new, green bud surged forth, unfolding into a delicate leaf. And then another, and another still. The fresh growth spread across his cheek, exploding into beautiful white flowers with yellow stamen, and purple daisies with deep black centres, and small, pink bleeding hearts that bobbed as he stumbled back again. In seconds, endless beauty erupted from the filth that was Aodhan, consuming him with life and promise. He fell back, but before he hit the floor, it was only a cascade of flowers that spilled across the stage, making no more sound than a whisper.

I wrenched my hand from the nail and grasped my key. My hand was bloody but had stopped hurting; was that a bad thing? The Queen looked at the pile of flowers that was Freckle Freak and then looked at Eleanor. "The time for sport is over. Bring me Luke Dillon."

I stopped breathing.

"With pleasure," Eleanor said, sweeping over the petals as if they meant nothing to her. I crept over to James's side, crouching protectively between him and the Queen, though who knew what I could do against her if she tried to kill him. She had my name. The power to stop me in my tracks. A small part of me wished that Luke would whirl in and rescue me again, but I didn't really think it was going to go down like that.

The Queen looked at me, her eyes flitting over the bloody key and over James, behind me. "You aren't strong enough, you know. Not to kill me. Not to rule Them."

I cradled my hand in my lap, shoulders hunched, and gazed back at her. "I don't want to rule Them."

She shrugged. "Then They will kill you. Haven't you heard the legends? Don't you know what happens to cloverhands who cannot control the fey? Eyes gouged out. Paralysed. Killed."

Her words rang true, echoing faerie tales from my childhood. But my mind slipped away from her, escaping into a memory of Luke's – him playing a wild reel in a circle of faeries who bent bows and pounded drums. I recognized Brendan, saw Una's smile, heard the feral beauty of the tune. It was one of the most beautiful memories I'd got from Luke, the only one I'd wished I'd been there for.

"Deirdre," snapped the Queen, and my attention focused back on her. "You have already given up. Lay down your key and I promise it will be quick."

I frowned at her. Something in her words reminded me of that breathy voice singing the legend of the other Deirdre – the third Deirdre – in my ear this morning.

But before I could think why it was important, the

Queen looked at Eleanor, who had returned to the stage alone. God. Where was Luke? Dead?

Eleanor's expression was unfathomable. "The *Daoine Sidhe* are outside, my Queen." She raised a delicate eyebrow and I could have sworn that she nearly smiled. "They demand an audience."

The Queen looked surprised, but then scoffed. "The *Daoine Sidhe* are nothing. They have no power to demand anything."

"And I told them that, my Queen. But they said the cloverhand saved the life of one of theirs, the *tarbh uisge*, and that the law demanded she be given a gift in return."

My eyes darted to the Queen.

Her expression was dark, but she didn't disagree with Eleanor. "The *Sidhe* are too weak to come here without being called, even on this night. Who has called them? It is forbidden. *Who has called them?*"

"I have."

A shiver ran through me – my body telling me who had spoken before I even turned to look.

"Luke Dillon!" If I had thought the Queen's expression was dark before, now it was awful to see.

Eleanor stepped aside, letting Luke step up on to the stage. His eyes found me, and I saw pain in them. I couldn't stop staring at him standing there, his hair bright under the stage lights, his face pale against his black T-shirt, his shoulders square but his eyes defeated.

"Luke Dillon," the Queen said again. "It is forbidden to call the *Daoine Sidhe*. Would you see your soul in hell?"

"It's over," Luke said, and dropped his dagger on to the stage. It clattered across the shiny floor with ringing finality. "I'm done doing your bidding. Do with me what you will, but I am done."

The Queen glowed with fury; I saw the setting sun in her eyes. "Gallowglass, you have so much to lose. How can you deny me?"

Though Luke spoke to her, he looked at me as he said, "*T mo chr i istigh inti.*"

"How can you love her?" screamed the Queen. "She is *nothing.*"

And then, with Luke's pale eyes soaking me up, saying *sorry, this is all I can do,* I remembered – *God, I'm a moron!*

"I'm not nothing." I stood up. "I'm not nothing, Deirdre O'Brien."

The Queen turned her perfect face to me in disbelief.

"That's your name, isn't it?" I took a step towards her. I didn't need her to answer; I could feel the truth of it. I could feel the power it contained. Power over her. Combined with the thundering darkness outside, I felt invincible. I *knew* I was stronger than she was. It was well past sunset.

I looked at her old snake-eyes, and as I did, I saw

one of Luke's memories behind my own eyes. This Luke, hundreds of years younger but wearing the same face, stood before the queen, his clothing strange. The Queen, too, was unchanged, her eyes already the ancient ones that I saw today.

"I will not love you," Luke said. "I won't lie. I will not love you."

The Queen didn't look surprised. Instead, she circled him once, her massive dress dragging behind her and catching on his ankle. He stood stock still, silently waiting for her anger. If he was afraid, I couldn't feel it in the memory. The Queen ran a finger around his biceps where his torc now was, her face calculating, and then she smiled at him. "You will wish that you had."

Anger pushed me from the memory to the present. I could hurt her. I could let myself remember every cruel thing she'd done to Luke, and I could use the darkness to absolutely destroy her.

I wanted to. I wanted to stomp on her and then say something pithy as she curled up and died like a spider.

As if reading my mind – maybe she was – the Queen said, scornfully, "You are still not strong enough to control the fey. You are weak unless it is full dark. But we don't have to do battle . . . I can teach you. I can teach you how to find the darkness that hides in the corners of rooms. To harness the night that is caught beneath the tangled branches of a tree. To find the darkness that's in you all the time. I can make you more than you are."

As she spoke, I saw the evening unfolding in her eyes, the summer folding flowers along her skin, ever blooming but not consuming her as they had Aodhan. Her hair cascaded in rivers of laughing summer waterfalls, never reaching the stage. Her fingers reached towards me, vines and roots striving for the stage lights through the tips of them.

"No." I held my hand out towards Luke, and he walked wordlessly over to me, twining my fingers tightly in his. God, his hands were cold. Like he was already dead. "No, I don't think so. I want to see the *Daoine Sidhe.*"

The glorious evening retreated into the Queen abruptly. Fury rolled off of her in vicious waves, but she couldn't refuse – we were two equal pieces circling on the chess board. She turned to Eleanor. "Get Luke Dillon's soul."

Twenty-One

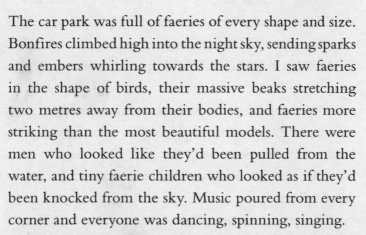

The car park was full of faeries of every shape and size. Bonfires climbed high into the night sky, sending sparks and embers whirling towards the stars. I saw faeries in the shape of birds, their massive beaks stretching two metres away from their bodies, and faeries more striking than the most beautiful models. There were men who looked like they'd been pulled from the water, and tiny faerie children who looked as if they'd been knocked from the sky. Music poured from every corner and everyone was dancing, spinning, singing.

We stood just outside the propped exit door to the auditorium, for all the world like a dysfunctional family. Luke pressed against my arm, his features hawk-like as his gaze flitted around the car park. The Queen stood a few metres away from us, supremely out of place on the dirty tarmac, and looking the more impressive for it.

Thomas Rhymer emerged from the crowd, curls bouncing, and stood before the Queen.

"Good Solstice, my lady." His voice was solicitous, if not sincere.

"Get away from me, Rhymer. You have chosen your side." Casually, the Queen lifted a hand, not looking away from the crowd, and Thomas tumbled next to my feet. "I will deal with you and your tongue later."

Luke held out a hand; Thomas accepted it and pulled himself up. His eyes met mine, but he didn't say anything as he stepped slightly behind me. *Damn, I think I'm getting a retinue.*

"I do not see the *Daoine Sidhe*," the Queen said to me. "I believe they have forgotten you."

Perhaps they had. I didn't know what my move was now.

"Not so quickly," whispered a voice, equal parts song and chant. Eleanor's eyes widened as Una slid out from behind her, moving soundlessly.

"You needn't look so shocked," Una said. "It was only a pinch."

"Keep your distance," the Queen warned, and lifted a hand. "I will snap you in two."

"Come here!" Brendan's voice conveyed the worry that was absent in Una's face. He looked nearly as regal as the Queen, winding his way through the revelling faeries astride a dapple grey horse draped in bells. Bells around the horse's hooves jangled with each step, and bells hanging from the reins trilled as the horse spooked at a ring of dancing faeries. Behind him, a half dozen more horses pushed their way through the crowd, all dapple greys with coats reflecting the colours around them. All of their bells should have made a cacophony, but instead there was an endless rippling chord of stunning melody. Despite everything, I caught my breath, struck with wonder.

Una spiralled over to where Brendan had stopped, tweaking his mount's reins to hear the bells again. "Did I not *tell* you it would be this door? Don't you look a fool now?" She wiggled her fingers towards the Queen and Eleanor, who stood behind the Queen holding a covered cage. "Behold the peacock and her handler."

I wasn't sure whether the Queen or Eleanor was the peacock, but neither of them looked pleased with the comparison.

"Say your bit," the Queen snarled. "Since you must."

Luke bowed slightly towards Brendan, as much as he could while still keeping his fingers in mine. "Good Solstice, Brendan. Please hurry. We haven't much time."

Brendan nodded back and glanced at the other *Daoine Sidhe*. They urged their horses forward until they stood in a row of seven, shoulder to shoulder, the faeries' bare feet touching the toes of the faerie next to them.

"Deirdre," Brendan said. "You have saved the *tarbh uisge*, one of ours, on this night, and that binds us." He sang,

> *The bird that flies across the fields*
> *Eats the seeds of the meadow grasses*

The seed that falls from the beak yields
More than the meadow's losses.

I stared at him. He was looking at me expectantly, and I'm sure I was supposed to say something clever.

Thomas leaned in and touched my shoulder. "A life for a life," he whispered. "It's a song of balance. They'll give you a life for the life you saved."

Oh.

Oh.

In my head, Eleanor was pressing a dirty-pigeon soul into Aodhan's chest and he was falling to the ground, dead, wearing Luke's face. But it didn't have to end that way. I could ask for Luke's life. I could win his soul back and save him. This wouldn't be the last time I held his hand. My story *would* have a happy ending.

"Save his life," Luke whispered, his lips on my ear. "Hurry. He doesn't have much time left."

Guilt rocked through me, pricking immediate tears in my eyes. I didn't know how I could've forgotten James, back on the stage, gasping for life. What kind of a person was I? Of course, I had to save James. What was I thinking? I half-turned my head towards Luke, swallowing more tears. "But then – but when – if I – if you get your soul back—"

Luke kissed just in front of my ear, so brief and light that it was almost just his lips forming words. "I know. I know, pretty girl. I knew all along."

I wanted him so badly it hurt, a dull ache somewhere below my ribs. I wanted to say, "Save Luke." It would be so easy.

It would be so wrong.

I looked at the ground, at every little jagged crevice in the tarmac. If you stared at it long enough, you could see little flecks of some sort of shining rock mixed into its surface. Two glistening drops splatted on the tarmac, and I looked up at Brendan and wiped my cheek.

"Thank you for the favour. Truly, you are very kind. Please – please would you save my friend James? If you can?" I almost choked on the last words, but I got it all out before another tear escaped.

"Good girl," Luke said softly.

"Where is he?" Brendan asked.

Una whirled past us. "I know. I can hear him dying in here."

Brendan dismounted and followed her through the door, giving me and my iron key a wide berth, even on Solstice. He said over his shoulder, "It will be done."

And I burst into tears. I didn't care who was watching – the Queen, Eleanor, all of the faeries of the world, whatever. I didn't care. Luke squeezed his arms around me, letting me bury my face in his shoulder. I felt him staring at the Queen as he kissed the top of my head.

"Let go of her." The Queen's voice was stony.

Luke's arms tightened around me as I pulled up my

face to look at her. Again, the red setting sun was blazing in her eyes. *Please don't let go of me.* He didn't.

"*Let go of her.*"

Eleanor's lips curled into a smile at the anger in her Queen's voice.

"I will when she asks me to," Luke said. "I told you, I'm done doing your bidding. If this is the way I die, so be it."

If he was afraid, I could not feel it. The Queen whirled to the cage at Eleanor's feet, and tugged off the cover. Beneath it, a doorless birdcage with wire-thin bars surrounded a dove so white it hurt my eyes. It flapped its wings in terror, crashing off the sides of the cage and tumbling to the bottom. Luke sighed, his eyes fixed on the bird, his body firmly pressed against me but the rest of him somewhere else.

"Foul, isn't it?" the Queen asked. "Seems only fitting that the essence of a killer should manifest as a filthy, ordinary pigeon."

The words burst from my mouth. "Are you kidding? It's the most beautiful thing I've ever seen." I stared at that brilliant form in the cage. It *felt* like the promise of what people could be, before we started to screw ourselves up. It felt like a beginning.

The Queen crooked an eyebrow at me, disbelieving. "One last chance, Luke Dillon. Tell me you will love me and I'll spare you."

Luke just shook his head, a slight movement against

my cheek. I stepped out of the circle of his arms, towards the Queen. "You can't force someone to love you – don't you get it? You can force them to kill for you. You can force them to be your subjects. You can't *make* someone love you!"

The Queen shrilled, "My subjects love me! I do not force them to obey me!"

Eleanor's eyebrow raised.

I seized whatever meaning I could find in that little gesture. "Prove it. Prove it."

"You will die, cloverhand," the Queen snarled. Then, louder, she screamed to her subjects, so loud that her voice cut through every bit of music and laughing and dancing. They froze, and magic hung in the air on this weird night. "Do you see me, my lovelies? Witness my beauty? Now look at the cloverhand – look at how ordinary she is, how dull, how simple! She is nothing, but she claims that my subjects do not love me!"

A slow smile had started on Eleanor's face as she stood behind the Queen. With every word that the Queen spoke, it widened, until the beauty of her smile was agony to look at.

The Queen lifted her arms, and when she screamed, her voice was as fierce as summer lightning. "Choose your Queen!"

The night was quiet.

It was so quiet that I could hear the cicadas buzzing in the field across the road, and the frogs chirping in the ravine behind the school. A car's tyres hummed on the distant highway and, above me, in the absolute silence, I heard the streetlight buzzing faintly.

Then the faeries rushed towards the Queen, one crazy mass of shimmering bodies and wings and beaks and claws, and I was forced away from Luke by the press of the throng. The noise was unbearable: cries and laughs and growls. I didn't know what was happening, and I couldn't see Luke or the Queen or anyone for all the bodies shoving past me.

But one cry could be heard above all of them – a high, reedy wail that went on and on, freezing my blood with its wildness. And then I saw a tall faerie, with shaggy fur growing on his shoulders, stalk by me holding a handful of blonde hair in his huge fist. Long blonde hair, with a clump of red on the end. I still didn't get it until I saw a collection of lithe, willowy she-faeries tossing a hand between the three of them. I saw blood drip from it. Then I saw two faeries the colour of the sky tugging on either end of a long stretch of fabric from the Queen's dress.

"Oh my God." I pushed my hand to my mouth. Next to me, Eleanor made a small, vaguely amused sound.

A hugely tall faerie with the pricked ears of a horse lifted some gory prize above his head, and the wild crowd cheered, primitive and delighted with their kill.

They killed her.

"Dee," Luke pushed by Eleanor as if she were nothing and gripped my arm. "Are you all right? I thought—" He broke off as he watched a dragon-like creature slither by with an arm in its long, toothy mouth. His pale eyes followed its progress through the strange crowd.

"I didn't think they'd kill her."

"I thought it was you." Suddenly I realized that Luke, for the first time, looked shaken. "I saw them carrying a hand and—"

"Shut up. I'm OK. Nothing happened." It felt good to be the one to comfort him for once; to hold him together. "What's going on?"

A tall, beautiful male faerie had caught everyone's attention, and he held the Queen's bloody circlet above his head. His voice was like one thousand voices together as he said, "We have chosen our Queen."

He walked through the crowd, the faeries making a path for him, heading straight for me with the horrible crown – still covered with the Queen's blood. I couldn't even begin to imagine its awful weight on my head. I shivered; Luke's hand tightened on my arm.

Oh God! No!

Still the faerie came, his path unerring, through the crowd towards me.

No. Not me. Not me, I wished fervently. *Anybody but me.*

The faerie stopped before me, and I saw blood dripping down his arm from the circlet.

Not me.

He stepped forward, closing the space between us, and then he placed the circlet on Eleanor's head. "Long live the Queen."

"Oh, that I will," said Eleanor.

Book Six

All you who are in love
Aye and cannot it remove
I pity the pain that you endure.
For experience lets me know
That your hearts are filled with woe
It's a woe that no mortal can cure.

—"The Curragh of Kildare"

Twenty-Two

There was silence as Eleanor faced us across the car park. Over her shoulder, the moon moved slowly across the sky, the birds still fluttering and trembling on its surface. The silver glimmer they cast mingled with the ugly yellow of the streetlights.

"I have waited a long time," Eleanor said finally. She knelt and picked up the soul-cage with more grace than any human. "Luke Dillon, you served the last Queen, not this one. Take your soul, darling."

"Thank you," I said.

"It's not a gift," Luke said, his voice flat.

Eleanor smiled, both beautiful and fearsome. "You were always such a clever one. Do you want it or not, dear? You worked so hard for it."

Luke released my hand to retrieve the cage. He returned to my side and set the cage down between us, like it was something we both owned. "What happens to Deirdre?"

Eleanor shrugged. "Probably an extremely boring life. Ugly children. Midlife crisis. Bed pan. Death."

"You won't hurt her?"

Eleanor smiled at me as if the idea was pleasing, but she shook her head. "I doubt it, dear. So many other fun things to do." She looked around at her faeries and clapped her hands. "Speaking of which, pretties, where did the music go? Is this not Solstice?"

And with that, They whirled into the night around us, filling the car park with music once more. Eleanor smiled benevolently. "Now, Deirdre, are you not going to give the gallowglass back his soul? He cannot stop looking at it."

It was true. Luke's eyes kept going back to the bird, and the part of him in me tugged towards it as well. I almost hated it. I hated that it meant goodbye. But most of all, I hated that I didn't know what would happen to him after he had his soul back. Was Eleanor right? Would he have to pay for the Queen's sins?

"The hero always dies at the end of Irish songs, didn't you notice?" Luke's voice was barely audible. He crouched to look at his soul, and I saw the brilliance of the dove reflected in his pupils.

"Wait!" Una's voice carried as she danced out of the auditorium. Behind her, Brendan was carrying James's body as if it weighed nothing. He strode as close to me as he dared and laid James down on the tarmac.

"Is he alive?" I asked, rushing to him, thoughtlessly pushing Brendan back with the presence of my iron. I knelt and saw the rising of his chest; I put my hand above his mouth and felt his breath warm my hand.

"I still don't think it's a good idea." Brendan shook his head. "But for now, the piper lives." He jerked his head towards Luke. "What of Luke Dillon?"

Luke looked at me, across the million miles that separated us. I think he was afraid. "What of me, Dee?"

I took a deep breath. No matter what happened, I wasn't going to win. But maybe I didn't have to lose completely. I looked at Brendan and Una. "Do you remember what you said that first night I met you?'"

"He remembers everything," Una interrupted me. "He's like an elephant."

Brendan held up a hand. "Shut. Up." He turned to me. "What did I say?"

I stumbled over the words, not sure how to say what I wanted to. "You said that Luke had played with you – that he played with you in the past. You said he was like you, more like you than most people. And—" My eyes found Thomas Rhymer, watching from nearby. "And Thomas said that humans who live with the faeries don't die. If I give his soul back – do you think – so he has a chance to prove where his soul belongs—"

Luke's eyes darted to me, and then to Brendan. I didn't even know if he wanted what I was trying to get for him. Maybe he'd just think he was going from one prison to another. Then he looked from Brendan to Una. "Will you have me?"

Brendan frowned at him before speaking. When he finally opened his mouth, it seemed he was choosing his words carefully. "You've spent so much time among the iron."

"Indeed," added Una. Luke was frozen beside me.

Brendan frowned deeper. Slowly, disgust began to grow on his face. My stomach turned uncomfortably. "You stink of it. The filth of iron. I cannot imagine us—"

Una giggled, and Brendan elbowed her. He turned back to Luke. "I just do not think it will be possible. I'm sorry."

Luke started to say something, but then Una began to laugh, a beautifully silly laugh. She laughed so hard she had to crouch down on the pavement and rest her hand on the ground. She finally gasped, "Brendan, love, Luke Dillon *believes* you."

Luke made a face at Una and looked back up at Brendan. "Are you having fun with me?"

The disgust melted off Brendan's face, replaced immediately with an easy smile. "You and your flute don't have to ask whether you belong with us, Luke Dillon. We'd be honoured. You are far more faerie than you are human."

Una wrinkled her nose. "But also more gullible."

Luke made a soft little noise – whether sadness or appreciation, I couldn't tell.

It was so unfair. After all we'd done, after everything that had happened, I should have got to stay with him. But there was no way to make it fair.

"Do it," Una said. "Stop moping. You have the rest of Solstice with him. We're here as long as the music is."

I left James and walked back to the cage. Luke kissed my cheek, my forehead, my lips. Then he whispered against my skin, "Thank you for making it mean something."

Eleanor strode over to us, regal in her bloody crown, and pulled out her bone-white dagger. "Truly," she whispered reverently, "this was a wonderful game." She handed the dagger to me. It took me a long moment to realize she meant for me to open the birdcage with it.

Without giving myself time to second-guess, I sliced through the top of the cage. The bars sprang outwards like wires, and the dove flapped in the bottom, its eyes frightened. I could see its heart pounding through its fragile skin.

"Shhh," I whispered. Reaching in, I cupped its wings to its sides. It was unimaginably light, and I felt as if it would disintegrate in my hands if I pressed too hard. I looked up at Luke. His eyes were locked on mine, unmoving.

In my hands, the soul tugged towards Luke, and I let it guide my hands to his chest. I imagined Luke before me, young and vibrant and grinning, and everything we could have had. I wanted to say something like "goodbye", but in the end what was there, really, to say that we hadn't been saying all along? And then I let his soul flutter back into him.

Luke gasped – and when he blinked, he was alive. He was so alive, his eyes so bright, his face so light, that I realized I didn't know anything about him. He grinned at me, this strange, young, wild thing, and he kissed me, hard.

Una came over and gripped Luke's shoulder. "You're one of us now. You're bound by music. Music owns you. Music is your life."

Luke looked at me. "I'm here as long tonight as the music lasts, pretty girl. Get your harp."

Acknowledgements

This novel wouldn't have been possible without the help of several people: my generous and charming editor Andrew, who believed in this novel back when it was a fugly duckling; my friend Naish, who dropped everything for tireless editing sessions and fixed grammatical errors that even drunk monkeys speaking English as a foreign language wouldn't have made; my sister Kate whose intense enthusiasm for Luke and Deidre kept this story alive and who giggled with me over the plotting process (one word, Kate: "splat-shmear"); my sister Liz, who threatened me into beginning this story in the first place … no really, she did threaten me – I have it in writing; my mom, because without her I wouldn't be here; my cyber-chums for their enthusiasm, especially Wendy, who lives in a place where they stand upside down; and of course my husband/love-slave Ed, whose long-suffering expression hides a true heart.

About the Author

Maggie Stiefvater's life decisions have revolved around her inability to be gainfully employed. Talking to yourself, staring into space, and coming to work in your pyjamas are frowned upon when you're a waitress, calligraphy instructor, or technical editor (all of which she's tried), but are highly prized traits in novelists and artists (she's made her living as one or the other since she was  twenty-two). Maggie now lives a surprisingly eccentric life in the middle of nowhere, Virginia, with her charmingly straight-laced husband, two kids, and multiple neurotic dogs.

www.maggiestiefvater.com

Look out for more by
Maggie Stiefvater

The pack circled around me, tongues and teeth and growls.

When a local boy is killed by wolves, Grace's small town becomes a place of fear and suspicion. But Grace can't help being fascinated by the pack, and by one yellow-eyed wolf in particular. There's something about him – something almost human.

Then she meets a yellow-eyed boy whose familiarity takes her breath away...

The heart-wrenching sequel
to the best-selling Shiver

*I feel the weight of
the pack's gaze. . .*

Grace and Sam must fight to be together.
For Grace, this means defying her parents
and keeping dangerous secrets. For Sam, it
means grappling with his werewolf past . . .
and figuring out a way to survive the future.

But just when they manage to find
happiness, Grace realizes she's changing in
ways she could never have expected. . .